"NORRIS PUTS YOU IN THE COCKPIT FOR A GRIPPING FLIGHT."
Stephen Coonts

Randi caught sight of a single dark shape and broke the radar lock to let the Hornet's radar mode search for the second aircraft. Scanning the area, she caught sight of the smoke rising from a crash sight on a distant ridgeline.

"Hawk three-six is engaging the southern bandit. Wreckage bears one-eight-five for six from my position."

The carrier air group commander replied, "Your bandit bears one-seven-five, four miles. We've lost contact on both Lobos."

Randi adopted the old TOPGUN trick to locate the surviving Lobo. Using the nose of the MiG as a pointer, she scanned the ground until she found the shadow of the aircraft he was chasing. It had to be Dizzy trying to escape. The MiG was closing and would soon be in range. Randi had to take him out, but the set-up was terrible. She needed more look-down, but there wasn't time.

With no choice, she took a lock and launched a Sparrow . . .

Also by Bob Norris

FLY-OFF

CHECK SIX!

BOB NORRIS

AVON BOOKS

An Imprint of HarperCollins*Publishers*

AVON BOOKS
An Imprint of HarperCollins*Publishers*
10 East 53rd Street
New York, New York 10022-5299

Copyright © 1998 by Bob Norris
ISBN: 0-06-101353-6
www.avonbooks.com

First Avon Books paperback printing: April 2004
First HarperPaperbacks printing: October 1998

Avon Trademark Reg. U.S. Pat. Off. and in Other Countries, Marca Registrada, Hecho en U.S.A.
HarperCollins® is a trademark of HarperCollins Publishers Inc.

Printed in the U.S.A.

10 9 8 7 6 5 4 3 2 1

*For Pam, my wife,
who taught me that life is
a contact sport and whose
love inspires me to play*

Acknowledgments

I am deeply grateful and humbled by the wise counsel and support provided by Bob Campbell and Bob Irvine, two fine authors and wonderfully generous friends. Many thanks to Greg Neary whose unmatched skill as a strike fighter pilot is reflected in his legendary briefing cards, including those he contributed to this novel. And I must publicly acknowledge my indebtedness to Randy Roach, my backseater during those early Tomcat years, for keeping us alive during three cruises. Of course, I cannot omit my family and friends, though they are reminded of their promises to pay full retail. Finally, I bow to the men and women who are prepared to throw themselves at the pitching deck of an aircraft carrier in the middle of an ocean far away.

Author's Note

In the lexicon of American fighter pilots many words and phrases take on new meaning. While a "Bogey" is an unidentified aircraft, a "Bandit" is a confirmed enemy. And when a pilot is told to "Check Six!" the threat is lurking behind—at six o'clock—an aircraft's most vulnerable position. But when you're deep in enemy territory, trapped in a knife fight with a MiG, there's nothing more chilling than hearing your wingman transmit, "Yo-Yo, Baby."

It's like calling 911 and getting a busy signal.

CONTENTS

LINE-UP

-CALLSIGN-	-PILOT-	-IFF	A/A
HAWK 31	SLICK	5111	29X
HAWK 32	LUMPY	5112	—
HAWK 33	BANZAI	5113	—
HAWK 34	GUMBY	5114	92X
JESTER 61	SKI	5115	92Y
JESTER 62	BERT	5116	29Y

E.2 - STEELJAW 1   SWEEP - LOBO ½
TANKER - STEELJAW 2   TARPS - JESTER
                                  DEVIL 11, 12

- COMM -

①	②
STRIKE	TAC
249.8	302.0
FIGHTER	
318.5	

"DOLLY"
301.5

- RENDEZVOUS -

LOBO 51,52	31K
JESTER 63,64	30K
HAWK 31-35	29K
JESTER 61,62	28K
DEVIL 11,12	27K

250 KTS

- WAYPOINTS -

⓪ "MOTHER"

① "PUSH"   33 45 26   0'
           013 52 43

② "COAST" 32 59 02   32'
   IN   013 47 21

③ "IP"   32 28 40   860'
           013 40 12

④ "TGT"   32 50 21   271'
           012 17 21

⑤ "EGRESS" 32 25 33   —
           013 30 10

* BULLSEYE ⟷ TARGET *

- CODE WORDS -

MIG-29 "SHARK"
MIG-23 "BARRACUDA"
MIG-21 "TUNA"
SA-6   "UZI"
SA-3   "BARETTA"
SA-2   "COLT"

- TIME LINE -

PUSH - T-12+00

FEET DRY
COAST IN - T-7+00

TOT - T-0+00

Pilot's kneeboard card (slightly smaller than life-size). On the left is the "Admin" side; on the right is the "Strike" side. (Illustration courtesy of Gregory D. Neary.)

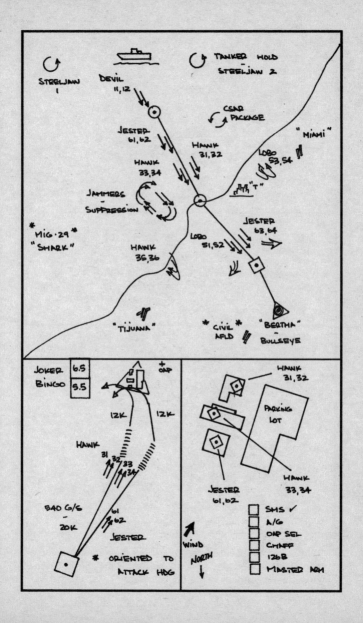

USS *Independence*, Eastern Pacific— Friday, 1 May

At 0900, precisely, the catapult fired, launching the first of twenty-two aircraft into the milk-bowl haze of the morning sky.

The blast deflector lowered to make room for the next jet in line. As crewmen scurried to reset the catapult, the pilot of Coyote 404 completed the final items on her post-start checklist. Like other rookie pilots—the old-timers called them nuggets—she'd mastered the basics of surviving on the flight deck the hard way. It had been a rocky road.

The challenges of flying day and night off the carrier had overwhelmed her classmates, decimating the first cadre of women F/A–18 pilots. All, save her, had washed out or quit. Today's flight would be her fifth since joining the air wing. She had prayed fervently not to make a fool of herself on this, her first bombing mission.

When the taxi director gave her the breakdown

signal, she checked her brakes and returned a thumbs-up.

"Tower, four-zero-four is up and ready, thirty-five," she transmitted, confirming her launch weight in thousands of pounds.

"Roger, four-oh-four."

Her teeth clenched, hands sweating, and shoulders rigid, she tried her best to match the director's rapid signals. It was a bitch. The twenty-year-old director had impatiently gestured for her to get the power up and execute a tight turn, and then, obviously unhappy with her response, he signaled, with sarcastic deliberateness, for her to stop and begin again.

Passed to the catapult officer, she swore when he disappeared in a cloud of billowing steam from the previous launch. Straining to see him, sweat stung her eyes.

There was movement on the left side of the airplane. A sailor was holding a weight board that incorrectly read thirty-six thousand pounds. She was torn. The extra thousand pounds would make for a faster end-speed, and thus a safer launch, but it was hard on the airframe. Following the book, she reluctantly corrected the weight with a hand signal, then looked up to find the director giving her the unofficial, but universally understood, flight-deck gesture to pull her head out of her ass.

"Four-oh-four, are you having a problem?" the Air Boss asked over the radio.

"Negative, sir." Beneath her oxygen mask, she flushed.

"Then follow your director. We've got to get you launched before we can recover your shipmates."

"Shit!" Her hands shook. Her leather flight gloves felt slick with sweat.

With the aircraft finally in position, the catapult officer gave her the signal to run up her engines. She pushed the throttles forward to the first detent. The Hornet hunkered down. Giving the flight controls a full wipeout, she remembered to cycle the rudders this time. Then she nodded to signal her readiness. Next came the afterburners.

Pumped up for the shot, she shoved the throttles hard against the fire wall. The aircraft lurched against its holdback.

After one last glance inside, she saluted with her right hand, then grabbed the handgrip on the windscreen instead of the control stick. Procedure required it. The Hornet was the Navy's first "hands off" aircraft, requiring pilots to let the jet's four computers manage the flight controls during catapult launches.

The cat officer returned her salute and, with a flourish, knelt, touched the deck, and then pointed toward the bow. A waiting sailor hit the fire button.

With breathtaking acceleration, the pilot and her thirty-five-thousand-pound, forty-million-dollar jet were blasted from a standing start to 140 mph.

She felt the first thump halfway down the stroke. It came from the port side. A huge jolt of adrenaline burst through her.

The second thump, just after the aircraft became

airborne, was more severe. It was followed by a series of rapid, banging compressor stalls from the left engine.

Instinctively, she snapped both throttles out of burner. The aircraft immediately began to settle into the wave tops. Realizing her mistake, she pushed the right throttle back against the fire wall, stepping hard on the right rudder pedal. The Hornet's low-altitude warning sounded.

Her mind raced. Remembering procedure, she located and pushed the emergency-jettison button that would explosively separate the bomb racks and the external fuel tank.

Freed of the weight of the one-ton fuel tank and two bomb racks, the aircraft pitched nose-up. The flight-control computers programmed the twin rudders and deflected the horizontal stabilators, flaps, and ailerons to compensate. A second before the computer's commands took effect, the stall warning sounded.

The harsh alarm shattered her confidence in the airplane and her ability to control it. Reaching between her legs, she grabbed the yellow-and-black-striped ejection handle and pulled.

Even as the canopy blew off, the aircraft was recovering. The ejection seat followed, in split-second sequence, rocketing up the rails and clear of the cockpit. By the time the pilot's parachute blossomed, the Hornet's flight-control computers had overcome the severe changes in thrust and weight induced by its former occupant.

The flight-deck crew watched incredulously as Coyote 404, looking for all the world like a rodeo horse pleased to have dumped its rider, halted its gyrations, assumed a modest climb angle, and established a steady course toward the distant horizon. Meanwhile, the dismounted Hornet pilot floated toward the ocean beneath the linen-white canopy of her parachute.

With little choice, the ship's captain reluctantly gave the order to shoot down one of his own aircraft. "Yes, of course. Splash the damn thing."

Disgusted, he turned to watch the ship's helicopter rescue the nugget. Speaking to nobody in particular, he added, "And then there were none."

PART ONE

Rendezvous

CHAPTER 1

Washington, DC—
Monday, 14 Oct/2000 EST

The pilot has already started our descent. Only now do I realize that not only haven't I made a hotel reservation, but I don't have enough cash to cover the fifty-dollar cab ride from Dulles to the city. Meanwhile, back in my dirty apartment, sitting next to a pile of unpaid bills and a loaded answering machine, is yet another houseplant about to make the ultimate sacrifice. And I'm sure I forgot to take out the garbage.

This, my ex-wife would tell you—and anyone else in earshot—is par for the course. My name is Jack Warner; I'm a journalist specializing in military affairs, particularly those involving the Navy. You've read my work. I was nominated for a Pulitzer for my coverage of the Tailhook scandal. Truth is, I'm still pissed off that I didn't win.

Covering Tailhook made me a whole slew of enemies, particularly among the Navy brass; getting that award would have made the aftermath worthwhile. In those first couple years my name triggered a gag reflex among the Navy faithful, not unlike the mention of Charles Manson or, worse yet, Jane Fonda. Of course that's part of the job, but being a pariah, unwelcome at any base or function, made reporting on the Navy downright challenging.

So while every media type in the country lined up to take a whack at the Navy, I started a new series titled, *The Other Victims of Tailhook*. Scores of good officers, despite having been cleared of wrongdoing, had their careers devastated by congressional pundits who smelled votes. After that, the invitations and leads started rolling in.

In retrospect, it was inevitable that I encounter the Secretary of the Navy. You might remember from civics class that the Secretary is a civilian and the Navy's gold-stripers take their orders from him. It turns out that I was a line item on his daily briefing. You know: so-and-so aircraft carrier is steaming here, our nuclear attack subs are deployed there, and oh yeah, Warner is at it again. A guy without a clean pair of underwear to his name, attracting the same level of attention as where our Trident nuclear missiles are hiding? Kinda scary, if you ask me.

Anyway, just this morning my editor, a cynical, cigar-chewing slave driver, gave me the word that not only was the Secretary of the Navy, the Honorable Gerald R. Carroll, in San Diego on an unpublicized fact-finding trip, but he had requested a meeting with yours truly.

Her orders were typically blunt. "Get your ass

over there most ricky-tick, buster. And don't you dare piss him off until *after* you get the quote!"

Intrigued, I hustled over to Miramar Naval Air Station. After being escorted to the commandeered office of the base commander, I met the man himself.

"Jack," he said, after asking his staff to leave us alone, "there's not an organization in the world that scrutinizes itself with more diligence than the United States Navy. When a problem surfaces, we confront it by mobilizing the finest experts in their fields, and we investigate the matter fully, without prejudice, until we reach suitable closure."

My puzzled look made him chuckle.

"Good Lord, would you listen to me? I've definitely been in this job too long. I'm starting to sound like those nonsensical reports I have to wade through every morning." He motioned me to a chair, pulled one up for himself, unbuttoned his jacket, settled in, and peered over his glasses at me. The effect was disarming, a technique he'd no doubt perfected during his career as one of the world's top corporate negotiators.

"Let's get down to business, Jack. I've asked you here to discuss an exclusive."

"Exclusive"—now there's a word to make a reporter's heart race. It was tough keeping my expression neutral.

"As you know," he said, exchanging the official tone for a collegial one, "though we've successfully integrated women into most of the Navy's combat roles, we're a bit behind schedule in the Hornet community."

I couldn't let that one slide. "I take it that's Navy-speak for having all ten women pilots in the first class either quit, wash out, or crash?"

He flinched as if I'd poked him in the chest, but quickly recovered. "Point taken. Of course our official position is that, while it's been less than optimum, the task of flying Hornets off a carrier is unforgiving and demands exceptional talent. Yet, we're completely confident that we'll soon have perfectly capable women pilots joining their male counterparts."

"And what's the unofficial position?" I asked, fishing for that quote.

"Off the record?" He paused, eyeing me while waiting for my acknowledgment of the distinction.

Since I've always found that those three nasty little words tend to stick in my throat, I just nodded.

"Off the record, Jack, it's been a fiasco. I thought we'd lose a couple, maybe even half, but all ten? It makes even the most ardent pro-Navy supporter wonder what's going on."

"Surely you've investigated?"

"Yes, we have. The Navy has conducted a full investigation into each and every case. I've even had my own investigative resources take a look."

"And?"

"And we've uncovered no evidence of organized resistance—it appears as if these young women were just in over their heads."

"But you have your doubts?"

He nodded. "If there is something going on, it's well concealed. One thing for sure, regardless of whether the training was fair or not, the effect has been catastrophic for the gender-neutral movement. The naysayers are coming out of the woodwork claiming that this experience serves as proof that women don't belong at sea." He paused to check my reaction.

I didn't. Better to let him fill the silence.

"This is a volatile issue on the Hill, Jack."

"You mean a threat to certain careers?" I asked.

This time, he didn't smile at the jab. He cut his eyes at me. "Believe me, son, the only place this job is taking me is into an early grave. More than careers are at stake here. This is a political minefield. The proponents of gender neutrality have seen that our budget and support for key programs are intricately connected to our progress on integration. We're being squeezed from both sides. It is not an understatement to say that the immediate future of the Navy is hinging on our ability to successfully put women Hornet pilots at sea."

"I'm struggling to see where I fit in, Mr. Secretary. I can't very well do my job if all of this is going to stay off the record. And frankly, if you want me to look into what happened to those women, the trail is ice-cold. Your investigations have sent anyone involved into hiding. Good hiding by the sounds of it."

He tapped me on the knee. "Jack, you more than

anyone should understand that, in Washington, perception is reality. No matter what we say in the Pentagon, we're perceived as self-serving."

"And your point?"

He laughed. "My staff was right—they said you were a tough guy. Look, I can't prove that those young women ran into some form of organized resistance, but like you, I've been around long enough to trust my gut. Conspiracy or not, women have made it into our other programs, including the F–14. It's clear to me that these women couldn't possibly have received the kind of help they deserved."

"You're the boss. Why not call the senior leadership in here and spell it out for them?"

He stood and walked to the window. A pair of fighters took off, the power of their afterburners rattling the windows. He spoke without turning. "Jack, we both have jobs where we can't afford to fool ourselves. I may be in charge of this organization, but I don't run it." Spinning on his heel, he pointed to the sleeve of his Brooks Brothers jacket. "See? I don't have the stripes." Then he tapped his chest, just above the heart. "And I damn sure don't have the wings. Whatever is going on out there, it's happening at a level that policy, speeches, even threats can't touch."

Walking back, he picked up a photograph from the desk, sat down, and handed it to me. "Let me tell you why I've asked you here. We're getting ready to send two more women pilots out to the fleet."

The eight-by-ten photo showed two young women in flight gear posed near an F/A–18. The smiling one was brunette, the other, fair-haired.

SECNAV said, "I'm told they're two of the best students we have, male or female. This pair may be our last chance before this situation is taken out of my hands. Jack, simply put, I want to put you on this story in hopes that your reputation and presence will buy them enough time to get their sea legs."

"You want me to follow them out to the ship?"

He nodded.

"For how long?"

"Two, three weeks, tops. C'mon, Jack, what do you say to getting a little fresh air and salt spray?"

Was he serious? A juicy exclusive on a carrier? Choking back the desire to jump on the deal, I kept playing it cool. "I'll do it, but I have a couple conditions that are nonnegotiable."

He sat back, appraised me for a moment, the veteran negotiator in him already certain he'd achieved his goal. "Let's hear them."

"I will be the only journalist aboard. I am provided written orders authorizing complete access and cooperation. And, Mr. Secretary, you will read my story in the paper, just like everyone else."

He didn't blink. "Done."

We stood and shook hands to seal the deal. Yet, instead of excitement, I had the sinking feeling that I'd just been completely outplayed by a master: game, set, and match.

As he escorted me from the room, he was gracious. "It's been a pleasure meeting you, Jack."

I stopped before we made it to the door.

"Yes?" he asked.

"Why are you so keen to have me on this job? There are other reporters out there, even ones who would be willing to spin the story any way you wanted to get this piece."

He put his hand on my shoulder and guided me the rest of the way out. "I think you just answered your own question, Jack. Now, please see my aide for those orders. He'll describe your travel arrangements and tell you about your appointment in Washington with the Chief of Naval Operations."

"CNO?" Only then did I see a hint of gloating in his eyes. He was clearly enjoying the surprised look on my face.

"I had to promise Admiral Russell that he'd have equal time with you." Smiling as the door closed between us, he added, "Enjoy your trip. I'll be looking forward to your reports."

The Chief of Naval Operations and SECNAV on the same story? As the aide droned on about administrative details, I scanned my memory for data on CNO. Admiral, that's four stars, Jonathan Russell, a tough, hard-nosed, five-foot-nothing, wiry bundle of ceaseless energy. Russell was reputedly brilliant, widely respected, and just as greatly feared. He was to naval aviation what Admiral Rickover had been to the Navy's nuclear power program. He was only the second CNO not to have attended a military academy.

A former single-seat attack pilot, Russell was a war hero and had been credited by many with rebuilding Navy pride and morale through inspired, old-school leadership. Considered a visionary, he was supposedly the most cantankerous personality in uniform. Russell didn't take crap from anybody, especially Congress. Inside the Pentagon, the betting wasn't on *if* he'd be relieved of command, but *when*.

I was packed, out the door, and on the red-eye before I called my editor from the air-phone.

"Pam, Jack here. I'm on my way to DC on a hot one."

"Jack? Jack who? This certainly can't be Jack Warner, because he works for me, and last time I checked, I still approve all travel."

"C'mon, don't be like that. I told you I've got a hot story for you. And, besides, the Navy is picking up the tab."

"I don't suppose you'll be back to knock out those local assignments sitting on your desk, will you?"

"Give them to West. He needs the practice. Listen, I'll check in Wednesday after I see Russell."

"This better be good, buster."

"Trust me."

"Now, there's a . . ."

Not waiting for the insult, I disconnected and tried, unsuccessfully, to catch some sleep.

CHAPTER 2

Naval Air Station Oceana, Virginia— Monday, 14 Oct/2015

Lieutenant Miranda "Randi" Cole shared a table, in the back-room bar of the Officers' Club, with her flight instructor, Captain Joe "Hoser" Santana. There was enough noise from the jukebox and the medium-sized, Monday night crowd of aviators that they could speak without being overheard.

"I can't help it," Randi said. "I feel like a total idiot every time you kick my butt. I was counting on winning at least once before we were done." She pushed her untouched beer away while avoiding her instructor's glare.

"Great attitude for a fighter pilot." Santana's tone was scathing. "Ms. Cole gets her ass whipped, and she's ready to park the jet and go drive boats for a living."

"Hey! That's below the belt. I never said I wanted . . ."

"I heard what you said, sister. You're bellyaching because I don't *let* you win a fight. Go ahead, tell me that's not what I'm hearing."

When she didn't respond, he rapped the table hard with his knuckles, a signal for her to pay attention. With his student now focused on him, he finished the lecture. "I told you that I was going to make you reach down into your gut. Didn't I?"

She nodded, biting her lip.

"Now, listen up. You wouldn't be shipping out if you weren't ready for the big leagues. But, Randi, you're nowhere near as good as you *could* be."

He took another swallow, giving her some time for his message to sink in.

"Yes, sir. You're right; I just need to work harder," she said, sorry she'd brought it up.

Hoser drained the beer and set the mug down on the table with a resounding thunk. Then he reached over and tousled Randi's hair, like he used to when she was a ten-year-old tomboy.

She accepted the gesture as a peace offering.

Hoser smiled. "I remember sitting right here with your dad. I wish he were alive to see you now."

"Me too."

Bill Cole, Randi's father, had been Santana's best friend and squadron mate. Since the elder Cole's death, Hoser had been the father figure in Randi's life, though the inveterate bachelor was never comfortable with the role, particularly when she'd defied her mother's demand that she stay out of the Navy.

"C'mon, Randi, let's go get some chow. You can buy me a steak, and I'll tell you all about how I used to cream your old man."

She gave him a rueful smile. "No, thanks. I

scheduled some extra time in the dome tonight. I really need to work on my switchology. You showed me this afternoon that I certainly need the practice."

She stood up to leave. "See you tomorrow." Pausing, she leaned over, and whispered, "You'd better check-six." The threat implied that, the next time they'd meet, Randi would be camped out behind him, his jet in her gunsight.

"Not if I see you first, Missy." It was their traditional good-bye.

He watched her leave the bar area and noted the appreciative glances of the males in the room. When one young buck started to say something, obviously about her, to his buddy, Hoser caught his eye, and with just the faintest twitch of his head, left the youngster openmouthed and chagrined.

Not really hungry, and definitely not inclined to let good brew go to waste, Hoser reached across the table and snagged Randi's mug. Taking a long, appreciative pull, he settled back in his chair, surveying the comfortable surroundings.

The aviators, clad in their olive green flight suits, looked pretty much the same as had his peers, nearly thirty years ago. Except these youngsters were drinking lite beer, or even sparkling water, ate yogurt for lunch, and talked about their portfolios with the same enthusiasm his generation reserved for discussing motorcycles and women.

Nope, he decided. This was a different breed being trained to fly forty-million-dollar machines off carrier decks twice as long as the old wooden decks he'd first slammed into. These kids wanted the image of a Navy fighter jock, but they sure as hell didn't want to get their fingernails dirty getting it.

He'd miss kicking their butts.

Eyeing his empty mug, he decided to call it a night, the Navy's policy on DUI being another thing that had changed radically over the years. To a chorus of farewells and friendly insults, he walked into the chilly night, instinctively noting—as every naval aviator would—the size and position of the moon and the resulting visibility. This evening, a huge moon-ball illuminated the base with enough light to cast shadows.

"All the commanders will be flying tonight," he said to himself, reciting the adage that senior pilots finagled to get their night hours when the moon was up, leaving the pitiless, black-assed nights for the junior officers, known as JOs, to throw themselves at the back end of the ship.

Walking to his car, a vintage Corvette he'd bought new, Hoser cast an appraising eye at a lone F/A–18 Hornet as it launched into the night sky on twin tails of flame from its powerful afterburners.

He wondered, again, what life might be like without flying.

With the defiance of a twenty-year-old, despite the chill in the air, Hoser put the convertible's top down, zipped up his gnarled flight jacket, and gunned the sports car out of the parking lot into the night.

CHAPTER 3

**NAS Oceana—
Monday, 14 Oct/2045**

Randi locked her bicycle to a tree outside the simulator building. She flashed her ID card to the guard, signed in, and was given access to the darkened console room. A mission was just wrapping up.

She noted that the pilot had elected to fight against an F–16 foe, rather than one of the older MiG profiles. Interested, she pulled up a chair, exchanging smiles with the console operator. A fixture at the base, he was a former F–14 backseater, or naval flight officer (NFO), whose physical disability left him wheelchair-bound. Nicknamed "Wheels," he had helped train virtually every aviator going through replacement training for the last dozen years.

"So who's in the dome?" Randi asked.

"It's one of the newbies, John something-or-other," Wheels said.

"What level is he on?" she asked, referring to the five levels of difficulty the computer could offer.

"He's started on two, but had me bump him up to

three. He's about to regret that. Watch his knots on this next vertical." The digital display showed the disparity between the airspeed of the simulated Hornet and the Viper as they battled in a looping fight.

Clearly overmatched, and being crowded into a corner, the student pilot needed to sacrifice precious altitude for airspeed. But the F–16 mercilessly pressed its advantage. Within sixty seconds, the student was vainly dodging rounds from the Viper's cannon.

"Knock it off," came the frustrated transmission from the simulator.

"Roger, knock it off," Wheels replied.

"Were you flying that, Wheels?" The kid was challenging Wheels to admit that he'd taken over from the computer and flown the bogey from the console. After twelve years, there was nobody who could touch Wheels in a simulator dogfight, not even the computer on level five.

"You should know better than that, Lieutenant, but if you'd like to have a go . . ."

"Negative. I'm outta time. Maybe later."

Randi stayed in her chair at the console until the student, his blond hair sweat-matted and disheveled, exited the simulator dome. The look on his face, when he realized that she'd seen him gunned by the computer, was priceless.

Wheels laughed and turned to Randi with a smile. "Lieutenant, how long was it before you felt ready to tangle with an F–16?"

"More hours than I can count. How about giving

me a pair of bogies in combat spread, twenty-mile setups? I'm working on the finger drill."

"I guess I'm not ready for a Viper, yet," John said.

Randi entered the massive dome simulator.

The student pilot took a chair next to Wheels, and asked, "Mind if I stay and watch?"

"I'd prefer you stay and learn."

Closing the door behind her, Randi listened to her footsteps echo eerily from the perfectly round walls. The platform she was on would retract when the mission began, leaving her cockpit perched in the center of the golf-ball-shaped structure.

Randi lowered the canopy and got a radio check with the console. "Black Sheep one-zero-one is up and ready," she transmitted.

"Roger, one-oh-one," Wheels replied. "Your bogies bear two-zero-zero for twenty-five, angels medium."

"I hear she's pretty good," John said. "So how long was it before she fought a Viper?"

While Randi ran her first intercept, Wheels pulled up the student database on one of his screens and typed in her name. Up popped hundreds of entries. "Says here, for her first forty hours in the dome, there were no bogies at all. She's got over four hundred hours logged."

John was skeptical. "Nobody could fly that many simulator missions. There's way too many classes, and you gotta study and fly, too. Besides, half the time you can't get on the schedule, unless of course . . ." His expression changed to one of dawning realization. "Unless it's because they wanted to make sure she graduated."

Wheels shook his head. "You're way off course. Take a look at the time and date columns. While the rest of the students were out having fun, she spent her nights and weekends here."

"But what was she doing for all those hours?"

"While her classmates raged around in dogfights, and like you, usually found themselves overmatched, Randi flew a thousand loops, slice turns, and rudder reversals."

As John listened, he checked the screen displaying the current score for Randi's mission. She'd already scored two kills. The computer was on level five.

"So what did you have her do next?"

"It wasn't just me. She went to Captain Santana for help, too."

"Hoser Santana gave private lessons to a woman?"

"Sure. Hoser is always willing to help out a nugget. But they'd better be careful what they ask for—the man is absolutely relentless. To answer your question, once we were satisfied with her basic airmanship, we put a bogey behind her and had her fly the same maneuvers looking over her shoulder. That way, she couldn't use her instruments.

"At first, she couldn't even fly a simple loop. But the repetition had programmed her body to detect the subtle nuances of the airframe, flight controls, and engines that we've programmed into the simulation. Once she learned to tap into those senses, there was no stopping her."

"How long did that take?"

"About sixty hours."

"You mean she flew a hundred missions before she ever fought?"

"At least. By then, of course, she was chomping at the bit. So we raised the stakes again. We asked her to evaluate the bogey's energy package. It forced her mind, which was trained to track and compute her own aircraft's performance, to simultaneously become analytical and make guesses about the bogey's energy state, based on its maneuvers. It's like trying to simultaneously translate English into both Spanish and Russian. I think it almost broke her."

"What did she do?"

"Just what Hoser wanted her to, as it turns out. She was so desperate that she hit the books, studying the data on the various bogey aircraft, memorizing their optimum performance figures like turn-rate, corner velocity, acceleration, etc. Then she spent even more hours, cranked around in the cockpit, watching the simulated bogey fly on level five, knowing that, at its best, the computer would precisely match those numbers.

"And that's how it went. Hoser set the challenge, and Randi struggled to meet it. No sooner would she master one task, than she'd find herself facing a more daunting one. It was pure grunt work."

Wheels backed his chair up and deftly spun to

face the nugget. "So, John, are you ready to follow in her footsteps? With Randi graduating, I'm sure we'll have some time unscheduled this coming weekend."

John was suddenly eager to leave. "That sounds good," he said, quickly standing and heading out of the console room. "Let me check my schedule. I'll get back to you on that."

As the door banged shut, Wheels laughed and spun back to the console. "I didn't think so."

CHAPTER 4

**Washington, DC—
Tuesday, 15 Oct/1145**

I'd slept like a rock. The alarm reminded me that it was time to get to work. I connected my laptop to the Internet, accessed several commercial research databases, and downloaded several stories on female Navy combat pilots.

To date, dozens of women had become carrier jet pilots, or NFOs. Some had even flown the F/A–18 in shore-based assignments, but none had successfully stuck with a seagoing Hornet squadron.

In fact, four out of the initial cadre of ten women had completed their Hornet training syllabus. Each of the graduates had then struggled when they got to the fleet. There had been two mishaps, each blamed on pilot error. Neither woman had been killed, but both were permanently grounded. The other two had turned in their wings.

Department of Defense and congressional investigations concluded that none of the women candidates had demonstrated aptitude equivalent to their male counterparts.

Where less than one in twelve male aviators were selected for Hornet training, the ill-fated ten women were selected en masse. The reports concluded that handing out the choice assignment had been a misguided attempt by the bureaucracy to demonstrate the Navy's commitment to gender equality.

Under pressure from Congress, Secretary Carroll had initiated a program where assignments to combat aircraft were overseen by a group of senior male and female officers, using the same procedures as promotion boards. A search for highly qualified women was initiated.

According to one wire-service story, there were many disgruntled aviators and policy makers unimpressed by SECNAV's new plan. Men were quoted, anonymously, saying that the strike-fighter community was no place for a social experiment. They argued that for fifty years, the aircraft carrier was our country's first line of defense, and that Hornet pilots would be first to fly in harm's way.

There was a guest editorial in the *Post*, written by a former naval aviator. It was his contention that, since Tailhook, political correctness had enveloped the Navy. Along with sexual harassment, he claimed that something he called the warrior spirit was being censored by not allowing guys a safe haven to blow off steam.

"It is especially ironic," the editorial concluded, "that this loss of free expression is imposed on men who, living in one of the world's most dangerous environments, spend six months away from their loved ones, ostensibly to protect the freedoms Americans hold dear."

Next, I plugged into the Library of Congress, where I waded through the Department of Defense budget and acquisition plans. The Navy's stealth program, including a new class of destroyers and a controversial new attack aircraft, faced key committee votes before the Thanksgiving break.

According to the Washington press, there was a noticeable increase in the number of opponents who challenged the usefulness of having the Navy fly aircraft at all in the twenty-first century. SECNAV had more on his plate than women in combat. The Department of the Navy was up against a wall in more ways than one.

It was late before I finished putting my notes in order. I tried to find something interesting on the tube while choking down a rubber-chicken dinner from room service. Giving up on both, I crashed.

The next morning I grabbed a cab to the Pentagon. Despite having been there before, I quickly managed to get lost within the bizarre labyrinth. The Pentagon is famous for being the world's largest, and most confusing, office building. Despite my early start, I made it to Russell's office with less than a minute to spare.

CNO's secretary was upbeat. After welcoming me, she inquired about my trip and asked about the weather in San Diego.

I figured that she was buying time for her boss,

a suspicion that proved correct when the door to his office burst open and three red-faced men bustled out, obviously fresh from an ass-chewing—the Pentagon's version of a continental breakfast.

The ensuing silence was broken by a harsh bellow. "Warner? Where the hell are you?"

I entered his office through a mahogany door that closed discreetly behind me. He remained seated. Steel-gray eyes followed me from behind gold-rimmed glasses. There was no handshake, offer of a chair, or show of good humor.

"I don't have much use for the press, Warner. But I've read your work. Some of it is real horseshit. But some I've seen isn't all that bad."

"Thanks. I guess."

He continued as if I hadn't spoken. "When SECNAV told me what he had up his sleeve, I told him I thought he was nuts. We need a reporter out there like I need a kick in the nuts. But, as he keeps telling me, he's the boss."

I reached out to grab a chair and pull it over.

"Don't bother. You won't be here that long." He tossed a navy blue folder to my side of the desk. "Those are your orders authorizing you to embark on the USS *Ranger*."

"Where's the ship going to be?" I asked, figuring it wouldn't be too terrible to spend a couple weeks off the coast, preferably in the Caribbean.

"By the time you catch up to her, I'd say that *Ranger* will be about five hundred miles east of here." The corner of his mouth twitched.

I gulped at the distance. "Isn't that a little far for air-wing training?"

"Yes."

It dawned on me that the *Ranger* was going on deployment. "Hey, wait a minute! Nobody said anything . . ."

He cut me off. "Not only will you be going on cruise, Warner, you're going to take a ride in a Hornet. I may have no choice in whether you go, mister, but I can see to it how you get there. Since you're supposed to be an *expert* on the military, I'm going to see to it that you get to experience the dangers of carrier aviation firsthand. That is, unless you want to back out?"

I was speechless.

This pleased him. "Don't look so scared. I picked the pilot. Besides, they won't waste a good airplane to take out a pesky reporter."

"Who are *they*?"

"Jesus Christ, Warner. If we knew that, what the hell would we need you for?"

This was incredible. "Are you saying, Admiral, that you're aware of a conspiracy?"

He rolled his eyes. "News flash, Warner: Even a shavetail nugget knows that you don't screw with centuries of tradition without pissing off the old salts. Of course there are some assholes out there who'd like to see these gals fail. The question is, what the hell are they going to do about it?" He paused to gauge the impact of his words.

"Are these women in danger, Admiral?"

He snorted. "Danger? Christ, Warner, we pay them to throw themselves at the back end of a moving ship, in the middle of the night. I guarantee you, if they prove to their shipmates that they can handle that, the rest of this crap will disappear."

"Is that what Secretary Carroll meant by getting them their sea legs?"

"I suppose."

"So, just to make sure I've got this straight— If there are bad guys out there, I'm supposed to hold them at bay, with the power of my mighty pen, until these women have proven they belong? What is this, a college fraternity or the US Navy? I'm an investigative reporter, Admiral, not some PR hack."

"Don't go overboard on me, Warner. Do you really think you can sashay out to one of my ships, earn the trust of the crew, and ferret out an evil plot in a couple weeks? Wake up, young man. You're here because you blew the whistle on Tailhook and the bureaucrats have it figured that having your byline on a few stories will take the media heat off the Department of Defense long enough to get a couple key programs through the political loop."

"And what if I tell you to find another boy?"

For the first time he smiled; it wasn't an improvement. "That's the funniest thing I've heard in months. Now get the hell out of here and let me get some work done."

I was dismissed.

CHAPTER 5

Pentagon—
Wednesday, 16 Oct/0820

There was an aide waiting for me. After briefing me on the legal ramifications of divulging classified material, I was issued an ID card, given bio material on the two women, and instructed on how to contact the CNO's office in case of trouble. Then we drove to Andrews Air Force Base, by way of my hotel. Next, I was loaded aboard a luxurious corporate-type jet and flown to Virginia Beach. The ride took all of fifteen minutes. I was in the Bachelor Officers Quarters, or BOQ, by 10:00 A.M.

The VIP treatment quickly lost its appeal when I computed that my trip cost the government more than I had paid in taxes for the last five years.

I called the *Herald*. My editor explained that she'd already received a phone call from some polite Navy captain, thanking the paper for assigning me to this important story.

"Aren't you worried about losing your star reporter?" I asked.

Like any editor, Pam had a mean streak. "Of course not. Besides, we have insurance. But, come to think of it, if you could arrange to get maimed, now that would make a great story."

"Your concern is touching. I'll keep it in mind when I write my memoirs."

"I'd be worried if I thought anyone with a triple-digit IQ read your work."

"Ouch. Seriously, Pam, I'll be using the ship's satellite link to transmit my stories. They'll be encrypted. You have my code key, right?"

"Yes, we do. But, you'd better send me a test file tonight, just to be sure. We've tentatively scheduled you for six hundred words, every other day, unless something exciting happens out there."

"I'll see what I can do."

"Have you got the digital camera?"

"Yes. But, I'll have to get photos approved by their Public Affairs officer. That can take a while. You'd better pull the file copies of F/A–18s and the USS *Ranger* for the first one."

"Will do, but try to get us something with the women in it. Maybe you can get a shot before you head out. And, Jack?"

"Yes?"

"Be careful out there."

This was a switch. Pam rarely got sentimental. "I'll try."

"Now get off your butt and get me something to slap on page one."

So much for the kinder, gentler boss.

No sooner had I put the phone down than it rang again.

"Warner here."

"Mr. Warner, this is Lieutenant Commander Yunker. I'm the base adjutant. I wanted to welcome you to NAS Oceana and make sure you're settled in and comfortable with the accommodations."

The guy's voice made my skin crawl. I pictured a chinless, career bureaucrat. "Thank you. Everything is fine."

"The base commander wanted to welcome you himself, but I'm afraid we weren't given much notice of your arrival."

His tone insinuated that I'd sneaked onto the base instead of arriving, in plain daylight, on a military jet.

"Well, Commander, I thought that's why you folks used flight plans."

"Oh, absolutely, sir. I only meant that we like to personally ensure that our important guests are well treated."

Much more of Yunker, and I wasn't going to be able to stomach dinner. "Was there anything else, Commander?"

He seemed put off. "Yes, sir. I've been asked to inform you that you have an appointment to be fitted for flight gear at VFA–101 tomorrow, at oh-eight-hundred."

"That'll be fine."

I'd been through this flight-gear business once before, when I'd snagged a backseat ride in a Tomcat years before. Thursday would be a long day, and I was scheduled to fly out Friday. If I was going to interview the women pilots before they left for the ship, it would have to be today. The adjutant reluctantly agreed to track them down—*after* I explained who had signed my orders.

While I was waiting, I walked over to the Navy Exchange and bought six pairs of khaki uniform trousers and shirts; a pair of black, crepe-soled shoes; and enough underwear and socks to last two weeks. I planned to blend in like one of the civilian engineers who often travel on Navy ships. And I'd heard one too many horror stories about ships' laundries to trust that I'd ever get back what I sent down. That explains all the underwear.

Yunker called on my cell phone when I was heading back to the BOQ. He had found Lieutenant Mason, and arranged for us to meet in the lobby, as soon as she finished her transfer checklist. He was still looking for Lieutenant Cole.

An hour later, I was sitting in the BOQ lobby with Lieutenant Amy Mason. She was tall, maybe five-ten, kept her brunette hair in a bun, and had a fresh face and a ready smile. But she wasn't happy when I explained that I was going to follow her out to the *Ranger*.

"I really wish you'd hold off for a month or so, Mr. Warner," she said. "It's going to be tough enough for us to blend in, without the press looking over our shoulder."

I'd anticipated the objection. "I can see your point, Lieutenant. But, if you think about it, lack of press didn't seem to help those other women. Look at it this way. Maybe my presence will help keep the playing field level and give you a chance to prove yourselves."

After pondering my logic for a moment, she brightened. "Well, it's not like I can change your mind or anything. Orders are orders, right?"

"Last time I checked."

"Lieutenant Commander Yunker said you wanted to interview me today."

"Not really." People tend to freeze up when the word *interview* is used, but they usually open up when I tell them I just want to get to know them. "I just wanted to let you know what was going on, get to know a little about you, and then get out of your way. How's that sound?"

"Fair enough. Shoot." She was alert and obviously intelligent. My instinct was that it was important to her to be well liked.

"I hear you've been flying since you were a teenager. Tell me about it."

"I grew up in a farming community, back in Nebraska. My dad and uncles are crop dusters. I started riding along when I was eleven, and learned to fly when I was thirteen."

"You were a crop duster?"

"Absolutely not. That takes a commercial license."

Her eyes told a different story.

"You're not going to confess, are you?"

She shook her head and laughed.

"But, you will admit, won't you, to spending a lot of time flying at low altitude?"

"Yes, that's true. Heck, I was eighteen before I flew over a mile high. That seems so funny to me now."

"All of that experience at low altitude has to help you in the Hornet, doesn't it?"

"Oh, sure. I'm comfortable flying on the deck, but I've still got a lot to learn about using the F/A–18's weapons system to put bombs and bullets on target. Also, the type of aircraft I flew needed to be horsed around; the Hornet's digital flight controls require a very smooth touch."

"When did you decide to be a naval aviator?"

She laughed again, this time with a tinge of embarrassment. "It was that movie."

"You mean *TOPGUN*?"

"Guilty."

"How old were you when it came out?"

"I was in eighth grade. I know it sounds arrogant, but while all the boys talked about how they'd like to fly off carriers, I knew I was going to."

"That was before women were allowed to fly combat aircraft. Were you being naive, or visionary?" Asking a person to classify themselves is often revealing.

"That's a good question, Mr. Warner. I'll have to think about it and get back to you." She smiled, waiting for my next move.

It was obvious that Amy Mason, a young woman who tried to pass herself off as a simple farm girl, was far more astute than 95 percent of the politicians I'd interviewed. She had the rare talent of being able to appear open and innocent, while deftly avoiding trouble. I was impressed.

"I understand that you were the top student in all of your training squadrons. Did that cause you any problems with classmates who might think you were getting preferential treatment?"

"I'd be a fool not to acknowledge that the Navy is bending over backwards to make sure I'm treated fairly. On the other hand, I worked hard, and I had the advantage of flying for half my life."

"Didn't your classmates resent you?"

"Maybe, at first. I tried to turn that around by helping them whenever I could. It worked out for all of us. I've made some friends I'll have for the rest of my life, Mr. Warner."

"Is there anything you'd change, if you could do it over?"

She leaned forward, looked straight into my eyes, and said with conviction, "Mr. Warner, I'm the luckiest girl on earth. You don't know what landing on an aircraft carrier meant to me. It's been my dream since I was a kid. All I can tell you is that, if I don't wake up tomorrow, I'll be satisfied with my life."

CHAPTER 6

NAS Oceana BOQ—
Wednesday, 16 Oct/1530

Lieutenant Mason let me take a few photos and promised to get me a copy of a couple she had that showed her in flight gear. We said our good-byes, and she was off to finish her errands.

Yunker called, now definitely in a sour mood, to report that he'd finally tracked down Lieutenant Cole and had given her my number. He hung up before I could thank him.

While I was waiting, I put together my notes. When the phone rang, I was happy for the excuse to quit working.

"Warner here."

"Hello. This is Lieutenant Cole. I was instructed to call this number."

Noting the precise language, I asked, "Did Commander Yunker tell you why?"

"He said that you are a reporter working on a story for SECNAV."

"That's right. I know you're very busy, Lieutenant,

but I need a few minutes with you today."

She didn't answer immediately.

"You still there, Lieutenant? I promise I don't bite."

"Okay, Mr. Warner, you win. Listen, I've got a few errands to finish up. I'll meet you at the BOQ in forty-five minutes, okay?"

"I'm in the VIP suite. See you then."

Lieutenant Miranda Cole arrived right on time. A thin but muscular five-foot-six, she was very pale, with blond hair that was cut short. She quickly scanned the room, then gave me the once-over.

"Hi, I'm Jack."

"Miranda." She had a firm handshake. "Everyone calls me Randi."

"So, what paper do you write for?" she asked.

"The *San Diego Herald.*"

She nodded. "You reported on Tailhook, didn't you?"

"Who didn't?"

"Good point. I remember reading your stuff, though." She let it lie there without offering an opinion. "So, can I sit down?"

"Sure. Grab a chair at the table there. Want something to drink?" I pointed at the honor bar.

"Want to loosen up my tongue, Mr. Warner?"

"Jack."

"Want to loosen up my tongue, Jack?" The smart-ass was fencing with me.

"I want you to be comfortable. There's soda and fruit juice as well."

"I'll take some water . . . if you've got it."

Unlike Amy Mason, this woman couldn't care less about making a good first impression. Randi Cole was quick-witted and self-assured, bordering on cocky. Exactly the personality traits I'd learned to expect in a fighter pilot. I needed to rattle her a bit.

With my back to her, I fixed us each a glass of sparkling water. Surreptitiously watching her in the mirror, I said, "So, Randi, tell me why a twenty-six-year-old aviator, who didn't make the pilot cut the first time, has what it takes to be a combat Hornet pilot."

Her head snapped toward me. I'd found a sore spot. Pretending not to notice, I delivered the drinks and joined her at the table.

"You've been checking up on me."

"Does that surprise you?"

The bright smile transformed her face. "Fair enough. Why don't we cut the bullshit and knock out this interview?"

"Okay. Why didn't you become a pilot in the first place?"

"Bad timing. We had quotas for females then. There wasn't one for me."

"Did you resent it?"

"Yup. Especially when I had to fly with guys who had no business being pilots. But, once I got to sea, I was too busy doing my job to think much about it."

"You must have done well. You and Mason were the top choices for this assignment." Was there a runaway ego?

She shrugged. "It was a small group of candidates. Besides, it's not like I've done anything, yet."

Score one for her. "Were you given a hard time because you were a woman?"

"Here?"

I nodded.

"At first. I mean, there were a couple phone calls. A voice telling me to quit, 'or else,' and then a hang-up. Stupid shit like that. There's been nothing in the last several months, though."

"I know your dad was a Navy pilot. Is that why you wanted to fly?"

"That was certainly a big part of it. I grew up around jets, and I used to watch my dad do all those air shows."

"Was he a Blue Angel?"

"No. He flew Tomcats. To tell the truth, the crowd always loved him, even more than the Blues. You know how big and noisy the F–14 is, all that flame and the magic of the wings moving back and forth. You ask anybody who's been around for a while who flew the best air shows, and they'll tell you it was Bill Cole."

"What happened to him?"

"He was killed during an air show, Jack." She said this matter-of-factly, then finished off her drink.

I kept quiet.

She filled the silence. "He was flying a show, off the boat, for a bunch of dignitaries. It was a hazy gray day, what we call a milk bowl. The kind of sky where you can't make out the horizon. They don't know exactly what happened, but the official report concluded that it was probably spatial disorientation. Basically, they think he just flew into the water."

"Do you believe that?"

"I didn't. Like Mom, I convinced myself that Daddy couldn't make a mistake that killed him and his backseater. But, I gotta tell you, now that I'm a pilot myself, I see how a slight miscalculation, just a tiny moment of distraction, can lead to disaster."

"And?"

"And it doesn't make a rat's ass about what kind of person you are, or were. Mistakes happen. Most of the time we're lucky enough to recover from them. But, sometimes we don't. It doesn't mean Dad was less of a pilot or father; he just picked the black jelly bean that day."

"The black what?"

She laughed at the look on my face. "My dad used to tell us that life was like a big jar of jelly beans. Every day, when you wake up, you reach in and pull one out. If you're lucky, you get a flavor you like, if not, you get a yucky one. But, somewhere in that jar is one black one. When you grab it, your time's up."

"That sounds like it's as good a philosophy as any. So tell me, why the Navy? Why not the Air Force or a civilian flying job?"

"It's a long story. The *Reader's Digest* version is that I never felt comfortable anywhere else. Lord knows, my mom tried her best to keep me away from it. Right after Dad's death, she moved us to a little town in Pennsylvania, away from my friends and the Navy people we knew. It didn't work out. Neither of us was ready for life in a small town. We ended up moving out to California.

"I became very independent. Of course I had Daddy's insurance money for college. But something was always missing. I couldn't picture myself going to grad school, or getting married, and I sure didn't want to work in an office all day. One weekend, I went to see my uncle, and we talked about flying, my dad, and the Navy. Afterward, I decided to apply for flight training. You know the rest."

"Your uncle was an aviator?"

"Oh, that's right, you haven't met Hoser, yet."

"Your uncle's name is Hoser?"

"Well, he's not a blood relative. Hoser was my dad's best friend. He's also the best fighter pilot in the world."

"What's he doing now?" I figured the guy had to be nearly fifty; certainly too old to be flying fighters.

"Jack, he's right here. Hoser has been a Hornet instructor pilot for the last eight years. He's an institution. I'm surprised you haven't heard of him."

The synapses in my brain finally began firing. I remembered hearing about a grizzled old codger out on the East Coast who consistently kicked everybody's butt in dogfights. "I think I've heard about him, but I thought the pilot's name was Joe something."

"Yeah, Joe Santana. But everybody calls him 'Hoser.'"

"Did he fly with you, or is that not allowed?"

"We kept our relationship quiet. And yes, he flew with me. He's the slave-driver that's been making me work seven days a week since I got here."

This had the feel of a great story. "When can I meet him?"

"He's flying now, but will be done in about an hour. You game to go see what kind of monster I've had to put up with?"

"Absolutely."

"Hoser lives on the beach. I was on my way out there; you can ride along, if you'd like. We can grab a bite to eat while we're waiting."

I took advantage of the twenty-minute drive to question Randi further. When I asked about the previous women F/A–18 pilots, she was candid.

"Some of those girls weren't ready for the Hornet. I know several instructors who flew with them. There was a lot of concern about safety."

"What have you heard about the West Coast training squadron?"

"Well, I did hear that the cards are stacked against women pilots."

"In what way?"

"It's hard to describe, but it's like, when it comes to women, all the rules are enforced."

"Unfairly?"

"It's more subtle than that. I mean, nobody enforces *all* the rules. We'd never get anything done if they did. What if a traffic cop suddenly started writing tickets for every possible infraction? You couldn't drive three blocks without getting busted."

"Is that what happened out there?"

"That's what I heard. It would be a pretty effective strategy. Document all sorts of minor infractions and show a trend, so that when a big mistake was made, it would look inevitable."

Not only was it an insightful observation, it jibed with the results of the investigations. "What about the four women who made it to the fleet?"

"I gotta wonder if they were given the kind of support nuggets usually get. Don't forget, I've already done a cruise. Every nugget I know struggled at first, but most came around with some coaching and patience. Sometimes you've got to hold a pilot's hand until they gain experience. That's where having a veteran backseater really pays off. But, then again, the Hornet is single-seat. If those women weren't being supported by their squadron mates, they'd have nobody."

Hoser's house was built on stilts, like most of the beach dwellings. After turning into the long driveway, both sides were suddenly illuminated by twin rows of blue lights, just like an airport taxiway. As we parked underneath the house, floodlights bathed the area in amber. The walls of the carport were painted Navy gray and had shipboard markings painted convincingly on them.

"Isn't it the coolest?" asked Randi.

"I've never seen anything like it."

Despite the unusual nature of the house's exterior, I wasn't prepared for the decor. Two beautiful, vintage wooden surfboards were mounted on one wall and another was made into a coffee table. A fourth, propped in the corner, looked suspiciously like it had been used recently, which would be a remarkable thing to do. I'd surfed for years and knew each of those boards had to be worth at least ten thousand dollars, maybe a lot more.

A real jukebox sat near the bar. Randi walked over, grabbed a handful of quarters from a wall-mounted slot machine, and programmed a stack of records. Over in the corner sat a full Olympic weight set. Judging from the weight on the bar, the owner was an exceptionally strong man.

There wasn't one thing that looked like a woman had been involved in its selection. "This place is great," I said, meaning it.

"I thought you'd like it. Fix us a drink, while I rustle up some food. I'll take a rum and Coke."

I found the bar impressive. It was stocked with quality liquor, including several specimens of single-malt scotch.

"What's upstairs?" I asked, delivering Randi her drink in the immaculate kitchen.

"It's the bedroom. C'mon, this you gotta see."

I followed her up the circular staircase, surprised to find a thick manila rope hanging down the middle.

"What's he do with the rope, or don't I want to know?"

"That's how he gets up and down. Hoser's kind of a fitness nut."

While I puzzled over what kind of guy surfs on

wooden surfboards and climbs a rope to his bedroom, I arrived at the top of the stairs. The bedroom was lofted and had a commanding view of the downstairs. Outfitted like a ship's cabin, the walls and deck were done in teak and mahogany, the windows were port-holes, and the lamps were kerosene. Randi lit two of them, which provided a warm glow. I ran my hand over the trimwork. It was exceptional.

"Lie down on the bed, Jack."

It was a waterbed. While I was trying to figure out how he buttressed the second story to hold its weight, I lay back and found myself staring up into the night sky. The roof above the bed was an enormous skylight that provided a million-dollar view of the stars. With the lamplight, waterbed, and wood paneling, I felt like I was berthed in a real clipper ship.

Randi was standing at what looked like sliding closet doors. They were intricately inlaid with differ-ent types of wood to depict a view of a distant, moun-tainous island.

"Check this out," she said, as she unlatched and slid one door aside to reveal a balcony overlooking the ocean. I joined her outside. The sound of crashing waves from the moonlit Atlantic came to us on a fresh sea breeze.

"This is my favorite place in the whole world," Randi said. "Hoser bought it as a beach shack, with my dad and a few buddies, twenty-eight years ago, just before I was born. It was almost destroyed a few years later, during a hurricane. Fortunately, it was insured. By then, the other guys were all married and couldn't really afford not to take the cash. Hoser bought out their shares and rebuilt it.

"He built this?"

"All by himself. Hey, are you hungry?"

"Yeah."

"Let's go eat!"

She ran through the bedroom, jumped and caught the thick rope, and slid down it like she'd been doing it all of her life. I gave it a try and learned that it was a lot harder than it looked. The rope burned my uncallused hands. I landed heavily, only to hear Randi's laughter as she disappeared into the kitchen.

I joined her and she put me to work chopping onions while she heated some homemade chili. We took our bowls and a couple draft beers from the tap on the bar and went outside to sit on the porch. The chili was hot and tasty.

Our reverie was broken by the unmistakable sound of a small-block V–8 being downshifted, the headers filling the evening with a sweet-sounding rumble. "Don't tell me," I said.

"That's the man himself."

"What's he driving? A Vette?"

"Good guess. He's got a sixty-five frog-back. That's a balanced and blue-printed three-twenty-seven with a Holley double-pumper, a four-speed Muncie rock-crusher, and a four-eleven, posi-track rear end. And, Jack . . ."

"Yes?"

"It's cherry. He bought it new."

Envy is such an ugly emotion.

**Beach House—
Wednesday, 16 Oct/1830**

He killed the engine halfway down the driveway and coasted in. As before, the nifty lights came on automatically, the effect dramatic from our perspective. The Vette's top was down; its chrome and paint sparkled.

Before the driver was out of the machine, he was bellowing. "Cole? Where's my beer? A man could die of thirst around here!"

His voice was distinctive, raspy, like his vocal cords had been sandblasted. Not so much like a smoker, more like a football coach who was permanently hoarse.

Randi stepped out into the light, and said, "Get your own damn beer, you old goat. And while you're at it, get one for me and my friend here."

"Friend?"

I could see him squinting in my direction as he extracted himself from the car. Joe Santana was a big man. At least six-four, he had to go 230 pounds.

Dressed in a beat-up leather flight jacket, green flight suit, and boots, he was the biggest pilot I'd ever seen.

He covered the distance between us in quick, powerful strides, grabbed Randi under the arms, and lifted her straight up, effortlessly, above his head.

"Now, are you going to get me a beer, or do I toss your raggedy ass into the ocean?"

Randi was giggling like a schoolgirl. "Okay, okay, I'll get you a beer," she said, as he set her down.

As soon as he let her go, she punched him wickedly hard in the stomach, putting her shoulder and hips into the blow. With a sound like a basketball smacking into a wall, the punch would have put any normal man on his knees. Santana was unfazed.

He turned to me, held out his hand, and said, "I'm Hoser."

We shook. I could feel strength being restrained.

"Jack Warner."

His eyes were striking—sky-blue—and framed with permanent laugh lines.

As we entered the house he asked, "Did Randi show you around?"

"Sure did. This is an incredible home you've built. I think it's terrific."

Shrugging off the praise, he said, "Oh, hell, this is just a beat-up old beach house. So, what brings you out here, Jack?"

"I'm a reporter from the *San Diego Herald*." Somewhat nervously, I waited for him to make the connection to Tailhook. "I've been assigned to cover the transition of both Lieutenant Mason and your niece to the fleet."

His eyes narrowed. "So you're the one."

"One what?" Randi asked, listening in from the kitchen.

"Your friend and I are scheduled to go bag some traps on the *Ranger*. The skipper called me in today to tell me I was going to have to drag some VIP out to the boat. I thought I was going to have some pissant to baby-sit. But, actually, this is going to work out just fine."

He lowered his voice and whispered confidentially, "To tell the truth, my eyes aren't so good anymore, Jack." He squinted at me, with a contrived look of concern. "I was worried they'd find out and pull the plug on my flying, but you can help me out. If you can just get me pointed at the back end of the ship, I'll grease her in. What do you say?"

"I say you're full of it, Captain. Admiral Russell told me he handpicked my pilot."

"SLUF Russell? How is the old bird?"

"Crusty. What did you call him? *SLUF?*"

He chuckled. "Yeah, it stands for, *Short-Little-Ugly-Fucker*. Fits, don't you think?"

"Perfectly."

He stepped closer to the kitchen and spoke in a stage whisper, "Hey, you want to see some pictures of Randi—naked?" He winked before heading to a bookshelf stocked with photo albums.

"Hoser, no!" Randi flew around the corner and

hurled herself onto the big man's back. Unimpeded, Santana calmly walked over to me, despite Randi's attempt to strangle him with a mean-looking forearm, and handed over an album opened to two pages of toddler pictures. Randi on the beach, in the kitchen, in the park, all sans clothes. As a child, she'd been quite uninhibited.

"Yeow!"

When I looked up, Randi had sunk her teeth into Hoser's ear. He reached up and pinched her nose until she let go, then he dropped to a knee and flipped her onto the carpet. She jumped back up and tried to attack again, but he held her off easily with a big hand on her forehead.

"What do you think, Jack? Would the boys in her new squadron like to get hold of those?"

"Well, I could certainly use one or two in my story. With a little luck, we could get these published in a couple hundred papers across the country."

Randi ran herself out of gas. "Hoser, one of these nights, I'm going to come in here and burn those damn things. You're just a sick old man. And you, too, Jack."

Fun and games aside, it was time to get to work. "So, tell me what kind of teacher Hoser makes?" I asked, taking a seat on a barstool.

He plopped down on the couch. "Yeah, spill it. This ought to be good."

From the look of consternation on her face, I got the feeling that she was struggling to separate the teacher from the uncle.

When she finally spoke, she'd lost her playfulness. "For ten months, he's been hammering on me. It seemed like nothing, I mean *nothing*, I did met his standards. I had no idea how difficult it would be. It's been brutal."

Hoser started to protest, but she silenced him with a withering look. "We haven't been very nice to each other. When it comes to flying, the man is a perfectionist. It was hard to take so much criticism. There were times I went to bed convinced he was being an asshole because I'm a woman."

"And now?" I asked.

"Now, I'm convinced he's just an asshole."

"Hey!" said Hoser.

She walked over to the couch and curled up next to him. "But, I always woke up knowing that he loved me and that I was lucky to have him in my life."

Santana was quiet, but obviously moved.

To give them some time, I went to the kitchen, and jotted down some notes. Even if the story about Cole and Mason didn't turn up anything exciting, this angle about an old curmudgeon mentoring a young woman in the art of flying high-performance aircraft was pure gold.

Five minutes later, Randi called my name. I found her standing behind the bar, pouring Cuervo Gold into three shot glasses.

"Listen, you two, I'm leaving tomorrow for six months at sea. And I don't want to sit around crying in my beer. We've got to drink tequila."

Hoser shot up out of the couch, to join us at the

bar. "Goddamn, youngster, when you're right, you're dead right."

Over the course of the evening, we put a good dent in the bottle. We talked until midnight. Hoser and I swapped surfing stories, and Randi regaled me with tales of the man's legendary antics. There were plenty. He'd flown four combat deployments during Vietnam, the last two with his best friend, Bill Cole.

Randi fell asleep in an overstuffed chair. I followed minutes later, crashing on the couch. Just before I went comatose, I watched, unable even to lift my head, as Hoser climbed the rope.

Beach House—
Thursday, 17 Oct/0630

The aroma of bacon roused me. Randi, apparently immune to hangovers, was up and cheerfully cooking breakfast. Afterward, sipping our coffee, the three of us discussed the day.

"I'll take Jack with me and get him squared away with flight gear," Hoser said.

"Great. I've still got to put some stuff in storage. And can I leave my car here while I'm on cruise?" Randi asked.

"No sweat. Leave me the keys, and I'll crank it up now and then. Anything else you need?"

"Nope. Amy and I are scheduled to COD out to the ship fourteen-hundred. I guess we'll see you out there tomorrow."

"What's a COD?" I asked.

"Carrier Onboard Delivery," Randi answered. "It's a prop airplane that hauls cargo and people out to the carrier."

"How come you have to go by COD, and I get to go by Hornet?"

"Well, we're just nuggets. You're a big-time VIP reporter. I think someone wants to impress you, and besides, Hoser never passes up a chance to bag traps."

I knew that bagging traps referred to an aviator collecting multiple landings on the carrier during one flight. This raised their personal trap count, a totem that all naval aviators cherish. "How many traps do you have, Hoser?" I asked.

"About fourteen hundred and eighty-nine, but who's counting?"

Nearly fifteen hundred was a staggering number. There probably weren't five active aviators with over a thousand traps left in the Navy. He had to be setting the record.

"Is there a chance they'll let you get eleven traps on our flight?" I asked, another story sliding into my sights.

"I don't think so. This is a fleet boat, going on cruise. And this jet isn't configured for a lot of action."

"I don't understand."

Randi stepped in. "What I think the big guy is getting at, Jack, is that he's a single-seat fighter pilot."

She was diplomatically letting me know that my presence was not desired. "Oh, of course."

Hoser nodded his agreement. "No offense, buddy. I just want to hit that number the way I started out: solo."

To change the subject, I asked, "Hoser, what kind

of advice do you have for Randi as she heads out to sea?" I asked.

"Yeah, Uncle, let's hear it," Randi added.

He got up, walked to the shelf with the row of photo albums, picked one out, and came back to the breakfast table. After thumbing through it and finding the right page, he turned the book so that we could see. Hoser tapped a black-and-white picture of a pilot, still in flight gear, standing by a jet on the deck of an aircraft carrier. The pilot was smiling and pointing to a hole the size of a bowling ball in the tail of his plane.

"Daddy," Randi whispered.

"Yup," said Hoser.

Breathing softly, she obviously was taken by surprise. "I haven't seen this in years. You took it, didn't you?"

"Yup." He carefully pried the plastic covering off and slipped the photo out of its holder. "Everything you need to know is contained in this picture, doll."

Randi held the photo carefully by the edges, staring deeply into the past. On impulse she turned it over and read the back. Her jaw clenched, she nodded, and offered it back to Hoser.

"You keep it," he said.

Randi glanced at me. "Here." She handed me the photo. Written in faded, but still-legible ink was the inscription:

"When the shit hits the fan, you gotta jink, or die!"

—Wild Bill, 21 Oct 1969

"Have you ever told me about that mission?" Randi asked.

"No, I don't think so. It wouldn't have made any sense to you then, anyway." He sipped his coffee, pausing long enough to worry me that he wouldn't continue.

Finally, in a quiet voice, he began the story. "That was a tough one. Your father and I were flying cover for a strike when some MiGs popped up, east of us. We lit the burners and separated from the pack. At ten miles the MiGs turned north and dived for the deck, but we had a lot of smack. We followed them down into a valley and closed to about three miles, just outside of missile range, when our EW gear went crazy."

Hoser's right hand clenched and unclenched. His eyes closed. When they opened, he was back in the cockpit, nearly thirty years ago. "The wily bastards had led us into a flack-and-missile trap. We were taking fire from both sides of the valley. We couldn't climb without taking a missile up the ass, and we sure as hell couldn't turn around without getting clobbered. But, if we kept heading northbound, we'd run ourselves out of gas and into God knows what. It was definitely shit city."

"What else could you do?" Randi asked.

He blinked, then turned to answer her. "That's exactly what I asked your dad over the radio." He laughed. "The schmuck radioed back, 'Jink, you sonuvabitch, or die!' And, that's exactly what we did. We horsed those jets all over the sky—lots of Gs—right down on the deck. Their gunners were good, but we kept them from drawing a bead on us. I never worked so hard in my life; we both overstressed our aircraft. But staying unpredictable saved our lives."

"How so?" I asked.

"There was a break in the western ridgeline, but of course that was the wrong direction. We needed to head east. Yet Bill called a ninety-left, and we were out of there before they knew it. Later, we found out there were MiGs waiting to ambush us, but we'd surprised them. They were waiting on the eastern side."

"Weren't you low on gas?" Randi asked.

"Hell, yes. We were on fumes. And both of us had taken some hits. Your dad was worse off, though. He was losing hydraulic fluid, and his rudder was shot to hell. Anyway, we got in touch with a tanker. Luckily, it was a Whale driver we both knew, and the crazy bastard met us right over the beach. Your dad plugged first, took five hundred pounds, then let me in. I took a squirt, and we swapped again. We nursed those broke-dick airplanes out to the boat, and that was that. I always carried a camera in the jet. I snapped that photo before we went below."

Randi slipped the photo into her purse and, after wishing us a safe flight, drove off to finish her errands.

Hoser and I rode to the squadron with the top down. He drove the Vette with effortless precision. I asked him if he thought there was a conspiracy to keep women from flying Hornets.

The near-permanent smile left his face. "Why would you bring that up on a gorgeous morning like this? Looking for another Tailhook, Jack?"

"No. That's not . . ."

"Don't look so surprised, Jack. I knew who you were as soon as I heard your name. Listen up. I was at Tailhook, mister. That was some bad shit the press pulled on us. Especially since we just got back from winning a war."

"I understand your resentment, Captain. But that's ancient history. Right now, I've got a job to do, and I didn't dream this assignment up. It was handed to me." I held up the folder with CNO's seal on. "And judging from the amount of time and effort spent on investigations, and the fact that they're sending me to the ship, the Navy brass must think there's a threat to these women. The question is, are you going to help me out, or what?"

He didn't speak for several minutes. In the meantime, I was left to ponder the wisdom of pissing off the man who was going to fly me out to the carrier. Visions of being violently airsick had me ready to beg forgiveness, when he broke the silence.

"What do you want to know?"

"Has there been any sign of trouble?"

"There was some harassment when they first got here. Late-night phone calls, I heard about some graffiti on their lockers, that kind of puppy shit."

"Randi told me about a couple phone calls, but nothing about graffiti. And Amy didn't mention anything about it."

He glanced at me. "It was Amy that drew most of the flack. I think someone thinks she's the weaker of the two. Randi came to me because she was concerned about her."

"What did you do?"

As soon as I heard about it, I held a men-only pilots meeting where I laid down the law."

"The law? What kind of law?"

"The kind where I bust the head open of the first guy I find pulling a chicken-shit stunt like threatening somebody over the phone. I told everybody in the room that I'd flown with both women and that they could fly circles around any student we had, and kick the butts of a few instructors, as well. After that, the girls weren't bothered again; they both think it was just one moron who gave up. The last thing they want to do is stir it up again."

"So, why do you think that there's going to be a problem on the ship?"

"Because, it's more than one or two guys . . . hey, goddamn it, I didn't say I thought there was going to be a problem out there!"

"You have now." It's an old lawyer's trick to phrase a question so that a person instinctively defends a hidden belief.

He glared at me. This was disconcerting, as we were on a two-lane road lined by ditches and trees on both sides. Thankfully, the car never wavered. "Screw this. I don't have the patience for these word games. So here's how it's going to go down from now on between us. Go ahead and ask away; I'll answer if I feel like it.

But if you quote me without my permission, I'll rip your head off and spit down your neck. Got it?"

Despite the threat of decapitation, I found it a refreshing change from "off the record." I knew this wasn't the time or the place to trot out arguments about journalistic integrity and the First Amendment. Yet I still made the egotistical mistake of going for the last word. "We'll both do what we have to do, Captain, but if you've read my stuff, then you already know how I work."

Santana grunted, glanced in the rearview mirror, then downshifted the Vette and punched the accelerator. With a bark of tires and a quick flick of the steering wheel, we pulled into the opposite lane and accelerated alongside a seemingly endless line of morning commuters. The speedometer swept past one hundred without pause. He appeared completely relaxed.

The combination of noise from the wind and the engine made talking impossible. When a large truck crested the small hill in front off us, I could see no place to get back into our lane. I grabbed his forearm; it felt like a piece of cordwood. Still, his expression remained impassive. Just when I was sure we were going to die, with the truck's lights flashing a warning, Hoser cut left instead of right—through an unmarked break in the trees—onto a skinny blacktop road angled to parallel the main thoroughfare. A sign declared restricted access; we were heading toward a back gate onto Navy property.

After checking our ID cards, the sentry saluted

Santana, who drove sedately until we came to a small clearing. Gravel crunched under the tires as he pulled the car over, parked, and shut off the engine.

I didn't trust myself to speak.

He twisted in his seat to look at me, and said, "Now you know how I work. Any questions?"

"Yeah. Are we done playing games? Because I don't have time for this shit. Besides, if you think that bush-league stunt impressed me, you haven't seen San Diego's rush hour."

He chuckled while pulling up the sleeve of his flight suit. His forearm bore a set of welts that clearly outlined my grip. Soon he was laughing: a great, rocking, belly laugh. Still giddy from the adrenaline—unable to help myself—I joined in.

A couple of minutes later he gathered himself, wiped his eyes, and said, "You're okay, Jack. So what is it that you want to know?"

There was no sense being subtle. "Do you have personal knowledge of a conspiracy to keep women out of the Hornet community?"

"No."

"Do you suspect that one exists?"

He nodded. "I don't have a feel for how widespread it is. There may just be isolated pockets of resistance. Or there may be something more organized."

"If it is a conspiracy, why hasn't evidence surfaced?"

"Who said it hasn't?" he asked.

I tapped the folder in my lap. "Several investigative teams."

"Maybe the proof is staring everyone in the face."

"How so?"

"Well, you're the expert investigator. I'm just an old stick-and-rudder man, but it seems like sometimes the best evidence is not what's been found, but what hasn't."

He had a point. "Give me an example."

"I saw some of the grade sheets for those West Coast gals. They were too perfect, not a smudge, not one misspelled word. That's not normal by a long shot. Most flight instructors write like doctors. And then there's what wasn't in there."

"For instance?"

"There were no positive strokes. Every write-up was bone-dry. See, instructors used to be students, too, Jack. When a youngster is having trouble, you always try to soften the blow, by highlighting something good, even if it was just the way the kid preflights the jet. Anything to give the student a little ray of hope. There just wasn't anything like that in the packages I saw."

The implications, if he was right, were severe.

"Are the girls in danger, Hoser?"

He cut his eyes at me. "Jack, you're either not listening, or you're playing games again. You can add it up just as easily as me."

"Humor me."

He ticked the reasons off on the fingertips of one hand. "The guys who pulled off the West Coast stunt had enough authority and organization to make sure the students flew with certain instructors. Yet, somehow, they avoided detection. Then, before I stepped in, Randi and Amy were catching grief right here. It's possible that there's a group spanning both coasts, that communicates without being discovered, and has the balls to risk their careers. You put it together. Are they likely to knock it off just because I raised some hell? The way everything stopped cold, as soon as I threatened to blow the lid, makes me think they've just gone to plan B."

"What's your best guess about plan B?"

"Get those girls out on the boat and hang them out to dry. As you're about to find out, flying off a fleet boat is a whole different world. There are a hundred chances to screw up. Lose your confidence, and it can all fall apart in a hurry. Hell, just taxiing around the flight deck can be lethal."

"What do these people gain by waiting until the women get to the boat? Isn't that too late?"

"Not for Amy and Randi. They were too solid to get bumped in training. But if these two fail at sea, it makes a convincing argument that no woman can hack it."

"Lieutenant Mason told me she has dreamed about this for years," I said. "As for Randi, I'd bet my next paycheck that she won't give up while she's got an ounce of fight left in her."

He tilted his head back and looked up at the sky for several seconds, a fist tapping lightly on the steering wheel.

When he spoke, his voice was deadly serious. "That's exactly what scares the living shit out of me."

CHAPTER 9

NAS Oceana—
Thursday, 17 Oct/0815

The first time I'd gone through the cycle of getting fitted for flight gear, learning to use the survival equipment, flying the simulator, and memorizing the list of do's and don'ts—mostly don'ts—I found it exciting, despite all the sweat and an almost over-whelming sense of clumsiness. This time, the novelty was absent. It was more like work.

One-time flyers make do with small, medium, or large. I was torn between wearing a too-tight, headache-inducing helmet, or a loose, floppy one which, I knew from experience, would slide down to the bridge of my nose and cover my eyes as soon as Hoser decided to put on a few Gs. I begged the parachute rigger for some help, and with the aid of twenty bucks' worth of persuasion, we added enough padding to keep the big one in place without squeez-ing my head like a grape.

From the paraloft, we went to the survival school, where I was instructed on the ejection seat, how to use it, and what to do if I ended up hanging under a parachute.

Next up was the simulator. Hoser proved to be an excellent teacher. He managed to distill a million details to a few, very important ones. And those he explained in simple, understandable terms.

"See that long, yellow-and-black-striped handle? If you grab it and rotate it aft, the canopy is going to come off, and it's going to get very noisy. If that happens, you'll want to lower your seat to get out of the windblast. See that red handle, there? That's the gear handle. I'll tell you when I'm lowering or raising the gear. When they come down, we want to see these three green lights. If one is out, test it first, like this, then tell me."

In that fashion, we went through all of the airplane's major systems. He talked me through a take-off and had me fly the aircraft through several basic maneuvers. With his coaching and the eye-popping displays, it wasn't too hard. Everything about the cockpit layout seemed to be designed for convenience and usefulness. I could understand how somebody might make the mistake of thinking that, because it was so easy to fly from point to point, it would be easy to use in combat.

When I mentioned it to Hoser he laughed and proceeded to give me a little example of what the Navy calls "task saturation." He had me fly the simulator at one thousand feet and then had me select a tactical navigation mode. I was supposed to follow the computer's commands for specific headings and speeds, while trying to adjust the radar and select a weapon. In less than a minute, I crashed and had to endure the ignominy of flashing red lights and a blaring alarm. There were just too many things to track.

"How in the world do you teach students without killing them?" I asked.

"We work up to it gradually. But, even so, it can be overwhelming. I had one student tell me that it was kind of like trying to rub your belly and pat your head, while riding a bicycle in rush hour."

After we finished with the simulator, Hoser took me out to the flight line. Aircraft were coming and going. Young sailors were scurrying over, under, and around the jets.

Santana was extremely popular. Everywhere we went smiling sailors hailed him. He knew all their names and more than a little about their personal lives. I watched him talk with at least twenty individuals, knowingly inquiring about spouses, babies, and new motorcycles.

He also knew the status of every jet in the hangar and the flight line. We stopped to kibitz with a crew of engine mechanics who were swapping engines in one of the aircraft.

"So, Chief Martinson, what the hell was wrong with that AB fuel pump?" Hoser asked.

"It was programming too rich, just like you said, sir. We've swapped the whole assembly, and I'm sending this one off to the Tech Rep. That was a good call, sir. Saved us a whole night of troubleshooting."

The young mechanics clustered under the jet nodded their agreement.

"Lucky guess, Chief. Even a blind squirrel finds a nut once in a while."

Again, the humble response to a compliment. The man was a fighter pilot; therefore, he had a big ego. But he managed to keep it well hidden.

After we checked me out of the BOQ and stashed my gear at the squadron for tomorrow's flight, we drove over to base operations and tracked down Cole and Mason as they were boarding the COD aircraft. Hoser pulled them aside and, out of my earshot, conducted what looked to be their last lecture. Both of them were smiling when he handed them identical packages. After saluting smartly, each gave him a hug. Then they were off. We watched their lumbering aircraft climb to altitude and disappear over the horizon. Hoser was unusually quiet.

"Are you sad to see them go?" I asked.

He waited several moments before answering. "Yes, and no. You see, Jack, I just sent off two of the best students I've ever had. One of them, I love like a daughter. Yet, part of me can't help but think that sending women to sea is basically wrong."

He started the car and drove slowly out of the parking lot. "It's a man's world out there. Nothing anybody says is going to change that."

A few moments later, he shook his head and let out a sigh. "Listen to me. I sound like a dinosaur. It's just complicated, that's all. They'll do fine. The Navy has changed; it's time I did, too."

"What did you say to them?"

"I told them that every swinging dick out there started out as a nugget, and I could personally provide embarrassing stories about ninety percent of them. I told them to expect to make mistakes out of ignorance, but not to get down on themselves. That the most important thing is to learn something every single time they touch an aircraft. And I told them to expect people to be cold at first, to let their flying do their talking, and to keep a smile on their faces."

"What was in the packages?"

"Today's paper, some new magazines, and a bunch of candy." He answered my puzzled look. "It's bribery. The boat's already been out for a while. They're to give the candy to the troops, the magazines to the chiefs, and the paper to the Operations officer. It's a small thing, but it'll buy them a little breathing room."

"Why the Operations officer? Why not the CO?"

"For crying out loud, Jack, use your noggin," he said, tapping me on the head as we headed out to the beach. "You can't walk in and start sucking up to the skipper. Besides, the ops officer signs the flight schedule, buddy. If you're going to suck up, do it to the guy who can keep you flying!" He laughed and downshifted the Vette, which responded by leaping forward with a bark of rubber and a full-throated growl.

A little while later, he said, "I'm counting on the fact that with you out there, the bad guys will keep a low profile and the girls will get enough time to build up some self-confidence. Trust me, they're both damn good pilots. Amy is a helluva fine bomber, and Randi can kick ass in a dogfight. They both fly smooth formation and know their weapons systems. All they need is to get a dozen or so missions under their belts, and they'll be fine."

He turned to look at me, again. "Jack, I need you to keep those assholes off their backs for a week or two. Can you do that for me, buddy?"

It was time to set the record straight. "Hoser, my job is to report what I see—period. I can't do that and be a baby-sitter."

Again the frown.

"Listen," I said. "I've got to remain objective. Without that, my work is useless. If you want to help, give me an idea of who these assholes are."

Grunting, he pulled a folded piece of paper out of his jacket pocket and handed it to me.

"What's this?" I asked.

"A couple names. If there is a plot, they're the types that might be involved. They might not be the only ones, but you'll want to watch these guys."

This was more like it. "What made you settle on these two?"

"I've been flying in this man's Navy for more years than you can count. I've heard these two yap about what they think of women pilots. That first guy there is definitely slimy enough to do something about it. Just remember that if they are dirty, you're a threat to their careers, their reputations, and their families. Don't get caught alone on the ship with them. By the way, there's someone out there who can help. His name's on the bottom of that paper."

It was a name I knew. "What's Master Chief Cardone doing out on the *Ranger*? He was back at Point Mugu last I heard."

"You know Art?"

"Sure. He's a legend. I did a piece on old-fashioned leadership in the new Navy, and he was my crusty chief petty officer."

"They were having some readiness problems in one of the Hornet squadrons on the *Ranger*, VFA–305. That's the one Amy is joining. Cardone was brought out to straighten up the maintenance department a few months ago. If you have any problems, get to him. Tell him what's going on. He'll know what to do."

"Thanks for the tip. By the way, how long will you be able to stay out there tomorrow?"

"I probably won't even get out of the jet. After you hop out, and they download your gear, I'll be a dot."

"A dot?"

He laughed. "Yeah, as in a dot on the horizon, heading back to my hooch and a cold brewski while you're bunking down with some Sasquatch Tech Rep, rubbing your shins, and wishing you were back on the beach."

I couldn't begin to decipher what he meant, but I knew I'd find out soon enough.

"Hey, could you pull over at that supermarket?" I asked.

"Sure, but I probably have whatever you need at the house."

"I don't think so. I want to pick up a bunch of magazines and some candy."

"You're learning fast."

CHAPTER 10

Beach House—
Thursday, 17 Oct/1800

I spent the rest of Thursday afternoon drafting my first article. Since it was going to be a series, I used it to introduce the readers to the main characters, Cole and Mason.

After a brief background description, I laid out the recent history of women in the Hornet community, the ensuing controversy, the new pilot-selection process, and the performance of the two women to date. Instead of plunging into the shadowy conspiracy theory, I focused on the challenges awaiting them on the carrier.

Women Combat Pilots Tested At Sea
Page 2

Though both women have excelled in every facet of training, it remains to be seen how they'll fare when the training wheels come off. Based on their grades, Lieutenants Mason and Cole are fully qualified to assume the duties of rookie fleet strike-fighter pilots, or nuggets, but as they readily admit, they each have a lot to learn.

"Sure I'm nervous," Lieutenant Cole said. "I've been out there, I know how tough it can be. Up till now, I've been able to focus on individual phases of flying the Hornet. Starting tomorrow, I'll be expected to put the whole package together. To fly complete missions, I'll have to tank, drop bombs, maybe dogfight, and then come back to the carrier and land. Then I'll debrief, work on my other duties, and probably fly that night, with little or no break. And that goes on seven days a week at sea."

Lieutenant Mason added, "I know I have a lot to learn, but this has been my dream since I was a kid. I'm prepared to work my tail off; I'm just thankful for the chance."

While there is no guarantee that any pilot will successfully make the transition from shore-based aviation to flying off the ship, veteran fighter pilots cite common personality traits of exceptional nuggets.

"You want to see self-confidence, but not arrogance," says one F/A–18 Hornet instructor. "Ideally, a nugget has a steep learning curve. They're able to avoid catastrophic mistakes by listening and staying focused. What mistakes they do make are small and only happen once. It helps if they have a sense of humor, because it doesn't matter how much talent you have, for the first part of the cruise, you feel like an idiot."

Yet, these are women aviators. Clearly the Navy has not yet discovered what traits successful women Hornet pilots share.

What is known is that the first 10 women selected to join the F/A–18 community were unsuccessful. According to the Navy, Lieutenants Mason and Cole are more talented and better prepared than were their predecessors. What remains to be seen is how they will be received and supported by their new shipmates, and how well they'll adapt to the dangers of flying off a ship.

Today, this reporter will join the two women on the USS *Ranger* as it steams across the Atlantic. For the next two weeks, through a series of on-scene articles beamed back to you by satellite, you'll be able to follow their efforts to join the elite realm of US Navy pilots. Stay tuned. The next installment will appear (editor, pls fill in, JW).

I compressed and encrypted the file on my laptop and sent it, along with a half dozen digital photos, across the Internet to my editor in San Diego. I expected it to be published Friday. That would give me until Saturday evening to submit the next installment.

The time difference was working in my favor. I planned to get some new photos and maybe interview the ship's captain and the squadron COs. Cole was going to VFA–303, the sister squadron of VFA–305, where Mason was being assigned. In addition to the two Navy Hornet squadrons, the *Ranger* hosted a Marine Hornet squadron and a Tomcat squadron. Also on board was an E–2 Hawkeye squadron that provided airborne radar support, an S–3 Viking antisubmarine and aerial refueling squadron, an EA–6B Prowler squadron specializing in electronic warfare, and the ship's helicopter squadron, which handled search and rescue and joined in antisubmarine patrol. All together, the eight squadrons comprised Carrier Air Wing Thirty, or CAG–30, under the command of Captain Ted Andrews.

Before disconnecting, I pulled backgrounds on the squadron COs of VFA–303 and VFA–305, the CAG, and ship's CO, Captain Paul Morganelli. I was less successful with the names Hoser had given me. He was strangely closed-mouthed about them. He did say that one was an aviator and the other a staff officer. When I pressed, he said he didn't want to prejudice my investigation.

I raised the bullshit flag. "Give me a break, Captain. First you point these guys out, then you clam up. What's up with that?"

"I can't help it. I feel shitty about siccing you on these guys. I mean . . . hell, nobody has done anything—including these two—and now, thanks to me, the press is breathing down their necks. Look at you, investigating them using the Internet. It's Tailhook all over again."

Informant's remorse—an occupational hazard. "This morning you said you were scared for the girls' safety. What's changed?"

"Nothing. Everything. Damn it, Jack. You'll never understand the bond among shipmates. But I broke it when I gave you those names. And I have no proof! If you uncover anything, take it to the CO, and he'll have the bastards arrested. That's the best I can do."

I let it drop and went back to my notes. While I was working, Hoser cooked up a feast. The aroma of seafood gumbo was overpowering. I was drawn to the kitchen, my mouth watering.

"You are a man of many talents."

"Nothing to it, pardner. Consider it a peace offering. Grab a couple bowls. This stuff is ready to go."

The gumbo was phenomenal, but my long day was catching up to me. After reviewing the key points of my Hornet training, I collapsed on the couch. I don't remember my head hitting the pillow.

CHAPTER 11

NAS Oceana—
Friday, 18 Oct/0710

The aircraft sprang to life when he turned on the battery. Listening in on the intercom system, or ICS, I could hear Hoser and the plane captain (PC), who was plugged in with her own headset, conversing as they ran through the start checklist.

"Pre-start checks complete. Firing up the APU," Hoser said.

"Roger, APU clear."

The Auxiliary Power Unit, or APU, is a mini–jet engine built into the Hornet that provides enough power to start the big engines. Together, Hoser and the PC stepped through the start checklist until both engines were up and running and the APU was secured. Then they moved quickly through the flight-control checks.

Hoser took a minute to type in coordinates for our route of flight and ran several tests on the aircraft's navigation, radar, and avionics. He also contacted base operations to put our clearance on request. We were ready to taxi in less than fifteen minutes.

Ground control cleared us to taxi to the main east–west runway. As we made our way out, he ran through the takeoff checklist and we armed our ejection seats. After going through final checks at the end of the runway, Hoser called for takeoff. The tower cleared us for an "unrestricted climb."

Having no idea what that meant, I prepared myself for something painful.

We didn't even come to a complete stop before he ran the power up. And he was so smooth on the controls that he had the gear up before I realized that we were off the deck.

Hoser kept the aircraft low as we raced, flat out, toward the end of the runway. Just as we passed over the last inch of concrete, he brought the stick back and stood the jet on its twin tails. Surprisingly, it wasn't the least bit uncomfortable.

"Look behind you," Hoser said over the intercom.

The Hornet's cockpit visibility was incredible. I turned in the seat and watched the base grow small directly beneath us. In about a minute, we were leveling off at our cruise altitude, over four miles above the Virginia coast, and proceeding to the last reported position of the USS *Ranger*. She was supposed to be 470 miles east, steaming toward the Straits of Gibraltar.

Once we left US-controlled airspace, Hoser let me fly the aircraft. It was surprisingly easy. Unlike earlier fighters, the flight-control computers constantly trim the aircraft. The pilot rarely has to manhandle the machine. Further, I found that the aircraft responded identically to the simulator. Hoser said that it was because both systems were digital. Within a few minutes, I could bank, turn, and roll out on the right heading and altitude. We tried a few mild acrobatics and those, too, were fairly easy to perform. All except the barrel roll, which I found to be impossible.

"Don't worry about it, Jack. I know guys with two thousand hours who can't do a decent barrel roll." Then he demonstrated a couple of perfect ones.

"Well, I think we'd better put the needle on the nose and go find your new home."

I followed his instructions and settled down to fly the next three hundred miles, happy to still have the controls.

In five minutes a remarkable thing happened. I was bored.

"Hoser, how much of flying is like this?"

"Oh, you mean drilling holes in the sky?" He laughed. "Pretty dull, huh?"

"Well, not dull, exactly. Just not exciting."

"When you're on cruise, you do a lot of this, particularly at night, because fuel is always tight. You're right, dull isn't the right word, it's tedious. The problem is that you can't afford to let your attention drift. Think about it. You're sitting four miles up, two hundred miles from anything, over the ice-cold ocean, in a complex machine filled with five tons of jet fuel. Wild Bill used to say flying on cruise was eighty percent boredom, fifteen percent fun, and five percent sheer, stark terror." Hoser chuckled at the old joke.

I didn't have much trouble concentrating after that.

Once we were inside a hundred miles, Hoser was able to get a lock on the ship's TACAN navigation beacon.

"That's a first, buddy," he said.

"What's that?"

"The damn ship is just where it's supposed to be. Usually, those pinheads take great pleasure in playing hide the needle in a haystack."

I had a hard time imagining a thousand-foot, hundred-thousand-ton ship as a needle, but I kept my mouth shut while Hoser checked in.

"Guntrain, this is Black Sheep three-one-zero, checking in on your two-six-five for ninety-five, angels two-eight, squawking six-one-four-niner, over."

"Roger, three-ten, change squawk to six-five-one-five and ident."

I watched over Hoser's shoulder as he changed the transponder code. By tracking our IFF, the ship had our precise position, speed, and altitude to back up their radar display.

"Three-ten, ident observed. Pilot's discretion, descend and maintain three thousand, altimeter two-niner-niner-eight. Mother's weather is VFR, visibility seven miles in haze, wind is one-eight-zero for fifteen knots. Expected BRC is one-niner-zero. You'll be joining five Hornets for CQ."

"Roger that, Guntrain. Please advise, is there a recovery tanker?"

"Affirmative, three-ten. Tanker is currently overhead at angels eleven. Say your state."

"Three-ten is seven-point-oh, max trap."

In the interim, I noticed that Hoser, who now had the jet, had put us in a shallow, speed-building dive. We were inside seventy miles and closing rapidly.

"Three-ten, your signal is buster. Descend to angels three and call ten miles."

Hoser let out a whoop and plugged in the afterburners. In seconds, we were doing over 600 mph.

"Jack, check your harness and stow any loose gear."

He went through the descent checklist and configured the aircraft for shipboard ops.

"Check out our neighbors. Looks like two groups orbiting at three thousand."

Hoser had found the other Hornets on our radar. As we closed to within twenty miles, he took an offset to the north. Seconds later, the controller called.

"Ninety-nine Guntrain, Mother's in a turn, expected BRC is one-niner-zero, wind twenty-eight knots."

"'Ninety-nine' means that the message applies to everyone. BRC is the Base Recovery Course," Hoser explained. "The ship will head in that direction and try to get the wind to come right down the angled deck. Look down. There's the wake."

We were fifteen miles out, doing about five hundred knots. When I looked down, I could plainly see the track the big ship left in the ocean. Hoser kept our offset heading in for a few more moments before turning to parallel the wake.

"Mother, three-ten's at angels three. See you at twelve," Hoser transmitted.

I still couldn't see the ship.

"Roger three-ten, switch three-five-four-point-five."

"Three-ten's at eleven-six-point-four."

"Three-ten, Charlie."

During our brief, Hoser had told me that the term, *Charlie*, meant that an aircraft was cleared to enter the pattern.

"Hook's coming down. Jack, get ready for a break turn at the bow."

The next two minutes will forever be ingrained in my brain. Hoser took the aircraft down to eight hundred feet above the waves and aligned us behind the ship, which I could now see over his left shoulder. We were doing 450 knots, over 500 mph, an insane speed for entering the landing pattern.

"Three-ten, three miles," Hoser called.

"Roger, Charlie now."

In less time than it takes to tell it, we closed on the ship. I could see the froth of the churning wake, and strangely, the rear end of two jets poking out through a hole beneath the flight deck. We were over it in a flash, just as a plane on a catapult was launched beneath us. Hoser snap-rolled the Hornet to the left and put on an enormous break turn. I had once been the victim of a break turn and prepared myself by straining against the incredible strength of the G forces. Despite my efforts, I lost my vision. The world went gray.

As my vision returned, amid swirling black-and-white spots, I could hear Hoser reciting the landing checklist and felt the aircraft's flying qualities change dramatically as the gear and flaps came down.

The ship was steaming away from us, but it felt as if we were turning at an impossibly tight angle. Our altitude was below four hundred feet. I was certain that Hoser had screwed up by trying to show off. There seemed to be no chance that we could recover from our poor start. The flight deck looked impossibly small. There were at least a dozen aircraft parked on it, making it even less inviting.

It felt like every muscle was stretched taut. I wasn't breathing.

Just as we started to cross the wake, Hoser called, "Three-one-zero, Hornet ball, six-point-oh, manual."

"Roger three-ten, Sierra-Hotel break, good start."

Good start? Couldn't that LSO see that we were impossibly tight and too damn close to the water? As I pondered those, and other mysteries, Hoser smoothly rolled the aircraft wings level. Again, I was staring into the massive rear end of the ship, with its strange opening, churning wake, and the name, USS RANGER, cast in raised letters.

"Hold on, Jack," Hoser said.

A second later, we flashed over the ramp and slammed down with incredible, teeth-jarring force.

Hoser pushed the throttles to full power, in case we missed the wires, but it was never in doubt. We were caught as soon as our wheels hit the deck and stopped as if snagged by a giant rubber band. I was hurled, hard, into my harness. Coming to a sudden stop from 130 knots made it clear why aviators call shipboard landings traps.

Before my rattled brain could register that we'd survived, Hoser had already folded our wings, and after we rolled backwards a few feet, raised the hook and followed the director's signals to taxi clear of the landing area.

"Three wire," he said, matter-of-factly. I knew that the three wire was the target wire. Somehow he'd salvaged a perfect landing from that horrible start.

"Welcome aboard, three-ten. Guntrain says that was the best break and pattern he's seen all year. He wants to know if you have time to download that baggage pod and collect a few more traps."

"You keep talking to me dirty, Boss," Hoser transmitted, "and I'll sign up for the cruise." As we taxied, Hoser flashed a thumbs-up toward the tower, where I could see a row of faces staring out of the thick glass panes.

I was stoked to hear that Hoser had a chance to reach the fifteen-hundred-trap milestone. It would make a great balancing piece to the story of the two nuggets.

Meanwhile, the bustling activity on the flight deck was disorienting. As we taxied aft, toward the fantail, another Hornet slammed into the deck just a few feet to our right. I looked up to find yet another turning on final, what the aviators call "rolling into the groove." A woman called the ball with side-number three-one-two.

"That's Randi," Hoser said over the intercom. As he followed the director's hand signals to park our jet, I watched Randi fly her Hornet into the deck.

"What did she get?" asked Hoser.

"The third wire from the back," I answered.

"Good girl."

With Hoser locking one brake, the jet swung in a tight arc until we were pointing at the landing area. The yellow shirt–clad director signaled two sailors wearing brown shirts to chain us down. Each of them carried several thick-linked chains, with heavy-duty turnbuckles, and used them to tie our jet to metal pad-eyes built into the flight deck.

"This will take just a minute, Jack. The grapes are going to fuel us before downloading that pod. So, how did you like your first trap?"

"I think my brain is still back in the break." Sailors in purple shirts connected a fuel hose, and my fuel gauge began to climb.

He laughed.

"Hoser?"

"Yeah?"

"I didn't think we were going to make it, we seemed so close to the ship after the break."

"Yeah, we were tight, but remember the boat is pulling away from us while we're turning. Besides, a tight pattern is the mark of a good aviator. I'm a little rusty, but that was a reasonably good pass for an old blind guy."

"What's going to happen next?"

"They'll break us down, and we'll taxi to the catapult."

"That doesn't sound too good," I said.

"Of course it's good. How else . . . oh, I see what you mean. 'Breaking down' is a term we use to describe taking the chains off. I never thought of it that way. I guess it is a strange phrase to use. But don't sweat it; our jet is fine, buddy. Since they're using the two bow cats, we'll be taxiing all the way forward. I think you'll find the cat shot interesting. After we're airborne, I'll find our interval and take separation on him, or her. Then we'll do it again, except this time, no break."

"That's okay with me."

"When we get down to hold-down fuel, which is five-point-five, they'll bring us back here for some more gas, and I'll shut down the left engine and you'll hop out. Put your torso harness, G suit, and helmet in the pod. They should have it loaded by then. The plane captain will come up and tidy up your cockpit and you'll follow one of the sailors below. Then I'll blow this Popsicle stand."

"Do you think we'll get ten more traps so you go over fifteen hundred?"

"Can't say. Depends on how the deck's running, how these other aviators are doing, and what kind of mood the captain is in."

"Who is Guntrain, by the way? Is that the captain?"

"Yeah, that's the call sign of both the *Ranger* and the skipper. Morganelli is an old friend; he might let me run the deck a little."

"Does he know how close you are?"

"Can't say. He might."

"What was it the LSO said? Sierra, something?"

"Sierra-Hotel break."

"What's that mean?"

"It's radio code for the letters, S and H. You know, like alpha, bravo, charlie, and so on. It stands for, shit-hot. They like seeing us come in fast and break at the bow. It raises the degree of difficulty."

We were interrupted by the return of the yellow-shirt, who signaled the brown-shirts to unchain us.

Hoser called the tower. "Boss, three-one-zero, up and ready, eight-point-five."

"Roger, three-ten."

I was amazed at how close the director had us taxi to other aircraft. Scant inches separated us. The yellow-shirt coaxed Hoser's control inputs with a variety of signals, using little head nods, almost delicate hand gestures, and body language to impart his desires. When he passed us to the next director, he flashed Hoser a thumbs-up, apparently happy with the captain's responses.

As we continued to taxi toward the bow, our cockpit filled with acrid fumes from the jet exhaust of other aircraft. Even with the oxygen mask on tight, I found my eyes watering.

There was a jet in place on the right-hand or number-one catapult. With no warning, a huge, three-part metal blast deflector rose out of the deck only a foot in front of us. Almost immediately, the jet on the cat went to full power. Despite the blast deflector, our plane shook violently. About ten seconds later, there was an explosion, the shaking stopped, and the blast deflector lowered to reveal that the jet was gone, already airborne. We taxied forward as clouds of steam rolled aft.

The horizon lowered, then rose uncomfortably high as the bow plunged downward. The ocean was impossibly close. Surely, there wouldn't be enough room to get us airborne. Even if the catapult worked, it would merely shoot us straight into the water.

"Hoser?"

"I'm busy."

He unfolded our wings as he followed the director's precise directions. I heard him recite the takeoff checklist as our jet thumped solidly into place on the catapult. The next second the power came up, and he cycled the flight controls.

"Remember, Jack, don't touch the stick."

I started to answer, glancing down to make sure I had my hand on the ICS switch, when Hoser saluted. In the next microsecond, the catapult officer touched the deck and pointed toward the bow, which, thankfully, was on the rise. Somewhere, a sailor pushed a button, opening valves that fired a big steam-powered piston.

I felt a monstrous slam in the back. The acceleration was staggering. My body was crushed into the seatback. The flesh on my face was pulled back into a maniacal grin. Somebody was screaming.

Suddenly, we were clear of the ship, flying peacefully, as if we'd never landed. The screaming stopped. The whole effect was eerie.

"Jack."

"Yes?"

"Are you all right?"

"I think so."

"Okay, try not to yell like that, okay?"

"That was me?"

Hoser just laughed and laughed.

CHAPTER 12

Mid-Atlantic—
Friday, 18 Oct/1100

We flew around the pattern, alternating crash landings with mind-numbing cat shots. In short order we'd accumulated seven more traps and run ourselves low on gas. After our eighth trap of the day, we were pulled out of the conga line of jets waiting for the cat and sent aft.

"Well, that's it, Jack." Hoser said. "Get ready to hop out after we're chained down."

"But, you're only three traps from fifteen hundred."

"Yeah, but the pounding has taken its toll. The bosun signaled that we have a hydraulic leak. It looks like we're done. After they fix it, I'll need to take this machine home."

It seemed unfair to me, but Hoser took it in stride. After we were chained down, a troubleshooter came on the ICS and had Hoser cycle the flight controls. Together they tracked down the source of the leak to a bad actuator seal, whatever that was. Hoser was told to shut down and stand by for a two-hour delay.

After de-arming my ejection seat, I unstrapped and climbed stiffly out of the backseat. Perched on the side of the aircraft, face-to-face with Captain Joe Santana sitting in his cockpit, I was struck by how perfectly he filled the role of carrier pilot. His salt-and-pepper mustache and rugged, lined face, framed by the helmet, could have been a statue.

On impulse I pulled the digital camera out of my G-suit pocket and took his picture. Then I shook his hand. It was too noisy for words, but the thumbs-up he gave me was special.

On deck, I struggled out of my harness, and a brown-shirt gave me a flight-deck helmet to swap for my flying helmet. My time as a tailhook aviator was over. But Hoser wasn't finished. A yellow-shirt was pointing him at a jet as it taxied past us. Hoser grinned like a five-year-old, pounded the director on the back, and scrambled back up the ladder of our jet to retrieve his knee board and helmet bag. Back on deck he pantomimed to me that he was going flying in aircraft five-zero-one. I held up three fingers and he nodded enthusiastically. Apparently some other pilot was getting pulled in favor of Hoser.

My guide yanked on my sleeve and led down below. When the hatch closed behind me, the noise of the flight deck was replaced by the quiet hum of ship-board activity. A young lieutenant, dressed in khakis, was waiting for me and introduced himself as one of the ship's Public Affairs officers.

"Welcome aboard, sir. I'm Lieutenant Irvine. After we get you out of that gear and let you make a head call, I have orders to take you up to the bridge to meet Captain Morganelli. I'm having your baggage stowed in your stateroom."

With that, he led me to a cramped paraloft, where I struggled out of the bulky antiexposure suit. It felt great, even better than taking off ski boots after a long day on the slopes. I then made a much-needed head call. While washing up, I noticed red marks imprinted on my face from the helmet and mask, lingering signs of my baptism.

Remembering my digital camera, I went back to the cramped paraloft to retrieve it.

"So how was it?" a familiar voice asked.

I turned to find Amy standing behind me, still in her gear.

"It was awesome!" I was happy to see a familiar face. "Are you done, too?"

"Heck no. Thanks to Hoser, I only got two traps. Can you believe he just took my ride? And he didn't even have the good grace to apologize. In fact, he accused me of stinking up the cockpit with perfume." Her anger was clearly feigned. "I hope he gets a no-grade on his last trap."

Before I could ask, Lieutenant Irvine interceded and explained that we had to hustle up to the bridge. Amy waved good-bye after saying she'd watch Hoser's record trap with her new squadron mates.

Irvine led me on a circuitous journey through the length of the ship. Passing an open hatch near the paraloft, we were assaulted by an incredibly loud crashing noise, followed by a sound much like a big fishing reel being stripped by a monster tarpon, but a hundred times louder. My guide explained, by shouting into my deafened ear, that we were directly beneath the landing area, and were next to the arresting-gear machinery.

The lieutenant was moving gracefully through an endless series of open hatches, each of which required a person, stepping through, to negotiate a twelve-inch metal lip. On about the tenth one, I caught my shin. It hurt like hell, but Irvine kept right on walking. On the next one, I made the mistake of stepping on the lip itself, smashing my head painfully into the steel top of the hatch.

"Shit!" I stopped to massage my aching scalp. A knot began to swell. I was surprised when my hand came away blood-free. Meanwhile, my shin still throbbed.

"Oh, I'm sorry, sir. You've got to watch these knee-knockers. It's an unwritten rule that nobody steps on them. See how shiny they're kept? Also, there's etiquette for meeting someone coming the other way. Always yield to someone of higher rank. As a VIP, your rank is equal to a Navy captain, so there aren't many people you need to yield to, though it's a courtesy to let aviators in their flight gear through. And when you hear someone call, 'Clear a path!' you'd better flatten against a bulkhead, because it could be the Marines responding to a security alert. They have the authority to run over anyone who gets in their way." He smiled. "And they love to do it."

He pointed out the frame numbers that marked

each hatch. He said they marked each horizontal frame, starting with number 1 at the bow through 255 at the stern. Walking forward, more slowly this time, he pointed out maps posted on bulkheads and the numbering scheme used to label every room on the ship. There were muffled concussions coming from the bow, cat shots, accompanying the crashing landings from behind us.

By the time we got to the captain's ladder, I was beginning to comprehend just how huge this ship really was. We climbed up a gleaming staircase, or ladder, its rails covered by intricately knotted ropes, like fancy macramé. After several levels we came to the entrance of the bridge, where we encountered an imposing Marine guard. The corporal's dress uniform reminded me how disheveled I looked in my now-baggy flight suit with my uncombed mop of hair.

Nevertheless, we were admitted to the bridge. The view was spectacular. Captain Morganelli greeted me warmly. He offered a cup of coffee, which I gratefully accepted. He asked for my thoughts about flying from his ship.

"Captain, I'm rarely at a loss for words, but that was the most incredible experience in my life. Your people out there are so skilled and competent, well, I've never seen anything like it."

"Thank you, Mr. Warner. We're happy to have you aboard. I understand that you will be writing specifically about the assimilation of women into two of our Hornet squadrons."

"That's right. How are they doing?"

"From what little I've seen thus far, they're doing fine. But, of course, those questions are best aimed at their respective COs and maybe CAG Andrews." He paused to take a phone call, using one of several handsets installed above his swivel chair. After giving a few instructions, he turned back to me. "Why don't you plan on joining me for dinner tonight? Lieutenant Irvine, will you make the arrangements?"

"Yes, sir."

Captain Morganelli then pointed to the bow. "I called you up here, Mr. Warner, so that you could witness a historic event."

I looked down and saw a Hornet, with side number five-zero-one, taxiing into position on the number one cat.

"So you're going to let him get those last three traps?"

"He's already logged two while you were finding your way up here. You almost missed out." Irvine flinched from a darting look of disapproval. "This next one will be for the record. I'll let you in on a secret, Mr. Warner. SECNAV, himself, set this whole thing up. It's going to be a very big deal. Nobody has ever logged this many traps. Hoser doesn't know it, but when he lands back in Oceana, he's going to be met by the media, brass band and all." He smiled. "And there's a surprise in it for you, too. I understand that, even as we speak, the wire services are waiting for your firsthand story. Isn't that right, Lieutenant Irvine?"

"Yes, sir. Mr. Warner, our Communications Center is standing by for your story. If you need any background info or technical help, just ask. Will you be able to get us something in a couple hours?"

"No sweat." For a wire-service lead, I'd write the damn thing standing on my head. Tomorrow morning several million people would be reading my work. Yet my good fortune didn't stop me from feeling like an idiot for not seeing it coming. SECNAV had adroitly set the stage so that the first report in the series would be overwhelmingly positive.

Beneath us, Hoser's jet went to full power; its exhaust actually shook the bridge a little. After the control wipeout, the cat fired. Hoser was airborne once again.

The captain reached up, pulled down a phone, and said, "Build a triple interval. I want the photographers to get plenty of time."

Then he grabbed another handset and nodded at one of his sailors, who produced a small metal whistle, a bosun's pipe I was told later. He played a few notes over the ship's PA system. After the whistle, the bosun's mate said, "Aboard the *Ranger*, stand by for the captain."

Captain Morganelli's eyes followed the flight of the Hornet as he spoke. "Attention *Ranger*, this is your captain. In just a few seconds we are going to be privileged to witness a historic event. Captain Joe Santana, in Hornet five-zero-one, is about to make his one thousand, five hundredth trap. That's right folks, I said *fifteen hundred*. This aviator is the most experienced fighter pilot in this or any air force in the world. Believe it or not, Captain Santana has more combat flight time than every pilot on this ship combined.

"I urge you to take a moment and find a television to watch this landing. It is something you'll be able to tell your grandkids about. It's only appropriate that *Ranger*, the oldest carrier in the fleet, will be part of this event. Join me now in saluting two legends, Hoser Santana and the grand lady herself, USS *Ranger*."

We turned to watch the approach. I glanced at the "plat camera," really just a monitor displaying a view from a camera built into the landing area. It had crosshairs depicting the optimum glide path.

"Captain," I asked, "what's a no-grade?"

"That's one of the grades a landing signal officer can award. A no-grade means it was pretty ugly, almost dangerous. Most pilots collect a handful in a cruise. I don't know if it's true, but the rumor is that Hoser has never had one. But that seems impossible. Now I'm curious. Why do you ask?"

I didn't want to get Amy in any trouble. "I just heard the term and wondered about it. Thanks for explaining it."

Five-zero-one rolled out perfectly centered in the plat, and remained glued there as Hoser called the ball and flew his last pass. It was a perfect approach all the way. From the bridge, we had an unimpeded view of the aircraft as it passed over the ramp and flew into the wires, its tailhook again snagging the third wire from the back.

In that frozen moment, a cheer for Hoser's accomplishment poised in my throat, something strange about the aircraft's attitude grabbed my eye.

Throughout the ship, thousands of people watched as the Hornet's right wing continued unchecked in its downward flight, crashing hard into the flight deck. The right landing gear had collapsed, and now was splayed awkwardly, like a broken leg pinned beneath a giant bird. Sailors scattered as the jet skidded down the flight deck, sparks and debris flying. Several were pushing and dragging shipmates.

With its tailhook no longer held by the thick metal cable, the F/A–18 slid past the bridge, spinning clockwise until it was pointed right at us. Fuel spewed from ruptured tanks.

I heard someone say, "Eject!" but it was too late.

Lobo five-zero-one, its underbelly exposed by the angle of its tilt, crashed with startling abruptness into the steel jet-blast deflector behind cat two. Hoser's helmeted head whiplashed cruelly into the Plexiglas canopy and sagged forward, his body restrained only by his parachute harness.

Fire erupted immediately and engulfed the back of the jet. Flames raced across the flight deck, igniting spilled jet fuel.

Amid the crash Klaxon and a series of rapid-fire orders from Captain Morganelli, I stood transfixed, witnessing the carnage below. Certain that Hoser would die, I silently prayed that he would not suffer in the inferno.

In less than five seconds, a small red cart manned

by sailors in crash gear arrived and began spewing white foam from a nozzle on its hood. They concentrated on the area around the cockpit. Two firefighters, in their bulky silver suits, moved toward the jet. One knelt, opened a panel, grabbed a handle, and moved quickly away from the aircraft, trailing a wire lanyard. When he pulled it taut, the canopy exploded clear of the wreckage, bouncing once off the flight deck before dropping over the edge.

By now, there were two fire hoses manned by dozens of sailors, none with fire suits. Working together they sprayed hundreds of gallons of foam into the retreating fire. At the wreckage, the two firefighters disengaged Hoser's body from the ejection seat and dragged him out of the cockpit. A stretcher appeared. He was placed on it, strapped down, and moved underneath the bridge, out of my sight.

I turned to find Captain Morganelli staring at me.

He nodded at the bosun's mate, who again announced the Captain over the ship's PA system.

"*Ranger*, this is your Captain. As you've seen, we've had a mishap, but thanks to some quick work by our flight-deck crew, we've rescued the pilot. But we still have aircraft airborne and must continue to operate. I am counting on each of you to perform your duties to the best of your abilities. That is all." He looked again at the bosun, and said, "Sound General Quarters."

For the next few minutes, the ship was in turmoil. The Marine guard entered the bridge and helped the captain into battle gear. The corporal searched the bridge, spotted me, and started to move in my direction, but the captain said, "Leave him alone. He'll remain with me." Then he said, "Mr. Warner, we're a ship of war, just beginning our deployment. I can't afford to pass up a chance to let the crew taste blood."

"Is Hoser alive?"

"Yes, but he's unconscious and seriously injured." One of the overhead phones rang, and the captain answered it, nodded once, and said, "Dump it."

I struggled to comprehend what I'd just seen. In less than three minutes, these people had witnessed a horrific crash, some barely escaping death themselves, and yet they'd responded in no time to put out the fire and pull the pilot from the wreckage. It was an impressive display of courage and expertise.

I snapped several pictures with my digital camera.

As the fire-fighting cart continued to spray the smoldering wreckage, a large motorized crane lumbered into view. Other firefighters moved in and secured the crane's cable to the aircraft. In the next minute, it lifted the fire-charred Hornet and moved it to the edge of the flight deck, setting it down almost gently. The firefighters disengaged the crane's cable.

I couldn't understand why the crane had set the wreckage on the edge of the landing area. There were still aircraft airborne. Wouldn't they have to land soon?

My answer came swiftly. The crane operator swung the boom out of the way and drove straight into the wreckage, pushing it unceremoniously over the side. Five-zero-one had been buried at sea.

Over the course of the next fifteen minutes, the flight-deck crew cleared the debris out of the landing area and the catapult tracks. There was a great deal of concern about the JBD, but it was soon repaired and working again. In less than twenty-five minutes, the ship started flight-deck operations again. Aircraft were recovered, refueled, and launched. The crash had been a mere speed bump on the big ship's schedule.

While waiting for Hoser to come out of surgery, I interviewed Morganelli.

"Captain, you've chosen to keep operating. Some people might say a mishap like this merits a pause so that people can catch their breath and figure out what went wrong. Would you disagree?"

"That's a fair question. We were fortunate that no flight-deck personnel were killed or badly injured. Normally, we'd try to preserve the wreckage so that we could conduct a full mishap investigation, but we're in the middle of the ocean, conducting blue-water ops. That means we don't send our jets away just because there's a problem. We have to take care of our own.

"*Ranger* is no longer on work-ups. We're on deployment. The situation allowed me to invoke combat rules, and that was too good an opportunity to pass up. Everyone on this ship, from the mess cooks to the pilots, just made the mental shift with me. I know it sounds cold, but you just can't buy training like that."

He lowered his voice. "And, Mr. Warner, I promise you, were Hoser in my place, he would have done the very same thing."

PART 2

En Route

CHAPTER 13

Friday, 18 Oct/1300

After General Quarters was secured, Lieutenant Irvine led me to the infirmary. Hoser was in a coma. He'd suffered several broken bones, including his left wrist, collarbone, and a couple of ribs. An emergency operation to remove a ruptured spleen had already been performed. I met the surgeon outside the ICU room.

"We don't know to what extent his brain has been damaged, Mr. Warner. We are no position, nor is he, to transport to a bigger hospital. Our only option is to monitor his progress, look for signs of brain swelling, and hope for the best."

"Was that the good news or the bad news?" I asked.

The surgeon smiled. "I can tell you that his remarkable physical condition is helping. His heart is as strong as an ox's, and I'm sure he'll heal quickly from the fractures. We were very lucky that there wasn't a catastrophic injury to the spine. The way the crash crew had to manhandle him during the rescue could have caused irreparable damage. I was also pleased to see that there were no other signs of internal injuries."

I was just about to leave, when Randi showed up, wide-eyed and ghost white.

"Oh God, Jack, how is he?"

After guiding her to a chair, I sat with her while the doctor explained the situation. He did his best to put a positive spin on it.

When the doctor left us, she spoke haltingly. "I was stuck up there, Jack. I mean, I was airborne when it happened. I could see the fireball." She touched my arm. Her eyes glistened. "I just knew that he'd been killed." Instead of crying, she straightened her back, glancing away momentarily. When she faced me again, her face was composed. "It was the hardest thing I've ever done, but I had to keep flying the damn jet. Hoser would understand."

"He's going to be okay, Randi. He's way too much of a hard-ass to let this stop him."

She nodded, struggling to be convinced.

I talked the doctor into letting us into the ICU. It was difficult for Randi to see her mentor unconscious amid an octopus array of tubes and monitors. She took his hand and told him she loved him. There was no response except that of the machinery.

Ushered outside by the nurse, Randi and I agreed to meet in her stateroom after my dinner with the CO. Lieutenant Irvine assured me it was within a couple of frames of mine, on the same level. While Randi headed back to the VFA-303 Ready Room,

Lieutenant Irvine led me back up the six ladders to my stateroom. It was tiny, but it had a sink and a small writing desk. There were towels, and someone had made my bed. The head was only a few steps from the door, a lucky treat according to my host.

"I'll be back at seventeen-forty-five to escort you to dinner, Mr. Warner."

Before he left, I asked him, "Are you surprised that the captain is still going through with that?"

"No, sir. Everyone still has to eat, right?" He patted my shoulder reassuringly. "Look, sir, I know it seems like the end of the world, but these things are part of our life out here. Nothing is going to stop the *Ranger*, Mr. Warner. We'll be flying again tonight. You look tired, sir. I suggest you catch some shut-eye. I'll call you at seventeen-hundred to make sure you've got time to take a shower."

"I appreciate your concern, Lieutenant, but I've seen much worse. I was just asking your opinion."

He wasn't buying it. "Of course, sir."

I spent the next few minutes unpacking. I was putting away my underwear when I noticed that my hands were shaking. My knees weakened. Suddenly cold, I lay on the bed, curling up under the rough wool blanket. I knew I wasn't ill. My body had processed its limit of adrenaline. I'd seen the delayed reaction before when interviewing survivors of violence. I closed my eyes and tried to shake the image of Hoser's flaming jet.

An incessant ringing jarred me awake. Temporarily disoriented, I almost struck my head on the top bunk. Through the fog I managed to find the ancient rotary phone and thank Lieutenant Irvine for the wake-up call.

I found the ship's phone book and called the infirmary. Hoser still lay in a coma, his condition unchanged. The nurse assured me that, at this stage in his recovery, remaining stable was good news. I was inclined to believe her.

Getting up, pain shot through my body. My back and neck, in particular, were sore as hell. The cats and traps had taken their toll. A nice, long, hot shower would be just the ticket. I gathered my toiletries, wrapped the skimpy towel around my waist, and flip-flopped out of my room toward the head.

Walking was difficult. Slipping repeatedly, I banged into the wall. Mystified at first, I felt silly when I remembered where we were. In the middle of the ocean, even a monster ship the size of the *Ranger* could still be tossed around.

The head smelled sour. Trying in vain not to inhale, I managed to squeeze into one of the metal shower stalls, bracing myself as best I could against the ship's rolls. There was no showerhead. Instead, I found a long, black rubber hose with a small plastic nozzle attached.

Fair enough, I thought. *This will allow me to point the spray where it needs to go.*

Holding the gizmo above my head, I turned on the water, making a guess at the right mixture of hot and cold. Nothing happened. Examining the nozzle, I found a button that presumably controlled the flow.

Certain that I had at last figured out the system, I mashed the button and was rewarded by a small stream of ice-cold water that lasted for no more than three seconds before my thumb was literally pushed off the button by back pressure. I turned it up and wound up spraying my chest with scalding water.

And so it went. Each three-second spurt of water was at a surprise temperature, flowing at the rate of a can of soda being poured down a sink. After lathering up with shampoo and soap, I found that, try as I might, I couldn't get all the suds off. Using both hands to hold down that cursed button, I slid, as the ship rolled, banging against the cold metal walls of the shower stall. Desperate to get the soap off my body, I became impervious to the sporadic bursts of hot and cold. After thoroughly cursing the engineering idiot who designed the diabolical contraption, I finally gave up. My skin drew leather-tight where the soap dried.

I headed unsteadily back to the room, my wet flip-flops slippery on the waxed tile. Reaching the door, my black mood was suddenly shredded by panic. I realized that I had not taken the room key with me. My mind reeled with images of having to flip-flop, wet, barely concealed by my towel, to find help. My only chance was if the door didn't automatically lock. When the knob turned in my hand, I felt nothing but relief and a warm regard for the brilliant designers of the ship.

After using my sink faucet to get as much of the remaining soap off as possible, I dressed in my new khakis. The effect, without any insignia, was fairly strange. I looked like a cross between a prison guard and a landscaper.

A few minutes later, Lieutenant Irvine arrived and led me to the captain's small, but well-appointed wardroom. Captain Morganelli again greeted me warmly and introduced me to his other guest, Captain Andrews. As the Carrier Air Group commander, Andrews was traditionally referred to as CAG. Lieutenant Irvine was dismissed.

"I just got back from the infirmary," CAG said. "Hoser is still unconscious, but the doc is happy with his vital signs and such."

"What do you think caused the mishap?" I asked.

"It's difficult to state conclusively until we analyze the video more closely, but if I had to guess, I'd say that the planing link failed on the starboard gear. It's a known failure mode; we thought we had a handle on it with an airframes change instituted a couple years ago."

"CAG is being diplomatic," Captain Morganelli said. "Because I chose to have the wreckage pushed over the side, we may never know what caused the mishap. In the meantime, we've contacted the Pentagon, and they've ordered a full inspection of every Hornet's landing-gear system."

"Did you take heat for disposing of the wreckage?"

"Not directly, but you can bet it caused some consternation in the five-sided wind tunnel."

That was as good a description for the Pentagon

as any I'd heard. Our discussion was interrupted by the arrival of dinner. My plate held meat loaf, salad, and mashed potatoes.

"Just like the diner," CAG said, digging in.

The skipper smiled. "I hope you're not too disappointed, Mr. Warner, but I make it a policy to eat what my sailors and Marines eat. CAG and I eat at least one meal a day on the mess decks, as well."

The meat loaf was okay, the potatoes were instant, and the salad wilted. I was surprised. I expected the captain of an aircraft carrier to dine like royalty. It made me want to learn more about these two men.

After dinner, I asked, "CAG, the captain told me I should ask you how Lieutenants Cole and Mason are doing. That is, after all, why I'm out here."

"No problems, so far. Cole is a fine ball flyer. Mason is solid behind the boat, too. Both seem to be learning the flight deck quickly. Cole flew well last night. Mason will be out there tonight. That's always the real test. Overall, Mr. Warner, I'd say that I'm quite satisfied with their performance."

"What kind of special arrangements did you have to make to bring these women into the air wing?"

"*Nada*. We've had women flying Tomcats and Vikings for a year. These two are just the first Hornet pilots. I'm treating them like any other nuggets. We'll give them plenty of time behind the boat and gradually phase them into tactical flights, where they'll drop bombs and fly ACM. I expect it'll take a couple more weeks of steady flying before they begin to feel comfortable, barring any unforeseen problems."

I decided to see what reaction I got by mentioning the top name on my list of suspects.

"Could either of you tell me where I could find Commander Holmes?"

They exchanged glances. CAG spoke. "Commander Holmes is my Deputy CAG. Why would you be looking for him?"

There was an edge of caution and concern in his voice. Captain Morganelli was tight-lipped. Pay dirt.

"I did a little research before I left. His name popped up. Would it cause a problem if I were to interview him?"

"No, Mr. Warner," CAG said. "We received clear directions from SECNAV's office that you were to be accorded access to anyone you wanted. I'll be glad to introduce you. He's usually in the CAG spaces after dinner."

"That would be great, if it's not too much trouble."

"No trouble at all." His eyes told a different story.

"One thing about living on a ship, Mr. Warner," the captain said, an effective diplomat. "When we're not flying, everyone is always within a thousand feet of each other."

We finished dinner while discussing the upcoming deployment. The *Ranger* was scheduled to turnover with the USS *America*, the off-going carrier, at Naples, Italy, in two days. *America* would be going home after being out for six months. I asked the CAG if he was envious.

"Envious? Hell, no. This is what we do. Sure, it'll be fine to be heading home in six months, but I wouldn't miss this deployment for anything. This is why I get up in the morning."

Maybe *his* shower worked.

CHAPTER 14

CAG Office—
Friday, 18 Oct/1850

Commander Holmes was a tall, dour man. He seemed none too happy to meet me.

CAG said, "Jim, this is Mr. Warner. He is that reporter SECNAV's office assigned to cover our two nugget Hornet pilots. He'd like to interview you."

"I don't really have much to say about that, Mr. Warner," Holmes said.

My ears perked up. When someone says they don't have much to say, you can be sure they have a load to get off their chest. The secret is in making them feel safe enough to talk. "That's okay, Commander. I'm just looking for background material. I probably won't need much of your time. Is there someplace quiet we can talk?"

I followed Holmes into his office, past a clerk who, after looking up and smiling, continued typing. I closed the door behind me.

His contempt thinly disguised, he asked, "What is it, exactly, that you want from me, Mr. Warner?"

"Commander, I'm interested in your opinions and observations, as a Deputy Air Wing Commander, about the inclusion of women pilots in the F/A–18 community."

"We do what we're told to do, Mr. Warner. They could send us trained monkeys to fly out here, and we'd try to make it work."

His clipped tone and dismissive attitude made me want to find the source of his anger. Maybe he needed a sympathetic ear. "But you've got a tremendous responsibility out here, Commander. Believe me, I saw firsthand how dangerous this environment can be. Surely, the Pentagon knows that you need the best pilots in the world out here."

He stared, appraising my sincerity. I kept my expression innocent.

With grudging acknowledgment, he said, "Yeah, I forgot that you bagged some traps today. That was too bad about Santana. Nobody deserves that kind of mishap."

I noted that he called Hoser by his real name, not his call sign, indicating that he wasn't a fan. In particular, his strange phrasing caught my ear. "Nobody deserves that kind of mishap." Did that imply that some people deserved some kind of mishap? Letting that question rest until another time, I pushed harder.

"You know, Commander, I've reported on the military for years, but until today, I never had an appreciation for what goes on out here, at sea. Now I think I understand why those women Hornet pilots on the West Coast didn't make it. I'm seriously questioning the logic of putting women on ships."

"Join the club." He bit off the last word, glancing sharply at me. I smiled and nodded agreement. After a pause, he spoke again, unable to contain his expert opinion on the subject. "The carrier is no place for a social experiment. We are always the first into combat, and hell, you've seen how dangerous our peacetime flying can be. But, even if they've got to put women out here, they just don't belong flying in a Hornet squadron. Look at that debacle on the West Coast. Those squadrons ended up critically shorthanded because the women couldn't pull their own weight."

"SECNAV's office told me that those were poorly chosen candidates and that the women in this batch, and the ones who follow, are and will be more talented," I said.

Holmes was in his element. He had a willing audience for his pearls of wisdom. "Of course they'll be more talented. They were handpicked, for Christ's sake. But, what you, and every one of those pinheads in DC, are missing is the fact that they just don't have the balls to be strike-fighter pilots."

On a roll, he slammed his hand down on the desktop. "Look what happened this afternoon. Santana goes and splatters himself all over the flight deck, and Ms. Cole rushes off to the infirmary in tears before she debriefed her flight. That's the kind of bullshit they expect us to put up with, Warner! What if she pulls that kind of stunt in combat?"

I'd found a headcase.

There was more. "You want to do something good?" He leaned toward me, pointing for emphasis. "Tell your readers that this is a man's game out here. We should keep it that way, unless they can stand to see their daughters come home in body bags."

He stood and walked to the door.

As I got up to leave, I took a shot in the dark. "By the way, Commander, what jet do you fly?"

His expression changed to a painful grimace. "I fly Hornets, but I've had this sinus condition." He sniffed for effect. "It's kept me grounded more than I'd like."

"Well, I hope it's nothing too serious. I know that those doctors are aching for a chance to ground you guys. I think they're all jealous."

He actually patted me on the back as I left.

"Let us know if there's anything you need, Mr. Warner." Nodding at his typist, he said, "Petty Officer Lawrence can help with any administrative needs you have, and I'll be happy to arrange any interviews, or a tour of the ship, if you'd like."

"That would be terrific. Thank you. I'm available anytime."

"Good. I'll be in touch then."

I got lost twice trying to find Randi's stateroom, which seems ludicrous when you consider that I only traveled about fifty feet, and every frame is labeled.

She opened the door, still in her flight suit, and gamely smiled a greeting. Her room was similar to mine, except that there were two desk units. One each, for her and Lieutenant Mason. We sat in straight-backed metal chairs, the ship rocking gently beneath us.

"Have you eaten?" I asked.

"No, but I'm not hungry. Maybe I'll go down to mid-rats and get a PB&J later."

"What's mid-rats?"

"Oh, they open the dirty shirt at twenty-two-hundred, that's ten P.M., to let you make a snack. You can usually get a slider, if you want one."

"Hold on. What's a dirty shirt, and why would I want to eat something in it called a slider?"

She laughed at my ignorance of shipboard life. "The dirty shirt is Wardroom I. It's on this level, just walk forward on the starboard side. They call it a dirty shirt, because we can go in there wearing flight suits. Wardroom II is on the second deck. That's right below the hangar deck, on the same level as the infirmary. You have to be in uniform to eat there. Aviators tend to avoid Wardroom II, unless there is a particularly good meal, and black-shoes never come up to Wardroom I. Remember, black-shoes are surface Navy officers. Aviators are called brown-shoes, because that's what we wear."

I cataloged all that information. "But, what's a slider? Or, don't I want to know?"

"A slider is a cheeseburger. They can get pretty greasy, but I've got to admit that they taste good, especially when you miss dinner. You can also get bug-juice and auto-dog."

"I'm not even going to ask."

"Bug-juice is this god-awful kind of Kool-Aid. I think I'll have to show you auto-dog. It'll be a surprise."

"Oh, joy. Listen, I had dinner with the captain and the CAG. It was meat loaf. You didn't miss much."

"So, the skipper really does eat what we eat. I thought it was myth when I heard it."

"Have you met the CAG, yet?" I asked.

"Just briefly. He's got a reputation for being a bit of a hard-ass, but fair."

"How about the Deputy CAG?"

She made a face. "He just about ran me over in the passageway yesterday. I was manning up, dressed in all my gear and heading topside. He came out of the CAG spaces and when he saw me, I swear he sped up to beat me to the knee-knocker. I had to press myself against the bulkhead to let him pass. Even so, he damn near knocked my helmet out of my hand. Then he looked back at me, and said, 'We make way for senior officers aboard *Ranger*, Lieutenant.' I don't think he's too happy to have me in the air wing."

"What's his reputation like?"

"I've just heard that he's a micromanager who doesn't fly much. Nobody has had much to say about him. Why?"

"I interviewed him. You're right. He's definitely antifemale. I suggest you steer clear of him."

"Thanks for the warning."

"So, how's your roomie doing?"

"Good. After tonight, we'll both have flown three hops and gotten a bunch of deck time. Amy is going bombing tomorrow. I'm scheduled for an ACM hop and another night fright."

"Fright?"

"Yeah, that's what we call them. It'll be good tomorrow. I'm going late enough to have a moonball. Last night the damn thing didn't come up until I was back on deck. It was severely dark out there."

"But you did well. Even CAG said so."

"He did? That's good to hear. Amy and I talked it over. We just need to get a few more hops under our belt, and the spotlight will be off us." She paused and looked at me meaningfully. "As long as you don't put us right back in it, Jack."

"I call it like I see it." A thought occurred to me. "Hey, can you find out who those guys were who rescued Hoser?"

"I guess so. You want their names for a story?"

"Sure. But, I also brought out some magazines and candy. It seems to me, those guys deserve them more than anybody."

"That's a great idea, Jack. Give me a minute."

She looked up a number and dialed. "Chief, this is Lieutenant Cole from VFA–303. There's a reporter on board who would like to interview the sailors who rescued the Hornet pilot this morning . . . Yes, that's right. If that wouldn't be too much trouble, that would be great. How about five minutes, then? Good. Thank you."

"They're off duty, but the chief said they're up in

the crash pad playing cards. I'll take you up there."

The trip to the crash pad was easy with Randi leading. I was starting to get my bearings, at least on the 0-3 level, which had the dirty shirt, most of the ready rooms, and our staterooms. On a whim, I stopped by the CAG spaces and let the clerk, Petty Officer Lawrence, pick out what he wanted. He surprised me by grabbing the *New Yorker* and passing on the candy. Interesting taste for a young kid. He seemed surprised and grateful.

Next, we stopped by the crash pad, really just a room in the base of the carrier's superstructure, where the fire-rescue crew hung out. It was full of sailors waiting for their next shift on the flight deck. Their silver suits hung on pegs.

The chief introduced us to Petty Officers Douglas and Cates, the men who had rescued Hoser. I asked Douglas, a handsome African-American, if he was worried about the aircraft exploding during the rescue.

"To tell you the truth, sir, I didn't have time to think of anything but getting to the pilot. You know, we were almost hit by the aircraft when it crashed." He nodded toward his partner. "Bruce grabbed me and pulled me back, just as a piece of the landing gear came flying past. From that point on, the adrenaline was pumping so fast we were in a zone. Heck, I just let my training take over." He smiled. "I guess it's kind of a crazy way to make a living, isn't it?"

Cates spoke up. "How's that pilot doing, anyway? He was a big sumbitch, we . . ." His face reddened in embarrassment. "Oh, excuse me, ma'am. I didn't mean that like it sounded."

Randi said, "He's in the infirmary, still in a coma. By the way, that man is my uncle." The room quieted. She reached out and grabbed his big hand in both of hers. "If it wasn't for you guys, that big sumbitch would be dead, right now. As far as I'm concerned, you can call him anything you want."

I snapped a picture of Randi and the two fire-fighters, and then took one of the whole crew. Then I put the bag of goodies on the table. The Christmas-morning looks on their faces when they saw what was inside were priceless.

"I was saving this stuff for a special occasion," I said. "I can't think of anything better than meeting all of you. I hope you don't mind that your families will be reading about you in the paper tomorrow."

"No shit, sir?" asked the chief, while the other men stared openmouthed at me.

"No shit, guys."

Sometimes, I really loved my job.

CHAPTER 15

Friday, 18 Oct/1945

The passageway was full of crewmen heading top-side. The carrier was cranking up for the night-flight schedule. Randi wanted to go to the infirmary, and, of course, I had an article to write. She agreed to call me when Lieutenant Mason would be in the landing pattern so that we could watch her approaches on the closed-circuit television monitor in the ready room.

With the time difference, I still beat Saturday's deadline. My editor would be thrilled with the extra story, especially a hot one. As it turned out, Saturday's installment was more upbeat than I thought it would be when I sat down at the computer.

Triumph and Tragedy
Record-Breaking Landing Ends in Fiery Crash

Experts say that flying a high-performance jet off an aircraft carrier is the most exciting thing a person can do with their clothes on. Yesterday, strapped into the backseat of a Navy F/A–18 strike fighter, myth became reality for this reporter.

It is also the most dangerous job in the world, no matter how much experience and talent a pilot may have. Less than 20 minutes after this reporter climbed out of the backseat of Black Sheep 310, Captain Joe Santana, a living legend at age 51, recorded his 1500th carrier landing.

Santana, a highly decorated combat veteran, flew his trademark perfect approach, as he had for nearly 30 years of accident-free flying, on that final landing. Every eye on the USS *Ranger* was glued to the landing monitors that showed the Hornet's tailhook once again picking up the coveted three wire.

But, as thousands of sailors soon realized, there was something terribly wrong. The aircraft's landing gear buckled, and in a split second, a routine carrier landing turned into a fiery crash. With its tailhook no longer ensnared, the jet slid across the flight deck, as sailors fled its path, and slammed into the upraised steel panels of the jet-blast deflector. Then it erupted into a fireball.

Captain Santana, unconscious and gravely injured, was trapped inside the flame-enshrouded cockpit. Somehow, before most observers could grasp what had happened, before the debris even stopped cartwheeling down the flight deck, the men you see in the picture, were on their way to save the pilot.

Petty Officers Glen Douglas, age 22, and Bruce Cates, 23, having barely missed being killed by the wreckage themselves, gave no thought to their own safety before moving in to rescue a pilot in peril.

"I just let my training take over," said Douglas, when asked how he mustered the courage to enter the flames.

They also trusted their shipmates to perform their duties. This reporter watched from the safety of the ship's bridge, while every man and woman on the flight deck, most without fire-retardant clothing, joined the battle against the flames.

After explosively jettisoning the Plexiglas canopy, Cates and Douglas managed to unstrap the stricken pilot from his ejection seat and move him to a clear area, where doctors were waiting.

The entire rescue took less than three minutes.

On its way to the Mediterranean Sea, the USS *Ranger* was operating in the middle of the Atlantic Ocean. Far from any airfields, there were still 10 planes airborne that needed to land. Among them was Lieutenant Randi Cole, one of the Navy's only two female Hornet aviators, and the subject of yesterday's article.

Fire at sea is a sailor's worst nightmare. Pilots fear being stranded aloft, without the ability to refuel or land. Following their captain's orders, the flight-deck crew hoisted the smoldering wreckage by crane and dumped it over the side, to clear the deck for landing operations.

Captain Morganelli and his crew never panicked. In fact, after they recovered their aircraft, instead of taking a well-deserved break, they continued flight operations throughout the afternoon and long into the night.

When asked why, Captain Paul Morganelli said, "In combat, we can't stop because we take some damage. Frankly, you can't buy training like that."

Which brings us to the status of the Navy's only two women Hornet pilots, Lieutenants Cole and Mason. How are they performing?

"They're doing fine," their Air Wing Commander, Captain Ted Andrews, said. "Both are extremely talented pilots."

A great deal has been made of the suitability of women flying combat aircraft at sea, even though women have been flying high-performance aircraft for years. Many Americans are wondering how they would perform in an environment where even the most experienced pilots can be killed in an instant. Some are convinced that they won't have the stomach for it.

For at least one woman pilot, that question has been answered. Lieutenant Cole was tested yesterday by the cruelest of circumstances.

Captain Santana was her mentor. The man she called Uncle was her father's wingman, and best friend, in Vietnam. Santana stepped in and guided the young girl after Bill Cole was killed in a crash at sea.

Airborne during Santana's mishap, Randi Cole watched, from three thousand feet above, as his aircraft burned on the flight deck. Short on fuel, certain that she'd—again—lost the most important man in her life, Lieutenant Cole had to contain her emotions and concentrate on her flying. Eventually, she landed her own F/A–18 on that same deck, in rough seas.

Tough enough, for you?

Captain Santana, critically injured, remains in a coma. Today, and tonight, while you're reading this article, Lieutenant Cole, and the rest of the *Ranger*'s crew, will continue to fly, honing their combat skills, as they prepare to take their place on America's front line of defense.

I downloaded the pictures from the camera, added annotations, zipped the files, and headed down to the CAG spaces. Petty Officer Lawrence was still at work and happy to help me. He made a couple of phone calls, persuasively explaining my need for satellite communications. Then he gave me directions to the Communications Center.

After showing my ID card to the duty officer, and waiting while she confirmed my status with the XO of the ship, I was allowed to watch while a technician linked up with the *Herald*.

The transfer was quickly performed. I added an e-mail message requesting that my editor confirm that the wire services had picked up the story, so that I could let the firefighters know they were famous. Next I arranged with the duty officer to have my name added to the access list. She explained that I had been given the highest noncombat priority. Sounded good to me.

Heading back to my stateroom, my chores complete, I heard the now-familiar thump and roar of an aircraft landing above my head. The deck beneath me vibrated as the ship's engines pushed the *Ranger* to make enough wind for landing. I was beginning to tune in to the rhythms of shipboard life.

CHAPTER 16

Friday, 18 Oct/2105

I met Randi coming toward me in the passageway.

"I was just coming to get you," she said.

"How's Hoser?"

Her mouth flattened into a line. "He's still in a coma. The nurse said his feet moved, though. That's good news, isn't it?"

"Hell, yes. Spontaneous movement is always a good sign, especially within hours of the injury." I was making it up, but it made sense to me, and she seemed to buy it.

She perked up. "That's what I thought." Another aircraft slammed to a stop above us. "Let's go watch Amy."

I followed her down to Ready Two, the home of the Hawks of VFA–303. We entered from the back. The room, large by carrier standards, held about twenty-five oversize, upholstered chairs. A cross between an airline seat and a recliner, each had a metal desktop that could be folded out of the way and a drawer for storage underneath. Many had flight gear draped over the back.

Plaques and photos covered one long wall, while the opposite wall held the Greenie Board. I knew that this marking board recorded each aviator's landing performance, with each trap represented by a colored square. The colors corresponded to the grade assigned by the landing signal officers, or LSOs. Randi confirmed for me that green depicted an okay pass, which despite its understatement, was the best grade. A fair pass was yellow, and a red reflected a no-grade. Pilots naturally wanted all green, but that rarely happened. Still, most of the board was green with a smattering of yellow, some white, and just two red squares.

"What are the white ones with the letter 'B' in them?" I asked.

"Those are bolters. You know, when we miss the wires and get to go do it again," Randi said.

I thought about how much pressure the system exerted on a pilot, especially a nugget. Checking out Randi's grades, I saw that most were green, though there were three yellows in a row. "Your grades look good."

"Yeah, well, I was going great guns until I ran up against Dizzy."

"Dizzy?"

"He's the VFA–305 LSO. I ended up in the pattern with the Lobos and he gave me three fairs on passes that were some of my best. The guys in my squadron say he's kind of a jerk."

"What's his real name?"

"Lieutenant Commander Bradley. Why?"

"Just trying to get a feel for the players out here. Has he been tough on Amy, too?"

"She's pretty frustrated. He talks a lot."

"What do you mean?"

"LSOs usually keep quiet on the radio, unless they've got something important to say. We're conditioned that when an LSO says something, we react immediately. The inflection in their voice is important, too. Dizzy's the kind of LSO who can talk a pilot into overreacting and screw up a perfectly good approach."

"Does he do it on purpose?"

"Who knows? I'm just glad he's not my LSO."

Randi introduced me to several of the pilots. A couple of guys joked with her good-naturedly. One asked about Hoser, and everyone listened with concern to her report. From what I could see, she was being openly accepted as another member of the squadron.

I noticed an interesting phenomenon. Conversations throughout the room paused at mid-sentence as an aircraft came into view on the monitor, and resumed, without a hitch, as soon as the aircraft was safely aboard. Even the guy who was quietly reading a book performed the odd ritual, pausing to look up, watch the pass, and return to his reading. These people were obsessed with landings. As an ever-present reminder, the Greenie Board would be a source of immense pride or public shame. Tough way to make a living.

Randi led me to her seat, and the empty one next

to it, which were located in the middle of the room.

"I figured the new pilot would sit in the rear," I said.

"Everything is done by seniority around here, and I'm not that junior anymore. But Amy is, so she's stuffed in the back of the Lobo Ready Room."

The squadron duty officer turned up the volume, so that we could hear the LSOs and pilots. Occasionally, the low-light camera would pick up the ghostly figure of one of the deck crew checking the wires. In the crosshairs, we could make out the flashing lights of the conga line of aircraft lined up, in one-minute intervals, behind the ship.

I watched, fascinated, as the largest group of lights gradually grew into an F–14.

"One-zero-three, Tomcat ball, five-point-two, manual."

"Roger, ball."

Almost immediately, the aircraft began to drift to the right side of the screen.

The LSO sounded calm. "Right for lineup."

The Tomcat started back toward center, but drifted low.

The LSO's voice was coaxing. "Power."

The Tomcat remained low, as it grew larger.

More insistent. "Power."

The Tomcat responded, climbing, but drifting again.

"RIGHT for lineup!"

The Tomcat's huge wings dipped awkwardly, and the aircraft dropped into the wires. Our room shook as the arresting gear paid out and the Tomcat's engines roared to full throttle.

A different voice said, "Light's on deck."

The Tomcat pilot turned off his external lights and taxied clear.

One of the pilots in the back summed up the pass. "Ugly!"

Another said, "Hey, Randi, how'd you like to be flying F–14s?"

"Not for all the money in the world."

The room erupted in laughter. I asked her about it.

"Tomcats are much tougher to bring aboard than Hornets. But not that tough. That guy"—she smiled—"or *gal*, was killing snakes in the cockpit."

"What do you mean?"

She grabbed a make-believe stick and pantomimed moving it violently.

"I get it. What kind of grade would that pass get?"

"Definitely a no-grade. I don't think it was bad enough for a cut. That's a pass that is graded as dangerous. Regardless, I'm betting that pilot is just glad to be aboard." She leaned toward me, and whispered, "I know the RIO is."

The next aircraft, a Hornet, flew into focus. By contrast, there wasn't a word spoken after the ball call as the aircraft stayed near the crosshairs all the way to touchdown. Nobody in the ready room commented. Again, I was struck by how hard it was to squeeze a compliment out of pilots.

Amy was up next. We heard her ball call. When the LSO answered, several guys groaned.

"Dizzy," someone said, with what sounded like disgust.

The Hornet was right in the middle.

"A little power."

The aircraft rose.

"Fly the ball."

The Hornet settled, coming back down to the crosshairs, growing larger on the screen.

"Watch your lineup."

The wings twitched.

Then, "Power." More insistent, "POWER!"

The aircraft flattened out, its descent rate stopped.

Almost as an afterthought, the voice added, "Easy with it."

The Hornet missed the wires, the hook leaving sparks as it trailed, clickety-clack, across the steel deck.

"Bolter! Bolter!"

Several pilots chimed in at once, angrily denouncing the LSO.

"Jesus, what the hell was that?"

"Let her fly the damn airplane, Dizzy!"

"What an asshole."

"What happens now?" I asked.

"She enters the bolter pattern. They'll have her climb to twelve hundred feet and turn downwind. Then they'll vector her into a hole built into the stack. It'll give her time to settle down." Randi didn't sound too convinced.

The front door opened and a commander walked in asking, "What's all the commotion?"

The duty officer answered, "Skipper, Dizzy just powered that nugget from 305 into a bolter."

Another pilot spoke up. "That guy's a menace, Skipper. She was flying a rails pass until he opened his yap."

The CO was about to reply when his eyes locked on to me.

He spoke to the squadron duty officer, or SDO. A rebuke was hidden in a matter-of-fact tone of voice. "You didn't tell me we had company."

The SDO's face reddened.

I stood up and introduced myself. He seemed wary, uncomfortable with a stranger in his ready room, unsure what kind of threat I posed. But he was polite and offered me a cup of coffee, pointing to the back of the room. He wanted to talk. I followed him back.

"Mr. Warner, I hope you don't take things literally. Lieutenant Commander Bradley isn't a menace, he's just, well, let's just say, cautious."

The CO's name tag said SLICK O'HARA. I glanced over his shoulder at the Greenie Board. All greens. "Would you like him to control your passes, Commander?"

"No comment." He was smiling.

I cut him a break. "Actually, I'm very impressed with how well your squadron seems to be accepting their new nugget."

He visibly relaxed. "Yes. That's really gone quite

well. Lieutenant Cole is a solid aviator. I'm very happy with what I've seen so far."

"I understand she'll be flying ACM tomorrow."

"That's right. In fact, I'll be her flight lead. I like to fly with all our new pilots. It gives me a chance to track their progress."

"And see how they act under pressure?"

He nodded. "That's important out here. Better to find out how a kid flies while the skipper is looking over his or her shoulder, in a canned scenario, than to find out when the shit hits the fan."

A voice from the front of the room. "Skipper, here she comes again."

We walked up, took our seats and watched Amy's second pass. Once again, the start was square in the middle of the crosshairs.

"Five-oh-four, Hornet ball, four-point-two, auto."

The LSO's voice was different. "Roger, ball. Good start."

"Who's that?" someone asked.

The SDO said, "Sounds like Pirate."

In answer to my raised eyebrows, Randi whispered, "They must have pulled Dizzy. Pirate is 305's senior LSO. He's real popular."

The difference was night and day. Amy flew a solid pass, catching a four wire. Randi said that Amy would be refueled and sent out for more. We watched for forty minutes as the pilots practiced their craft. There were no more bolters or scary no-grades. Landing after landing went textbook. Dizzy's voice never reappeared.

Soon after the last aircraft was recovered, pilots started trickling in, still in their gear. All were animated, talking in loud voices and laughing as their squadron mates critiqued their landings in unflattering terms.

"Geez, Snort, you looked like you were flying with your eyes closed out there."

"What are you jaw-jacking about, Ski?"

"Yeah, it was so ugly, we figured you couldn't stand to watch it yourself."

"Hey, you know what you can do with . . ."

"At ease, gentlemen," the skipper cautioned in a parental tone.

At first, I thought it was because of Randi, but I was wrong.

"We have a guest." He nodded at me.

The pilots debriefed the SDO with their flight time and landing totals and moved on toward the maintenance desk.

The one called Snort asked, "Hey, duty, what's the flick?"

I noticed all conversation stopped, obviously in anticipation of the answer.

"We've got a double feature. I got *Predator*"—there were some catcalls—"and, we're swapping with Ready One for *Trading Places*." This was met with a chorus of approval.

Randi leaned over and whispered, "Nothing changes. My last cruise, anything with Jamie Lee Curtis, especially with her naked, was a surefire winner. I bet the guys have each seen it a hundred times."

"Does that bother you?"

"Hell, no. It's not a skin flick, she just flashes her boobs. Boys will be boys. I'll be worried when they don't want to see it. You want to go talk with Amy, right? I'll take you down to our stateroom in a couple of minutes."

"She won't be too tired?"

"Not after night traps. She'll be jazzed for another hour, at least."

"Is that why everyone was so boisterous?"

"Oh, yeah. You really get a buzz from all the adrenaline. After you calm down, it's like falling off a cliff. I slept like a rock last night. It'll be Amy's turn tonight."

"How about you?"

"I don't think I'll be sleeping much as long as Hoser is still in a coma."

"Should you be flying?"

She gave me a quick, hard look. I got the message. The ready room was no place to talk about grounding a pilot, especially a woman pilot, who was still proving herself.

Still, it was a good question. I resolved to watch her for signs of fatigue. If we were home, I'd solve her sleeping problem with a bottle of wine, but not aboard ship. Alcohol was strictly prohibited. Which was damned inconvenient. I could use a scotch after the day I'd had.

CHAPTER 17

Friday, 18 Oct/2210

We caught up with Amy in the passageway. Her face still bore the imprint of the oxygen mask and helmet. Her eyes were wide-open, active, and her questions came fast and furious.

"Jack! Welcome aboard. How do you like it?"

Before I could answer, she asked Randi, "Any change in Hoser's condition? God, it was hard to keep my mind on flying, at least until I got in the pattern. Were you guys watching? Man, after that bolter, I was thinking, it might be a real long night, but then I settled down."

Randi said, "You looked good out there, roomie. How'd the LSOs call it?"

"Three okays, a fair, and a bolter." She smiled and shrugged. "I'll take it."

"Jack wants to get your impressions so far. I told him he could meet you in our room, is that okay?"

"Sure. Let me finish debriefing. I'll be down there in ten minutes."

Randi asked me to give her five minutes to

change, so I went to my stateroom. When I opened the door, the phone was ringing.

"Jack Warner."

There was no answer, but I could hear that someone was on the line. This wasn't uncommon for me. Sources frequently get stage fright.

"You've got me, but you'll have to speak up."

I had to strain to hear the low whisper. Obviously someone was trying to disguise his voice. "They're in danger."

"Who's in danger?" I grabbed my pocket tape recorder and turned it on.

"Those new pilots. The women."

I squeezed the lapel microphone in between my ear and the handset. Whoever this was, he wasn't trying to be intimidating. I had to be careful not to spook him.

"What do you recommend I do? How can I help?"

"Tell them not to fly anymore."

The more he talked, the more familiar his voice became, despite his attempts to mask it. "Why should they listen to me. I'm just a reporter. You'll have to give me something more solid."

"They've got to listen. You've got to make them."

"Then you've got to give me something more to go on, friend. I know you're a good citizen. Help me help them."

"I can't. They'll kill me."

"Who's going to kill you? Why are you in danger?"

"Just don't trust anybody." With a click, the line went dead. Maybe I'd pushed too hard. I sat down at the desk and ran the tape. The quality was grainy, but I'd caught most of it.

"They've got to listen. You've got to make them."

The guy sounded sincere, I'd give him that, and he sounded scared. My immediate problem concerned what the hell I was going to do with the tape. I could play it for CAG or the captain, if they'd listen to it, but if I chose wrong, and my source's voice was recognized, I might put him in jeopardy.

The more I thought about it, the tougher it was for me to accept the captain's decision to push 501's wreckage over the side. I'd once covered a Navy mishap investigation and knew that they'd go to almost any extreme to salvage wreckage for clues. Yet here was a captain who just pushed it over the side instead of moving it out of the way and saving it for the investigators. Was there something to hide? And before Hoser had climbed in, Amy had been flying it. Was there a connection?

Then there was CAG. His deputy was one of my leads. Even if CAG weren't involved, would he be willing to suspect his own deputy? There was also the danger that he'd let something slip in front of Holmes.

On the other hand, I couldn't just sit on it. Cole and Mason might very well be in danger; they certainly had a right to know about the call. I slipped the recorder in my pocket and went to their stateroom.

Amy was still on a high from her night hop. Randi was dressed in gym clothes.

"I'm going to go catch a workout," Randi said.

"Hang on a minute," I said. "I've got something you both need to hear."

When I pulled out the recorder, they glanced at each other and back at me with puzzled expressions.

"I just got an anonymous phone call. I was able to record most of it. There's a man on this boat who thinks you are both in danger."

I played it twice. Neither woman said a word.

"Well?" I asked.

Amy spoke first. "Jack, I've been getting phone calls like that since I first started flight school. I don't let myself take them seriously."

Randi said, "Same for me. I just hang up and feel sorry for the jerk. My bet is that he's a right-wing nut. Maybe someone who is convinced that having women on ships is morally wrong. In any case, what can we do about it? If we take this to our COs or CAG, we'll be grounded."

Amy was emphatic. "She's right. If that happens, this guy gets just what he wants. Jack, we can't stop flying because one idiot makes a crank call."

I thought they were dismissing it too casually. "Hold on a second. Aren't you the least bit suspicious that right after Amy is pulled unexpectedly from 501, the gear collapses?"

Amy sat up straight and spoke with conviction. "I don't want to offend you, Jack, but the suggestion that it was sabotage is ludicrous. Nobody out here would do that, and besides, the gear didn't fail until his third trap. Listen, I'm not saying that there aren't more than one or two guys who would rather see us on the beach." She glanced at Randi, then turned to face me again. "But, this is the United States Navy, and I'm not about to accept that someone would try to kill one of us just to get rid of women pilots. These men have sworn an oath to obey orders. They're patriots who sacrifice a great deal on behalf of their country. They may grumble about us being here, but they'll bust their butts to make it work, because it's their duty."

It was clear that, without a smoking gun, there was no way to convince either of them to stop flying. I nodded my acquiescence.

Randi said, "Jack, you've got to promise us you won't publish anything about this without hard proof."

Pissed off, I snapped at her, "That's right, Lieutenant, I'm spring-loaded to go to page one without any proof."

"I'm sorry." She looked contrite. "I didn't mean that like it sounded."

"Look, let's make sure we all understand the ground rules. As a reporter, my only assets are my skills at investigating and my professional integrity. I will write what I see as fact. And frankly, I can't be objective on this assignment and be your friend at the same time. Your best bet is to trust me to tell the truth, because that's what I do. When I'm done with this series, we can be friends, if that's something you still want. But until then I'm the press. Got it?"

Amy said, "That's fair."

"Randi?"

"I hate this, Jack. You can say what you want, but I consider you my friend, regardless of what you do for a living." As she stepped toward the door, she poked me hard in the chest. "Deal with it."

After Randi left, Amy and I discussed her first couple days of squadron life.

She was upbeat. "It's been great. I know a couple of the guys from flight school, and everyone has been helpful. I'm going to work in maintenance as a branch officer. I was worried that they'd stick me in Admin, because I'm a woman, you know, but the XO asked me where I wanted to work and then he gave me the exact job I asked for."

"How about the flying?"

"Oh, it's been terrific. We have solid jets. Apparently our maintenance department has improved dramatically in the past few months."

That reminded me of Master Chief Cardone. "Hey, do you know the number to maintenance? I know your master chief and would like to touch base with him."

"Sure." She dialed the number and asked for Cardone.

After hanging up she explained that he was out in the hangar bay supervising an engine swap. "Do you want to go see him?"

"Yes, but I'd probably get lost."

"No sweat. I'll take you down there. I need to meet my night-check troops anyway."

We meandered our way down toward the hangar

deck. Amy's natural friendliness drew smiles from just about everyone we saw.

The hangar deck was an immense cavern. Jets and equipment were shoehorned into every corner. We stopped and watched a team of sailors move a Tomcat into an impossibly tight space. The tractor driver was able to manhandle the big aircraft by using his tractor to push a tow bar connected to the aircraft's nosewheel. He carried off the feat with calculated nonchalance. Two brown-shirts quickly unhooked his tractor, and the yellow-shirt driver roared off in a cloud of diesel smoke to move another forty-million-dollar aircraft.

"What if he crunches one?" I asked.

Amy said, "They'll demote him, and he'll be lifting tow bars for somebody else. It happens, but rarely. Especially when you consider the dozens of moves they do each shift."

We found Cardone with his head buried in the belly of a Lobo F/A–18. He sounded in rare form.

"What the hell kind of connection is that, Pete? You guys stop using tools and decide to crimp the line with a rock?"

Apparently Pete started to disagree, but Cardone was ready. "Listen, you big oaf, I was swedging hydraulic lines when you were still in diapers. I told you when I made you night-check supervisor that I wanted you to vouch for every single job done by those hillbillies and lunatics in your shop. Now, cut that ugly-looking fitting off and teach your kids how to do it right, *capisce*?"

He was still muttering to himself when he ducked out of the jet's engine bay and wiped his hands on a rag. Built like a fireplug, Cardone was about five-foot-six, with Popeye forearms and no neck.

"Master Chief?" Amy said, trying to get his attention.

He turned toward us. Surprise, then recognition registered on his face.

"Well, look what the cat dragged in. What the hell are you doing out here?"

I explained that I rode aboard with Hoser.

His face sank. "Geez, I couldn't believe what happened. I've known that man for my entire Navy life and never seen him so much as scratch an airplane. I went by the infirmary, but they wouldn't let me see him. How is the old bastard?"

I filled him in, then asked him if he'd met Lieutenant Mason.

"Of course. She's flown my best birds. Hasn't broke one yet."

Amy laughed. "That's because you told me I'd be down here fixing it."

"And so you shall, Lieutenant. I make sure all of my JOs get plenty of time with a wrench in their hands." He looked at me and winked. "It keeps them humble."

"Well, my daddy had me draining crankcases and lubing landing gear before I was ten. I'd consider it an honor to be allowed to work with your team."

Amy knew how to butter up the old master chief. He spoke gruffly, just as he had to the mechanics. "For starters, why don't you head over to that shop of yours and introduce yourself to your crew of hooligans? I'll keep Mr. Warner busy for you."

When she was out of earshot, he said, "I like that gal. I think she's going to be okay. She listens and knows how to make the troops feel important." He elbowed me. "I'm glad you're out here, Jack. I never got to thank you for that write-up you gave me in the newspaper. My wife mailed the damn thing to everyone we know."

"No sweat, Art."

He took a moment to give me the once-over and fingered the sleeve of my khaki shirt. "Looks like you're trying to keep a low profile, buddy. This is more than a story about Hoser's trap total isn't it?"

"Afraid so. I'm out here to cover the Navy's latest attempt to integrate the Hornet community. Care to give me something quotable?"

"Yeah, right. What? You think I just fell off a turnip truck? You keep me out of this, *compadre*. I'm not tiptoeing in that minefield. Now, is there something special I can do for you?"

This wasn't the time to go into my suspicions. Looking around the hangar deck, I saw at least a hundred sailors and ten chiefs. "Is it always this busy, Art?"

"Not always, but you can bet there's usually going to be a bunch of broke-dick airplanes needing our attention."

"I heard you were handpicked to straighten out this maintenance department."

It was his turn to look around. "Yeah, they coaxed me out of retiring for this. Can you believe I'm that dumb?"

"I believe that there was an outfit in trouble. One that you knew you could help, and instead of taking a well-deserved break, you left Liz and came out here to work your magic."

His face turned beet red at the compliment, and he pretended to see something amiss. "I gotta get back to those idiots. I'll find you tomorrow and have you down to eat at the Chiefs' Mess." He slapped me in the stomach. "Looks like you could use a good meal, *hombre*."

Alone, I wandered through the hangar deck. It was separated into three bays, each of which could be sealed by giant sliding doors. Everywhere I looked was equipment for fighting fire. Overhead, spray nozzles and fire hoses were strategically placed around the perimeter. There were also firefighters stationed in a Plexiglas cubicle high above the deck.

I struck up a conversation with a couple of sailors who were on a break and asked if they thought someone could gain access to a plane without being seen.

"Not easily," answered one. "There's always someone here. Besides, we have roving watches all night. See that guy in the corner?" He pointed out a sailor I'd missed who was dressed in uniform and carrying a large black flashlight.

I'd seen enough. It was time for bed. Only then did I realize that I had to find my own way back.

CHAPTER 18

Friday, 18 Oct/2315

I managed to get lost, of course. I found that it did absolutely no good to try to remember a particular hatch or ladder by landmarks; they literally all looked alike. Somehow, I ended up standing in a small, dark niche lit only by the glow of a red lightbulb. A sailor came upon me and excused himself as he opened a hatch and stepped through. With no better prospects, I followed him, only to find myself outside, on the carrier's flight deck. As my eyes adjusted, I realized that I was behind the superstructure, or what sailors called the island.

Flight quarters must have been secured because there were no aircraft turning. I could just make out the silhouettes of dozens of sailors working on nearby aircraft. It struck me how odd it was that they kept the flight deck darkened except for very dim edge lights and hooded flashlights. Of course, it made sense when you think of the big carrier's vulnerability to attack, but it also made the flight deck dangerous as hell. Just walking from one point to another was difficult. Lurking obstacles were ready to trip, gash, or maim. Then there was the possibility of falling overboard.

Certainly in peacetime they could turn on some lights for safety's sake. Then it dawned on me that there was absolutely nothing sane or safe about running one of the world's busiest airports at night, in the middle of the ocean.

I carefully made my way to the starboard catwalk, a suspended walkway, running fore and aft, that was attached to the side of the flight deck. Its metal grating was an open mesh, allowing me full view of the churning ocean sixty feet below. If I fell overboard, I wouldn't be heard or even missed until morning. It was a sobering thought. Still the water was mesmerizing; its phosphorescence shone in swirling patterns as the ship's hull cut through the waves.

A gruff voice, coming from above me, interrupted my thoughts. "Where's your flight-deck gear, buddy?"

I turned to look up at the questioner. He pointed a narrow-beam flashlight in my face.

"I guess I don't have any."

I could only make out a shadowy figure behind the flashlight. The man's face was impossible to see. I was uncomfortable. "Look, I'm Jack Warner. A civilian. I guess I shouldn't be out here." I started to climb back to the flight deck.

"I know who you are." He moved in front of me on the top of the stairs, blocking my path. The light stayed in my eyes. The guy was purposely

being an asshole. "Listen up, Warner. You need a
float coat, a cranial, and ear protection to be on the
flight deck." He lowered his voice, and added with
deliberate menace, "Besides, you don't belong out
here."

Clearly, he was talking about more than my
unescorted walk in the night air. In the silence that
followed, I stepped back, reached behind me, and
grabbed the short guardrail, acutely aware that it
was the only thing between me and a long fall into
the dark ocean.

"This isn't a place for women and civilians,
Warner. It's dangerous out here. Things happen to
people who aren't careful."

Message delivered, the light snapped off. He
was gone before my eyes readjusted.

My heart was beating hard and fast.

For the next ten minutes, I wound my way
through the gray maze of passageways, eventually
finding my stateroom. After washing up, I
stretched out on the lower bunk, only to find that
my mattress was five-foot-ten. I'm six-two. It was
much less comfortable than I remembered from my
afternoon nap.

Pondering the encounter on the catwalk, I was
relieved to find that my reaction was enthusiasm.
The old juices were flowing. It was the feel of a
hot story. Both the phone call and the threat meant
that I was getting close to it. All in all, it had been
a helluva day.

Unable to sleep, I examined the graffiti written

on the metal bottom of the upper bunk. In the glow of the built-in reading lamp, I made out a few names, a couple dates, and examples of sardonic wit: NAVY = NEVER AGAIN VOLUNTEER YOURSELF!, and added beneath in a different hand, NAVY: IT'S NOT JUST A JOB . . . IT'S A BLOW-JOB!

Most notable were the marks denoting days of some long-past cruise. By quick count, I surmised that the tidy group of hash marks totaled 189 days, more than six months out of someone's life. From my position, sprawled bone-tired on that midget mattress, I was staggered by the realization that each mark was added one at a time. Every night, as the sailor laid his head down, he allowed his thoughts to drift away from work across thousands of miles of ocean toward his home and family.

The last mark was an exclamation point circled in red magic marker. The excitement of pulling into home port, knowing that he'd soon be embraced in loving arms, must have been overwhelming. I thought long and hard about the sailors aboard the *Ranger*, who tonight were carefully marking one more day done, albeit on a very short list.

Presumably, this sailor had made it home safely to his loved ones. But what had he missed? A first step? A home run? Or had the washer broken the day after he sailed? Then there were the darker questions. Had his wife been faithful? Had he?

It was easy to imagine the pulse of the ship beneath me. Five thousand souls uprooted from their lives and sent sailing abroad. Whatever it accomplished, the cost of sending this warship overseas was more than fuel, food, and paychecks.

I fell asleep to the sounds of chains being dragged across the flight deck and dropped with resounding clatter. It was oddly comforting to know that this floating city never slept.

CHAPTER 19

Ward Room I—
Saturday, 19 Oct/0600

I met Randi for breakfast in the dirty shirt. She was upbeat, having been down to the infirmary and told that Hoser had rested well and was showing signs of recovery, including spontaneous movement in all four limbs.

"The doctor was very encouraged by Hoser's brain activity. Apparently, the EEG is returning to normal. He said we might see him regain consciousness anytime."

Randi was eager to finish her meal and get to her 0615 brief. I asked her if she was nervous about flying with the skipper.

"A little bit," she said, then leaned toward me and spoke confidentially. "ACM is something I do pretty well. I know I can put up a good fight, and frankly, I'm eager to see how I measure up against these fleet pilots."

I had already decided against telling her about my encounter on the catwalk. It wouldn't be enough to stop her from flying, and it might be a dangerous distraction.

After Randi excused herself, I got a fresh cup of coffee and joined a group of aviators sitting at another table, one of whom I recognized from Randi's squadron. I introduced myself and sipped the strong brew while they bantered back and forth. This morning's hot topic concerned the news that Libyan leader, Moammar Gadhafi, was charged by the US State Department with building a chemical-weapons plant. This was a particularly big event, because the likely response from the US would include parking an aircraft carrier off the Libyan coastline.

There was lively debate whether the *America* or the *Ranger* would be given the mission.

"We haven't even in-chopped, yet," one of the pilots stated. "There's no way they're going to send us when the *America* is right there, ready to go." About half the aviators voiced agreement.

One pilot disagreed. "You're forgetting that we've got three Hornet squadrons and they've only got two, and *America*'s scheduled to out-chop in three days. I hear she's scheduled for yard work. With the way those labor contracts work, they don't slide yard dates."

"What do you think, Mr. Warner?" someone asked. "What's the news media say?"

I held up my hands. "Sorry, guys, my contacts out here are no better than yours. I wonder if the Air Force is being put on alert. Weren't they used on the Libyan raid in 1986?"

This brought several expressions of disdain. "The Air Force?" a Marine pilot challenged. "Those anal bastards would have to have three months' notice, and even then it might conflict with their long-range golf plans. Besides, what are they going to send?"

"How about the B–1s?" someone asked.

The Marine snorted derisively. "Now there's a fine weapons system. The whole fleet of the damn things, each costing more than my entire squadron, has never dropped a bomb in anger." He turned to me. "No, Mr. Warner. This is a job for tailhook pilots."

"Does that include women?" I asked, in hopes of provoking a reaction.

He didn't even pause. "As long as they carry their weight. Hell, yes."

There were nods of agreement around the table. I was surprised by their ready assent, and said so.

A brown-haired, sharp-eyed pilot wearing a TOP-GUN patch spoke for the first time. "Mr. Warner, most of us have flown with women since flight school. It's no big deal; we're used to it. We knew it was just a matter of time before they came to our community. As long as they're held to the same standards as the rest of us, I've got no problem with it. From what I hear, the two we got are the best students available, of either sex. What more can you ask for?"

There was no disagreement.

"What about combat?" I asked.

"Well, they're nuggets. You don't throw nuggets into the frying pan until they're ready. That'll have to be decided on a case-by-case basis, but someday, I fully expect to be leading a woman into combat as my wingman."

"Or, being led by one, as her wingperson," said the Marine, taunting his counterpart.

TOPGUN smiled in submission. "You're right. Or, being led by one."

I pushed it. "Are you trying to tell me that everyone out here shares your sense of fair play?"

There was a noticeable pause, while the men avoided eye contact with me. I'd hit a nerve. One of the older pilots finally picked up the challenge. "We've got our orders, Mr. Warner. I mean, it's not like we have a choice in the matter. We're part of a new Navy. But, to answer your question, there are some old heads, and probably a couple youngsters, who aren't thrilled with the concept."

"Then, what about them? Won't that present a big problem?" I asked.

He answered frankly, "Yeah, for them." His response generated a ripple of laughter. "The guys who don't get on board with the program are going to wind up pushing pencils, or out on the street. Orders are orders."

The group disbanded amid a flurry of friendly jibes. I was invited to visit the Marine Ready Room later in the day, which I agreed to do, and left alone at the table.

I pondered the problems faced by the men who conspired to rid the Navy of women Hornet pilots. Not only would they have to remain secretive, to prevent being discovered by Navy authorities, they wouldn't know whom, among their squadron mates, wingmen, and roommates, could be trusted. Officers were sworn to follow orders, as part of their code of conduct, and these men were violating that supposedly sacred oath. In breaking the rules, even to preserve the male-only identity of the Hornet community, these men also broke faith with their deepest obligations.

It struck me that it would take a powerful rationalization to overcome the stigma of violating the code of conduct. These men would have to convince themselves that their actions answered a higher moral calling. To find my conspirators, I needed to watch for men whose actions and demeanor revealed that kind of arrogance.

"Good morning, Mr. Warner."

I looked up into the looming face of Commander Holmes as he placed his tray on the table. We were soon joined by Lieutenant Commander Bradley, the VFA–305 LSO who had guided Amy's first pass last night. Holmes made the introductions.

Bradley was talkative, almost hyper. He spoke uninterrupted while shoving food into his mouth. "So, Mr. Warner, I hear you got a taste of flying behind the boat. Too bad about the crash, though. Have you heard any more news about the captain's condition?"

"Yes. Lieutenant Cole was told this morning that he is showing signs of recovery, though he's still unconscious."

"Very good," said Holmes. "By the way, did you

hear the news this morning about our friend in Libya?"

"The pilots were talking about it at breakfast. Do you think *Ranger* might be sent there?"

They exchanged meaningful looks, making it obvious that they were privy to info on the subject.

Holmes lowered his voice and spoke dramatically, "I would suggest that you ask Captain Morganelli if you can attend today's thirteen-hundred brief in CVIC. That's the Intel Center." Sitting back, he added smugly, "You might just want to sharpen your pencils. You could be in for a major exclusive."

"Well, that's why I'm out here. And I appreciate your keeping me up to speed." I made sure both of them thought me grateful and open to suggestion.

Again, the exchange of looks.

Bradley spoke. "Commander Holmes tells me that your experiences yesterday might have given you a new perspective on the importance of our job out here."

The bait was in the water. "Yes, they did. I had no idea how dangerous life on the flight deck is, not just for the pilots, but for the sailors, too. I told the commander that I now understand how important it is that you get only the best pilots available. I can see how affirmative-action quotas would be misplaced out here."

Bradley loved it. "Exactly! Like you found out, you've got to see our world, maybe even experience the danger firsthand, to understand. Mr. Warner, it's absolutely vital that you use this opportunity to share your revelations with the public."

"It's a touchy subject."

"You're telling us. Look, the cloak of political correctness has covered the eyes and ears of our leadership. They're all . . ."

Holmes cleared his throat. I figured he was warning the young zealot before he said anything quotable, but the signal came too late. I'd been a reporter too long to miss Bradley's use of the word, "us." That little slip was damning evidence.

"Mr. Warner understands all this better than we'll ever know," Holmes said smoothly. "He's been covering Navy brass since we were polishing it." Both men laughed heartily at the joke.

Bradley took another tact. "Seriously, Mr. Warner, we need to make sure that everyone understands that flying strike fighters off the boat is not an occupation where we should start correcting society's mistakes." He turned to Holmes, and asked, "Should I tell him about last night?"

Holmes acted as though he was giving due consideration to the decision, though I was certain it was prearranged. "Go ahead. He has a right to know."

Bradley said, "Last night I was waving the night recovery." His smile was self-deprecating. "I'm sorry, I've got to remember to stop using slang. Waving is a term LSOs use to describe controlling approaches and landings."

I nodded my understanding.

"Anyway, one of the aircraft was flown by Ms. Mason, our new nugget. Up till then, she'd been performing satisfactorily—nothing to write home about—but she's met the minimum standards. Until last night." He examined me with keen interest, gauging my response.

Playing my part in the charade, I remained glued to his narrative, as if I knew nothing of the event. I felt the scrutiny of Commander Holmes.

Encouraged, Bradley continued. "I don't know if it was nerves or lack of skill, but Mason was all over the sky on her first pass. I had to give her several calls, each of which she either ignored or overreacted to. It was an ugly approach, and she ended up boltering."

In response to his questioning look, I indicated I knew what a bolter was.

"Anyway, I was getting ready to talk to her on downwind, try and calm her down, you know, when the call came in."

"What call?"

Holmes answered, "The call to pull Dizzy."

"Why would they pull the LSO?"

"It came from CAG, and he's not saying why. But what remains is the fact that the first time a woman pilot gets herself into a bind, suddenly the LSO is to blame!"

I couldn't resist tweaking them. "So what happened to her after they pulled you?"

That was not the question they'd hoped for. Bradley said, "She eventually settled down and got aboard. But, that's not the point. The point is that she's getting special treatment. Do you think any other LSO is going to give either of the women bad grades?" He answered his own question. "No, sir. Not when the CAG himself is ready to pull the plug. No, Mr. Warner, it's not right, and I'm sorry to say it, but it's going to come back to haunt them."

"What do you mean?"

"I mean that last night was decent weather. Wait until one of those prima donnas ends up in a weak jet on a crummy night. She won't have the backbone for it, and CAG won't be able to kiss it and make it better."

"I see what you mean." And I did. I saw exactly how these two assholes had managed to convince themselves, and God knew who else, to believe that their cause was righteous. I needed to do some more background checks and keep an eye on their circle of friends.

Excusing myself, after thanking them again, I found my way down to the infirmary. The head nurse recognized me and led me in to visit Hoser.

"He's been active this morning," she said. "In fact, when I gave him his sponge bath, he was definitely responsive." She looked at me meaningfully.

Slowly, it dawned on me what she meant. "Oh, you mean . . . well, yes, of course, I see . . ." I tried to recover. "That would be good news, wouldn't it?"

"Well, I certainly think Captain Santana would think so. Don't you?" She was teasing me.

She laughed at my discomfiture and left me alone with Hoser.

"Well, you old goat. Not even a coma can keep

you down, so to speak," I told him.

He kept on sleeping. On the spur of the moment, I pulled up a chair and proceeded to tell Hoser about everything that had happened, from his accident, to the anonymous phone call, Amy's night fright, the catwalk encounter, even the news from Libya. He was the perfect listener, never interrupting, allowing me to go at my own pace. I found it very therapeutic.

All too soon I was escorted out, but told to come back in the afternoon. The surgeon was busy on the phone, but he flashed a thumbs-up when he recognized me.

Hoser was on the mend.

CHAPTER 20

Saturday, 19 Oct/1015

I had to visit *the man*. Not knowing the protocol, I meandered my way up innumerable ladders until I found the entrance to the captain's bridge. There I encountered a behemoth Marine guard. He was the size of a building, his mahogany arms each as big as one of my legs.

"I was hoping to see the captain," I said.

He remained absolutely immobile and equally impassive. I wasn't even sure he'd heard me.

"My name is Jack Warner. I'm a reporter."

His eyes ratcheted to my face, locked on mine, and his scowl deepened.

Remembering my ID card, I fished it out of my wallet and handed it over, as carefully as if I were feeding a lion.

He took the card, in a white-gloved hand, and eyed it suspiciously. Then, with begrudging acknowledgment, he turned slightly and keyed an intercom switch.

He spoke quietly, without once taking his eyes

off me, his voice clipped, yet professional. "Visitor to see the captain. Name, Mr. Jack Warner, a civilian."

"Wait one."

During the delay, I felt uncomfortable in the presence of this sharp Marine in his dress-blue trousers, me in my wrinkled pseudo uniform.

"Send Mr. Warner in."

The guard used a key to unlock the door and held it open for me. I wondered why a captain needed a bodyguard on his own ship.

Captain Morganelli was seated in his chair and waved me over. "Well, you must be getting your sea legs if you can find your own way up here, Mr. Warner," he said.

"I'm beginning to feel at home, though I may never get used to that shower."

He laughed good-naturedly at what must be an oft-heard complaint. "What brings you up here this morning?"

"I was hoping to get your permission to attend the thirteen-hundred briefing."

He gave me a look of mock surprise. "That's pretty good work, Mr. Warner. I called that meeting less than an hour ago. That must be why you're paid the big bucks."

"So I can go?"

He seemed to mull it over before saying, "I guess that will be okay. But we'll have to wait until your security credentials are confirmed before you can sit in on the strategy sessions and issue any reports. Of course you understand, don't you, that since you're not officially out here to cover this operation, there might be a problem?" He raised his eyebrows.

I started to object. "But . . ." I stopped myself when I noticed the grin tugging at his mouth.

"Relax." He reached up and patted me on the shoulder. "I've already contacted the Pentagon. You've been assigned as the wire-service pool reporter for the upcoming operation."

"Libya?" I asked, trying to appear nonchalant.

"Yup. We're on our way—do not pass go, do not collect two hundred dollars."

"Can I ask for how long?"

"You can ask, but I can't answer. Nobody can. I took the liberty of having Lieutenant Irvine contact your paper. They seemed quite happy with the turn of events."

"I'll bet they were."

"I've got to ask you to keep this under your hat until CAG and I have briefed the COs and they've had time to brief their people."

A thought struck me. "Yesterday you made a controversial decision to dump that Hornet over the side. You told me that you couldn't buy training like that. Were you thinking of us going straight into a combat situation?"

"Off the record?"

Did they teach this in school, now? "Yes, Captain, off the record."

"It was a spur-of-the-moment thing. Listen, Jack, I was devastated at what happened. Hoser and I have been friends for twenty years. It was a nightmare to see him crash on my ship, on what should have been the crowning achievement to a phenomenal career. But, I had to keep my cool, so I slipped into autopilot. My training took over, and my training has always been combat-oriented. In combat, you don't screw around. When you take a shot, you roll with it and strike back twice as hard."

He paused, seemingly lost in thought as he stared down at the activity on the flight deck. Jets were being towed to their launch positions. The catapult crews were inspecting their equipment. It was another day of cruise.

He spoke so quietly, I had to strain to hear. "To tell the truth, nobody was more shocked than me when the wreckage was dumped and we kept right on flying." He looked at me, wearing a half grin. "Such a good story, and you can't use it. Sorry."

One of his three phones rang. "That's my public." He answered it, then covered the mouthpiece, and said to me, "You're welcome to watch the launch from up here. I'd like you to see us under normal conditions."

What an amazing job. While I wandered the bridge, the man who was trained to keep his cool, under any circumstances, gave a quick series of orders that would send the next wave of aircraft aloft.

I found a seat overlooking the flight deck. From my perch I could see the bow, and most of the way aft, where a dozen or so aircraft were parked. Aviators clad in flight gear were conducting preflight inspections with the aid of their plane captains.

Hanging from the overhead was a black-and-white television monitor. It showed a Plexiglas grease board depicting the side-numbers, pilot names, mission, and fuel states of the airborne jets. Next to the name Cole was her side-number and an upward arrow, meaning, I surmised, that her jet was operational for the next launch.

The camera angle swiveled to the right and another board came into focus. I could make out the shape of a sailor standing behind the board. He was painstakingly adding all the information for the upcoming launch. I found it intriguing that he had to write backwards so that it was legible from the other side. The name, Mason, was written next to Lobo 509 with the notation, "L1."

"What does, 'L-one' mean?" I asked the sailor who was standing watch nearby.

"It means the jet is on elevator one, sir. You can see it if you move to the other side of the bridge and look behind cat one."

I thanked him for his help and walked to a window where I could peer down at cat one. There was a huge gap in the flight deck, because the elevator was down on the hangar deck. There were watches posted to keep people clear of the enormous hole. Lobo 509 was tied down with chains. The canopy was open, and a pilot was in the cockpit. A klaxon sounded, and the whole contraption moved swiftly up. Slipping into place as if it were the last piece in a giant jigsaw puzzle, the monster elevator made the flight deck whole once more.

Without her oxygen mask, Amy's profile was easily recognizable. I wished she'd look up, but she was intent on performing her checklist. I took a couple of photos; it was a great angle.

I could see why this woman was so happy with her life. At age twenty-four, she was paid to climb into the cockpit of a forty-million-dollar fighter on the hangar deck of a five-billion-dollar aircraft carrier. Then she rode it to the rooftop, where she was soon going to be catapulted off to go flying over her own piece of ocean. Just another day at the office.

In short order, a group of red-shirted ordnancemen swarmed around her aircraft. They uploaded two racks of blue practice bombs and cranked belts of ammunition into her cannon. Just as they finished, the Air Boss got on the address system.

"On the *Ranger*. It's time for the second launch cycle. I want everyone in the proper flight-deck uniform, helmets on, goggles on, sleeves rolled down. Take a good look around you for any foreign objects. Fly One, are you ready? Fly Two? Fly Three?" With the enthusiasm of a race-car announcer, he then called, "On the *Ranger* . . . Start engines!"

Every pilot must have had his or her finger on the switch. The flight deck erupted with the sound of APUs, and in a few seconds, the whine of jet engines spooling up joined the cacophony. The captain and I traded smiles.

He mouthed the words, "I love this."

I understood how it could get into your blood. God knew how many cruises Morganelli had pulled as an aviator, a squadron skipper, as ship's XO, and finally as the *Ranger*'s head man. By now it was programmed into his DNA.

Five minutes later pilots started calling in with their aircraft status and fuel states. Shortly after that the yellow-shirts started breaking down aircraft and taxiing them toward the waiting catapults. Right away, I noticed that they were using all four catapults, the two bow cats and both waist cats that are located in the landing area. This would be a covey launch, where the flight-deck crew cleared the deck of waiting aircraft in minimum time.

Working rapidly, the yellow-shirts had four aircraft staged on the cats. A line of waiting jets began to form behind each one. I watched Amy taxi off the elevator and take her place behind cat two.

Morganelli answered another phone call, listened for a moment, and said, "Launch 'em."

The catapult officers on cats one and three signaled their respective pilots to go to full power. The roar of jet exhaust rocked the superstructure. Both pilots cycled their flight controls, waggling ailerons and rudders, and within a nanosecond of each other, both catapults fired. As they reached the end of their catapult tracks it looked like they would collide, but the pilots executed sharp turns away, held them for a moment, and as if connected, resumed course. The two jets skimmed the wave tops as they raced away from the ship.

The aircraft on cats two and four were already up to power, under control of the same two cat officers.

After the pilots cycled their controls, they saluted and braced themselves for the shot. They, too, were airborne in moments.

With little delay, the jets on one and three rolled into place and ran their engines up. The launched jets executed their clearing turns and followed their predecessors. It was quite a sight. The pace I'd experienced the day before was slow motion compared to today's action. Within seconds, two more aircraft were airborne, and cats two and four were host to two big Tomcats. Each of them went into afterburner, bringing a new level of noise and power to the flight deck. They left together in a blaze of flame and billowing catapult steam.

Another two were launched, and then it was Mason's turn. She didn't get squared away in the catapult as fast as her peer on cat four. It highlighted the fact that this crew of aviators and flight-deck personnel had the benefit of months of work-ups under their belts. Amy Mason, no matter how talented, wasn't yet on their level.

It was the first launch not to go simultaneously. Her partner on cat four left as she brought the Hornet up to full power. She cycled her flight controls more deliberately than the rest. When the catapult officer signaled for burner, the Hornet's powerful engines spewed flame into the JBD. Amy saluted. The catapult officer returned it, knelt, and touched the deck before pointing toward the bow. A sailor in the catwalk made a final check and mashed the fire button. Amy's jet was catapulted with the same force as the other nine aircraft. Yet, there was something different.

Wanting a picture of her aircraft as it left the deck and became airborne, I had the F/A–18 centered in the camera's viewfinder. Sparks were flying out of the left engine. I heard the Air Boss tell her to check her engines. As soon as she was clear of the flight deck, both bomb racks and the fuel tank fell away. She must have used the emergency jettison button to lose the excess weight. The fighter pitched up for a moment, then the jet pushed over, its nose pointing down steeply, toward the water.

"Jesus," someone said.

The jet's nose rapidly came back up, but much too far. Even I knew the aircraft was out of control.

The Air Boss transmitted, "Off the cat, eject!"

The captain demanded something called a William's turn.

The helmsman responded, "William's turn, aye, aye, sir."

Though the nose of her aircraft pointed skyward, the plane was falling backwards into the ocean. In a puff of smoke, the canopy exploded clear. Then the seat rocketed out.

Underneath my feet, the deck tilted crazily to the left. Something behind me tumbled loudly across the room.

The seat hit the water like a missile. The jet followed, tail first, making a huge splash. I was fairly certain we ran over it.

There was no parachute.

CHAPTER 21

Bridge—
Saturday, 19 Oct/1105

For the second time in two days Randi's landing was delayed by the crash of someone close to her. This time she wasn't told who it was. Morganelli imposed an immediate ban on releasing the name of the pilot. He had the XO handle notifying the National Command Post in DC, who in turn activated the military's Next of Kin (NOK) notification system.

Less than ten minutes after the search-and-rescue helicopter recovered Lieutenant Mason's body, the duty officer and duty chaplain at Offet AFB in Nebraska were contacted. Theirs was the unspeakable job of driving to a stranger's home at midnight and waking two nice people to tell them that the child they had raised was dead.

I was prohibited from filing a story until the Captain received verification that NOK had been informed. In the meantime, I operated on my own form of autopilot. I've been a reporter for over twenty years. Like the firefighters and the captain, I let my instinct and training take over.

I sought out the only quiet place on the ship, Hoser's hospital room. To the steady rhythm of his breathing, I wrote down everything that had happened in the last two days. Then I read it.

Though I couldn't rule out sabotage on Hoser's jet, it could very well be a coincidence. But today's mishap smelled like a setup. And I wanted to find the bastards who did it. My best leads were Holmes and Bradley. Then there was that anonymous phone caller. If the guy called again, I'd have to be more convincing.

I also had Master Chief Cardone as an ally. Because they were both his jets, I'd have an inside track on the mishap investigations.

On top of that was the news that we were heading into a combat operation. As the pool reporter, I'd be given access to everything that wasn't classified. With luck, I could use the operation as justification for some serious snooping.

The door to Hoser's room opened, and Randi, still wearing her flight suit, stepped inside. She looked like hell.

I stood, and she walked into my arms. Her body shook with quiet sobs.

"Don't hold it back."

It was as if someone had opened a dam. Randi cried out in anguish, "Oh, Jack . . . they killed her, didn't they?"

In my gut, I knew she was right. But that was a far cry from proving it.

She sank to the floor, taking me with her. Her sadness turned to rage. Eyes ablaze with hatred, she spoke through clenched teeth. "Those bastards killed a dear, sweet person, for no other reason than she was a woman. I want them. Whoever they are, I want their asses. Promise me—you gotta promise me, Jack— that we'll get them."

"I promise I'll find the truth. That's all I can do."

She stared through me. I watched the emotions play across her face. Grief, anger, bitter revenge, then sadness. A deep wound had been opened. She ran out of steam and slumped against me, crying softly.

Eventually, her breathing slowed; she was asleep. My friend the nurse looked in, appraised the situation, and brought blankets and a pillow. After spreading the blankets on the floor, she helped me lay Randi down and cover her up. Without a word, she dimmed the lights, closed the door, and left us.

In less than twenty-four hours, a group of three, immensely talented, genuinely good people had been decimated. One was dead, one near death, and the last was overcome by grief and pain. For bad or good, I was here to witness their plight.

Never had being a reporter been more of a burden.

CHAPTER 22

CVIC—
Saturday, 19 Oct/1300

With military precision, the 1300 brief began as soon as the ship's bells finished. The assembled officers included all squadron COs and XOs, and several high-ranking members of the ship's crew. CAG Andrews opened the brief by acknowledging what everyone in the room already knew.

"We're proceeding at maximum speed to a position off the coast of Libya. When we arrive, we'll begin around-the-clock operations pursuant to our orders, which direct us to prepare for a contingency strike on Gadhafi's chemical-weapons facility."

He nodded to the Intelligence officer, who stood, had the lights darkened, and presented a synopsis of the situation in Libya.

Pointing at a satellite photo of a complex of buildings, he said, "We received indication, through our human intelligence resources, that Gadhafi was constructing a chemical-weapons-production facility. Our imagery analysts have concluded that this complex, which Gadhafi claims is an agricultural research laboratory, is actually being staffed to produce weapons-grade chemical agents. We believe these include, sarin, the chemical agent favored by terrorists. You might remember that sarin was used in the Tokyo subway attack a few years ago."

One of the audience asked, "What evidence do we have?"

The briefer shrugged. "Well, as you know, I'm not at liberty to divulge all of our resources or intelligence-gathering methods, but suffice it to say that we've tracked shipments of raw materials and production-related equipment. Further, we know that Gadhafi has contracted with North Korea to purchase one hundred Scud-3 missiles and twenty launchers. This variant of the Scud has a range of over eight hundred miles and uses an internal inertial-guidance system. With them, Libya could strike our ports as far north as Italy and Greece."

The group buzzed as the impact of this new threat was discussed.

"There's more."

The crowd hushed.

"We also know that Mr. Gadhafi has made arrangements to purchase a dozen MiG–29 Fulcrum fighters, some of which have already been delivered."

"Sounds like he wants to play," said one of the Hornet pilots.

"Well, it's too soon to tell if this is part of a master plan, or if he's just buying whatever he can get his hands on."

CAG asked, "Bill, what about pilot training? Are they doing it on-site, or in some other country?"

"Details are sketchy on that, sir. We haven't seen any evidence of a rush to get their pilots up to speed. We suspect that after he gets his jets, he will establish a maintenance-and-logistic-support system before beginning training in earnest. That should take another three months."

"What kind of weaponry did the Fulcrums come with?" asked the Marine CO. He was identifiable by his "high and tight" haircut, which left a small patch of hair, barely a half inch long, on the very top of his head.

"We don't know for certain. The airplanes are flying in without any weaponry. But missiles can be shipped in a variety of ways. Until we know for sure, it's safe to assume that the Fulcrums will have a full complement of air-to-air missiles, including Archers."

That elicited groans throughout the room. I made a note to ask Randi what an Archer was.

"So, what are we supposed to do when we get on station?" asked another officer.

CAG stood to address the group. "Gentlemen, our orders are quite specific. We are to buster over to our station and prepare the air wing for contingency operations. That means we construct a package of strike options: day, night, full suppression, and surgical."

As CAG spoke, the Intel officer was handing out packets of information to selected officers.

"I've assigned strike leads and planning teams to

these strike profiles. Bill is distributing planning materials. From this point forward, your top priority is to work up your briefings. We'll be on station in less than thirty hours. By this time tomorrow, I want to start receiving your briefs. There's a schedule printed on the back. Bill and his people will provide you with target data and the latest intel on Libyan air defenses. We've canceled the rest of the flight schedule to give maintenance time to prep the jets."

A hand was raised in the front row.

"Yes, John?"

"Do we have surface-to-air shooters of our own?"

"Good question. Yes, the Aegis Cruiser, USS *Arkansas*, has detached from *America's* battle group and will meet us on station. That reminds me. Bill, send off a message to her CO requesting their air liaison officer come over for a face-to-face. We'll send the SAR helo to pick him up."

"*Her*, sir. I'll arrange it."

"Good. Any more questions?"

The Lobo skipper said, "What about the mishap boards?"

CAG looked at Captain Morganelli, who stood and spoke for the first time. "I've been in contact with the Pentagon. Both mishaps are being classified as combat-related losses."

The pilots exchanged looks. I wasn't sure what that decision meant to the investigations that normally followed any mishap.

"Look, gents. If you needed proof that we're going over the beach, this is it. Unfortunately, we cannot stop our preparations to conduct as thorough an investigation as each of us wants." He glanced at me. Every pair of eyes in the room followed his. The point was made.

"CAG has assigned a small investigation team, headed by Commander Holmes, that will collect all records and conduct personal interviews. If there is any indication of material failure or maintenance malpractice that affects the Hornets or my catapults, we'll deal with it immediately. Otherwise, we'll wait until after this operation is complete. In any case, we're officially relieved of the need to produce a full MIR."

This brought the first smiles of the day to the group. I well knew how tough a Mishap Investigation Report, or MIR, was to produce, having reported on the process. The selection of Holmes to head the investigation team was a major setback. As team leader, he would be in the perfect position to alter or destroy any evidence pointing to sabotage.

"Any more questions?" asked CAG.

Someone in the back asked, "Has a date and time been set for the memorial?"

Morganelli stood, and said, "Yes, we'll be holding a nondenominational service on the hangar deck at ten-hundred instead of normal Protestant services. Given the nature of our assignment, attendance isn't mandatory, and the uniform is utilities. However, CAG has assured me that there will be representation from the air wing, and of course, VFA-305 will be there en masse."

He paused, seemingly pondering whether to go on. After taking a deep breath, he continued. "Gentlemen, I'm counting on each of you to help your squadrons put this tragedy in perspective. Learn what you can from it. Let us all honor the memory of our shipmate; she was a talented aviator—a pioneer, in fact. What happened to her could happen to any of us. Therefore, we must, each of us, vow to be ever vigilant, because we have a job to do."

He stepped forward, drawing the full attention of every listener. "After the service, I want every person on this ship to put this in our wake. I hate to say it, but before this week is out, we may very well have lost more of our shipmates."

Quiet descended on the room as Captain Morganelli glanced from face to face, making sure his message was received.

He walked quickly through the aisle, speaking over his shoulder. "CAG, please conduct the rest of the briefing. Mr. Warner, please join me."

"Attention on deck!"

As the men snapped to attention, I followed the captain out of the room, his hulking Marine guard shadowing us. I was curious as to the summons, but kept quiet. He led me to his ladder and then into his private stateroom, leaving the guard posted outside.

The cabin was surprisingly small, but well-appointed. At his behest, I sat in the spare chair.

Morganelli cleared a couple of items off his fold-down metal desktop, then turned his chair to face me. His expression was drawn. I could see the fatigue in his eyes. We weren't more than two feet apart in the tiny room.

"How's Hoser?" he asked, an obvious icebreaker.

"No change."

"I suppose at this stage that has to be considered good news."

"That's what the doctor tells me. I guess this operation means we won't be off-loading him to a real hospital."

"You're right. He's not stable enough to fly, and of course, we won't be pulling into port anytime soon." He smiled wanly.

I figured he was going to ask me to take it easy when I put this all on paper. It was a natural concern. It wouldn't hurt to put his mind at rest. He certainly had enough to worry about.

"Let me guess," I said. "You're concerned about how this is going to read, once I'm allowed to publish my reports."

He seemed taken aback, as if he hadn't given it any thought. "Well, that does concern me, a little bit, anyway. But, frankly, I can't let that affect my judgment out here, and that's not what I wanted to talk to you about." He picked up a pencil and twirled it in his fingers. "Sailors are a superstitious lot. You know that, don't you?"

This conversation was heading into uncharted waters. I shrugged, to let him know that I had no idea what he was talking about.

"Jack, this isn't easy for me."

Not only had he used my first name, these were

the exact words and much the same tone of voice I'd heard from my ex-wife the day she kicked me out. And I had the same sinking feeling.

"Just say it, Captain."

"Okay. I guess the best thing is just to put it on the table. Jack, it's come to my attention that members of my crew think you're a jinx."

My jaw dropped.

He leaned forward to explain. "You've got to look at it from their perspective. We go through nearly five months of work-ups without so much as scratching a jet. Then you come on board, and twice, within ten minutes of entering the bridge, we have a mishap. I'm going to have to bar you from the bridge during flight ops."

He wasn't joking; I couldn't believe what I was hearing. "I don't know what to say, Captain. I know you have to do what you feel is right for the ship. But seriously, Captain, you know that this is nonsense. And . . ."

"Perception is reality out here, Jack. If I let this go unattended, people will find a way to blame you for everything from a mishap to a stubbed toe. It *is* nonsense, I agree, but I've got take this ship into battle, and I can't afford any distractions. Surely, you understand that."

The pencil was tapping a machine-gun rhythm on the desk, clearly signaling his agitation.

I sensed that there was more. "Is there something else you haven't told me?"

He sighed and, catching himself, deliberately put

the pencil down. "I wanted to tell you, face-to-face, that I've asked that you be replaced with another reporter."

"But . . ."

"It's nothing personal, Jack. Please understand that."

Nothing personal? I'd just been accused of jinxing an entire aircraft carrier and kicked off the story. The guy was serious! I had to change his mind, and I had to do it fast.

"Captain, did you route that request through CNO?"

"No, through the Chief of Naval Information. Don't worry, I appended an explanation that said having a famous reporter aboard was distracting to the crew."

"That's not why I asked, Captain. As you know, my orders are signed by SECNAV, himself. Before I accepted the assignment, we had a frank discussion. I can't quote him, but he shared with me his deep concerns that there might be an underground movement to keep women out of the F/A–18 community. He sent me out here in the hopes that my presence would buy Cole and Mason enough time to acclimate before the bad guys, if there were any, acted."

I watched his face for a reaction. With luck, it would tell me what I needed to know.

He was genuinely surprised. But, of course, this was quickly followed by anger. "Are you serious? SECNAV sent *you* out here because he suspected my crew of conspiracy?" There was a pause, as his frustration peaked. He slammed his hand down on the desktop, scattering pencils, pens, and other items. "Listen to me, Warner. I want to know just what the fuck is going on!"

The door to the cabin burst open, and the guard entered, a 9mm automatic in his beefy hand.

"Sir?"

The pistol was leveled at my head.

The captain held up his hand. "Everything is all right, Corporal. I've just been told some distressing news. I'm sorry to have alarmed you. Now, please leave us alone."

The corporal's eyes scanned the room, finally coming to rest on me. With a silent warning, he made it clear that I was on very thin ice.

Speaking to his captain—the message intended for me—the corporal reluctantly agreed to obey the order. "Yes, sir. I'll be just outside." The door closed softly behind him.

Having regained his composure, Morganelli spoke with measured emphasis, "I assume you can prove what you're saying, Mr. Warner." It was more question than statement.

"Yes, sir. I had a similar discussion with CNO." I wasn't exactly lying—Admiral Russell and I had discussed it, Morganelli could draw his own conclusions on what was said. I fished through my wallet and found CNO's card. "He gave me his SATCOM number. We can call him right now, if you'd like."

He nodded and waved the card away, unwilling to call my bluff. "I don't understand your relationship with the Navy. I know that you covered Tailhook and that F–14 mishap. In fact, I've read your stuff off and on for years. Are you telling me that you are actually an agent for SECNAV?"

"Absolutely not. Though this is an unusual assignment, I don't run my copy through him, or CNO, for approval. The deal is that I print what I uncover as long as it's not classified."

"And just what is it, Mr. Warner, that you think you've uncovered?"

It was time to take the reins in this conversation. "Captain, how can you be convinced that it was simply a bizarre coincidence that both mishaps occurred to aircraft being flown by Lieutenant Mason?"

I could see he hadn't made the connection. He snatched the phone and dialed. "This is the captain. Who was flying Lobo 501 yesterday? No. Before Captain Santana." The answer shook him. "I see. Thank you."

He recovered quickly. "I'll be damned. Listen, I have to admit that I didn't remember she was in that machine before Hoser. But, as strange as it seems, it *is* just a coincidence. Think about it, Hoser logged two landings before that gear failed, and we have troubleshooters inspect it before every launch. And, besides, only a madman would do such a thing. Are you going to sit there and tell me that you suspect that Mason's mishap was sabotage?"

"Yes, I am."

I could see that he took that statement hard. It challenged every belief he held. "Do you have any evidence?" he asked, his voice betraying his fear.

"Not conclusive. Not yet. But I can tell you that I received an anonymous phone call yesterday telling me to warn the women to stop flying. And last night I was threatened by a man who followed me out to the flight deck."

He was incredulous that I hadn't brought this up before, and spoke slowly, the restraint clearly a chore. "Why is this the first time I've heard about these events?"

Given that it was his ship and his armed guard, I elected not to tell him that it was because I considered him a suspect. "Nothing was concrete. I told both Cole and Mason about the call. They said it wasn't unusual and laughed it off. The man who spoke to me on the catwalk didn't make an overt threat, he just implied one, and I can't identify him because I couldn't see his face. Look, Captain, what if I had told you? If you're having this much trouble believing me with Mason dead and two aircraft in the water, you would have thought I was off my rocker before her mishap."

With closed eyes, Morganelli chewed on what I'd told him. This was a man used to having absolute authority. How would he react to a situation beyond his control?

"If we have a murderer on this ship, I want him, or them. I'll call Naples and have some federal agents sent out here."

"That is certainly one option," I said, making it clear it wasn't my recommendation.

"I take it you disagree?" He smiled, but his eyes were humorless. "What then, Mr. Warner, would you advise me to do?"

"Concentrate on getting ready to fight. A full-blown investigation would be distracting. Let everybody think I'm being shipped home and am on a short leash because of this jinx business. Meanwhile, I'll be your eyes and ears. I'll find the bastards. We can delay my departure as long as necessary, and I'll keep a low profile. The crew will forget about me. By the way, who told you about this jinx issue?"

"Oh, I see what you mean. Like it could have been someone's cooked-up idea to get you out of here. Well, I'm sorry, but that's a dead end. It came from our chaplain. Apparently he heard it from some of the men."

I was disappointed. However, like any good reporter, I wanted to nail it down. "What's his name?"

"Hogan. Chaplain Brian Hogan."

Bingo. Brian Hogan was the other name on my list.

CHAPTER 23

Saturday, 19 Oct/1500

Morganelli reluctantly agreed to let me investigate on my own. I convinced him it was best that the conspirators believe that their plan had succeeded perfectly.

From their perspective, everything was running smoothly. The mishap investigation had not only been abbreviated, it was now under the control of Holmes. The pesky reporter was getting kicked off the boat and would presumably write a scathing article about Navy brass. And he would most certainly tell a harrowing tale of the dangerous business of flying off carriers, to boot. Meanwhile the last female Hornet pilot was on the verge of a breakdown with combat just around the corner.

This was all fine with me. As long as they thought there was no threat, they'd be likely to make a mistake, maybe even brag a little. I decided I needed to seek solace from a certain preacher.

Chaplain Hogan wasn't your garden-variety minister. He was tall, dark-haired, with an athletic build and an unsmiling face. He met me at the door with an air of indifference.

"Thank you for seeing me, Chaplain. I know you're busy. I'll only take a few minutes of your time."

"What is it that I can do for you, Mr. Warner?" He didn't budge.

Two could play at this game. "Chaplain, I'm not comfortable discussing this in the passageway."

"I don't have much time, Mr. Warner. I'm preparing for tomorrow's service. Can this wait?"

"No. It cannot."

"Very well, but please be brief. Come in."

I took a seat in a metal-backed chair while he positioned himself behind the desk. The walls of his office were covered with photos, plaques, diplomas, and certificates. It was what the aviators refer to as an *I love me wall*.

He waited for me to speak.

"I just left the captain's cabin. He broke the news to me about the crew's concerns that I'm somehow some kind of jinx. In fact, he's sending me off the ship because of it." I didn't say I knew he was the source of the jinx accusation.

"I don't know what to say, Mr. Warner. I'm sure the captain made the best decision he could under the circumstances."

"I was hoping you could help me convince the captain to let me stay."

"Why would you think I would do that, Mr. Warner?" He was alert, watching me closely.

"Well, you're a man of God, of course. You know that there's no such thing as a jinx. It's ridiculous."

Realization dawned on his face. "I see."

"So will you do it?"

"Do what, Mr. Warner?" The guy was purposely busting my chops.

"Tell the captain that it is silly to send me off the ship."

He nodded in understanding, but held his hands up in a gesture that conveyed the impossibility of his task. "Come now, Mr. Warner. I know you're not in the military, but surely you can't expect me to tell Captain Morganelli that his orders are silly, now can you?"

"No, I guess not. I'd just like to know how this thing got started."

"I'd say that's a mystery."

The guy, minister or not, was a liar. I took another angle. "I'm sorry to be complaining about my problems when here you are getting ready to deliver a memorial service for Lieutenant Mason."

He frowned. "Yes, that certainly is not a welcome part of my job. An unexpected death, particularly in one so young, can be a wake-up call for the living."

I lowered my voice to a confidential tone. "You probably know that I was assigned to cover her transition to the fleet."

He nodded.

"Before I came out here, I thought that women should be given equal opportunity in carrier aviation, but since Captain Santana's mishap and then that terrible experience this morning, I've changed my mind."

He leaned back in his chair and gazed at a wall full of mementos. He spoke with certainty. "I could have told anyone that it wasn't going to work. Mixing the sexes was a foolish idea. I know what I'm talking about, Mr. Warner." He pointed at a group of aircraft pictures. "You see, I wasn't always a minister. I used to be a naval aviator myself before I saw the light and devoted my life to serving the Lord."

News flash—Hogan used to be a Navy pilot. But he wasn't wearing wings. I was willing to bet my hat, ass, and overcoat that he'd washed out.

"That's fascinating. I'll bet you're one of a kind. What did you fly?"

"My last plane was the A–4. That's a jet."

The A–4 was a Vietnam-vintage aircraft that had been converted to a trainer. I was right: Hogan hadn't gotten his wings. But he still had the ego. "Really? A jet pilot. And now, you're a chaplain on an aircraft carrier. I guess you really can talk with these TOPGUNs out here. They probably trust you, since you've been there and all."

This was music to his ears. "I do enjoy a special bond with the pilots. My call sign is Saint." He flashed a quick grin and glanced upward, as if God were letting this little blasphemy slide, for the good of the ministry and all.

"So, do you think they'll get the message back at the Pentagon and stop trying to put women out here?"

This struck a chord. "I don't know what it will

take, Mr. Warner. But, if you're a Christian—a real Christian—you have to trust that Lieutenant Mason's death will serve a greater good. Maybe they'll stand up and take notice when we ship this child back to the States in a body bag. I hope so. I hope and pray that none of the rest of our nation's daughters will have to die before our leaders wake up. I pray that this is the last young woman over whose body I'll have to ask for God's deliverance."

"Chaplain Hogan, I'd like to hear more. I think I can use some of your perspective in my story. Maybe together we can help people to understand that Ms. Mason's death need not be in vain. Surely there are others who share those thoughts. I might be here for another day or so. Do you ever meet with the pilots, you know, to talk?"

"Well, we do have a small group. We call ourselves, The Brothers. But, we don't have another meeting until Monday evening." Thinking better of it, he backtracked quickly. "Actually, that's a private Bible study group. I wouldn't want to make them uncomfortable by bringing in a reporter. It would be a violation of their trust. I'm sure you understand."

"Yes, of course. I'll get out of your hair now. Thank you for seeing me."

He didn't bother to get up.

CHAPTER 24

Lobo Maintenance Control—
Saturday, 19 Oct/1535

On the way back to my room, I stopped by the VFA–305 spaces and left a message for Master Chief Cardone to call. I wanted to get his cut on how someone could sabotage a jet engine.

Coming out of the head, I bumped into Petty Officer Lawrence, the clerk from CAG's office.

"Excuse me, sir," he said, head down, submissively accepting the blame for our collision.

"Oh, I'm sorry. That was my fault," I said. "I shouldn't be allowed out without a keeper." I smiled, but he wasn't buying it.

His look was almost hostile, certainly different from yesterday's cooperative attitude. What had changed? Again, I got the feeling that a sharp intellect lurked behind the glasses and choirboy face.

I tried once more. "Hey, thanks for helping me get squared away with the Communications officer yesterday."

"Yes, sir." His voice was curt.

He made a move to slide by me, but I didn't move. I was several inches taller and a good deal heavier. Forced to look me in the face, his eyes flashed with anger.

"It's too bad about Lieutenant Mason, isn't it?" he asked, his voice conveying a mixture of sarcasm and bitterness.

I heard something else: the voice on my tape recorder. My caller was no longer anonymous.

My mind raced through the scenario. As the stereotypical, unassuming clerk, Lawrence would be privy to snippets of conversations. No wonder the kid played the innocent. He couldn't let on that he was astute, or he'd be a threat, and Holmes had enough horsepower to make him go away.

I didn't say anything at first. I stepped aside to let Lawrence by, but grabbed his arm, surprising him, just before he got out of reach.

"You and I need to talk. Call me. I know you know the number."

I dropped his arm and left him staring at me openmouthed. If he wanted to blame me for Mason's death, he was going to have to stand in line. Hell, I was already the ship's jinx.

Cardone called me about an hour later, after I'd put together a draft of my next article. He was in low spirits and in no mood for idle chat.

"I need to talk to you," I said.

"It's gonna have to wait. I spent all day on this mishap, and now we've got to prep jets for going over the beach."

"I know that, Art. I wouldn't ask if it wasn't absolutely necessary. It won't take ten minutes. I can't say any more."

There was a heavy sigh. "Okay, Jack. I'll be right up." He sounded like a man who had just had one more burden added to an already-unbearable load.

He was at my door in less than three minutes. The proximity of living on board ship was still surprising to me. Art's khakis were stained with sweat and grease. His eyes were red-rimmed and darted from my face to the room and back again. As he sat in the chair, his foot tapped incessantly. I recognized the symptoms of a long-term caffeine jag.

"Thanks for coming."

"What's this about?"

"Were you able to determine anything about the mishap?" I asked.

"No more than we knew. The port engine failed. I don't know why." He looked up at me with agitation. "I hope that's not why you called me up here, because . . ."

"No. I wouldn't do that, Art. Actually, I have some information for you. And then I've got to ask your advice."

"Go ahead. Just promise me it isn't more bad news." He gave me a rueful smile.

"That will be your call. But, first, you have to be sworn to secrecy. Nothing I tell you leaves this room without my say-so. Lives may depend on it."

That got his attention. "Okay."

There was no easy way of clueing him in. I had to

give it to him straight. "I'm convinced that your jet was sabotaged to kill Lieutenant Mason."

His reaction was total shock. The thought had obviously never crossed his mind. "What did you just say?"

"Hear me out. Captain Morganelli already has."

He raised his eyebrows, but didn't speak.

"I was sent here by SECNAV, personally, to monitor the transition of the two women pilots. He suspected that there was a conspiracy to prevent them from making it to the fleet."

I paused to let that sink in. "Art, last night I got a phone call telling me to warn the women not to fly."

His eyes bugged. "You didn't tell anyone?"

"Yes. I told both women. They said it had happened before, not out here, but during training."

"Well, you sure as hell could have told me!" He stood up abruptly, sending the chair skidding across the floor.

I stayed seated and spoke in even tones. "Yes, I could have. I could have come down to your shop and told you that an anonymous caller made vague warnings about Lieutenant Mason flying. Then I could have demanded that you ground your squadron until you'd gone over every jet with a fine-tooth comb, while the other squadrons flew. What do you think would have happened? I figure I'd have wound up in a bed next to Hoser's."

His hands were balled into fists. He turned around, grabbed the doorknob, but didn't turn it. I gave him time to work it out.

Eventually, he reached for his chair, carefully set it back in its original position, and sat down. He looked more tired than ever. "I see your point. It's just that, maybe I . . . well, hell, what else did you have to say?"

I laid out the facts, telling about the confrontation on the catwalk, the jinx ruse, and finally about Bradley getting pulled from the LSO platform.

"I never liked the sonuvabitch. He used to work in maintenance—arrogant as hell."

"Art, I want you to forget that five-oh-nine was your jet. If you were going to make an engine fail, how would you do it?"

He answered immediately. "Easy. A couple quarters."

"Pardon?"

"I'd stick a couple quarters to the back of the fan blades with duct tape. They'd stay in place until the cat shot, when they'd get sucked down the engine."

"Are you serious? Two quarters would do that much damage?"

"Yup. Jack, those engines are going at thousands of revolutions per minute. The tolerances are microscopic. I've seen a pebble no bigger than a pea destroy an engine. A quarter would tear a hole the size of a bowling ball through the turbine section. And once the blades start letting go, you've got white-hot shrapnel."

"Has this ever been done?"

"Yeah. Back in the dark ages, when judges used to tell criminals that they could go to jail or join the Navy."

"Would it be something you could spot on pre-flight?"

"Not a chance. Not unless you were looking for it."

"Now, the tough question. Could someone have done it to five-oh-nine? I know it was on the hangar deck last night."

"It would have to be somebody who wouldn't look out of place. Also, the Hornet intake is high and narrow. It would have to be someone who knew how to get in and out of there, like a plane captain."

"Or a pilot."

"Right, or a pilot. But, Jesus, what kind of ass-hole would do something like that just to get a woman out of the squadron?"

"Not *a* woman, Art. All women pilots. After the fiasco on the West Coast, this is the last chance for women to fly Hornets. And if it works, people are going to ask why women are at sea at all, if they can't carry their weight and fly the tough missions."

He let out a low whistle. "Well, that's over my pay grade. The only thing is that I wasn't on the flight deck for the mishap. I haven't seen the tape yet, but an engine that's been trashed by a metal object would be very distinctive."

"Sit still." I connected my camera to the laptop and turned it so we both could see. "I took photos from the bridge. Hopefully, I got at least one decent one of the crash."

It took a few seconds to download the five high-resolution photos. What we saw next would break a stone heart. I had two photos of Amy sitting in the cockpit on the elevator. She looked intent, like any other pilot, but there was a subtle gracefulness in the way her hand gripped the canopy sill. You knew it was a woman even with her face covered by the oxygen mask. It would be the photo I'd match to my story.

There was also one of her jet on the catapult, both engines in afterburner, but still restrained. The catapult officer was returning her salute. The next one captured the flaming debris emanating from the left engine, just as the Hornet got to the end of the stroke. I put the two photos up side by side on the screen.

"Look here," Art said. "In this one, there's no indication of a problem. The nozzle looks good, the flame pattern is good, and we can assume that there were no cockpit warnings, or she would have suspended the launch. Now, look at this one. The guts are coming out of it. The only thing that could make an engine self-destruct that fast is a sizable chunk of metal going down the gullet."

"Could it have picked up debris from off the deck?"

"Technically, yes. But, a bunch of other jets went off that same cat without a problem, and after the mishap, they inspected it and found no missing hardware." He leaned back in his chair, closed his eyes, and massaged his temples. "I can't believe it. Some bastard sabotaged that engine and killed that nice young girl."

I remembered a snippet of an article from my research. "Art, do you remember that Hornet mishap in the Pacific last year? The one where the woman punched out, but the jet kept flying?"

"Oh, yeah! They had to shoot it down. I'll bet that was the last time they let her in the cockpit."

"You're right, it was. Do you remember why she said she punched out?"

"Nope."

"She said she had an engine failure off the catapult. But, the jet sank in twenty thousand feet of water. Because it kept flying, the mishap board concluded that she had panicked. But, what if her engine was sabotaged, just not as badly?"

"Oh shit."

Art had to get back to his crew. He agreed to nose around quietly to see if anyone had noticed someone lurking around 509 the night before the incident. As a precaution, I made a backup of the photos onto a couple of floppy disks and gave them to Art for safe-keeping.

After he left, I started to shut down the laptop when I realized I hadn't looked at the last photo. I reopened the application and called it up. The photo was skewed badly, obviously taken as I was fighting to maintain my balance during the ship's wild maneuvering.

Even with the tilted horizon, you could tell that the aircraft was sideways, seconds from impact, the canopy already off. My eyes were drawn to a dark object frozen in space just above the ocean. I hit the zoom control, another benefit of having a digital photo.

A stunning picture emerged of the last instant of Amy Mason's life. Legs, boots, and helmet clearly visible, her body was still strapped into the rocket seat, captured for eternity a scant two feet above the wave tops.

Even as I was struck by the horror of what I was seeing, a part of me felt a thrill about getting the picture. It was a once-in-a-lifetime shot. I closed my eyes and wished it away, but I couldn't do it. The photo already had a life of its own.

Just as being a sailor was programmed into Captain Morganelli's DNA, being a reporter, for better or worse, was part of mine.

CHAPTER 25

Ward Room I—
Saturday, 19 Oct/1730

After making my way down to the dirty shirt, I loaded up on what could have been roast beef and potatoes. I found a seat at a table shared by several aviators. One of the guys noticed me looking askance at my meal.

"It's mystery meat, Mr. Warner. Best if you use a lot of steak sauce and don't think too much about what it could have been."

"Thanks for the advice. I had my hopes up that it might be roast beef."

Another pilot picked up the banter. "Close. It's actually *roast beast*. Like what the Grinch stole."

We had a good laugh at my expense while I tried to chew through the tough-as-shoe-leather slab of meat. The potatoes were instant, and the green beans must have been simmering since yesterday.

"Pretty yummy, huh?" asked a pilot I recognized from Randi's squadron. His name tag read, SNORT NEARY.

"I figured they wouldn't let you guys out of the planning room with all the work that's got to be done."

Snort laughed. "There's no room in there with all the commanders and department heads."

"They make the high-ranking guys do all the calculating and flight planning?" I asked, knowing full well that senior officers avoided grunt work like the plague.

"Make them? Hell, no, nobody makes them. They think this is a one-time shot, so they're down there making sure they get to fly and get their air medals."

The table erupted with hearty agreement.

I addressed the whole group. "But, if they aren't used to planning, won't they be liable to make mistakes?"

A Marine captain spoke up. "Give that man a cheroot. Hell, sir, that's what we're for. Along about twenty-two-hundred tonight, when the hinge-heads have all crapped out, CAG will have us come in and check every number, fix their dumb-ass mistakes, make them up some pretty charts and knee-board cards, and set up coffee for the morning briefs. We're like the brownies in that old fairy tale."

This prompted more hooting, and someone gave the orator a high five.

"Does that mean none of you will get to fly on the first mission?"

Snort said, "No. Some of us will fly as wingmen, or airborne spares. Unless, of course, there's a particularly nasty SAM system that needs to be taken out, then that'll definitely be one of us."

More raucous agreement followed. Snort got several thumbs-ups from the table.

"Hey, Mr. Warner, how's Hoser doing?" asked one of the younger-looking pilots.

Others chimed in, asking the same question.

I gave them the standard rundown, no change, but stable, which was good news.

"Now there's a hinge-head I'd love to go downtown with," said a pilot, who hadn't spoken yet.

"Hoser's no hinge-head, man," somebody argued.

"I give up. What's a hinge-head?" I asked.

Snort explained to the delight of the crowd. "Oh, you've probably heard that the Navy gives senior officers lobotomies so that they'll forget all about what it's like to be a JO, right?"

I played along. "Sure. We do that to editors."

"Right. But you know how the military worships efficiency. So we install a hinge. Each time someone gets promoted, out comes some more brain matter. They say, by the time you get to be CNO, all that's left is a brain stem."

As silly as it was, the way Snort told it and the thought of cantankerous old Admiral Russell hearing it, got me to chuckling. It was the first time I'd laughed since coming out to the boat. I felt much better and thanked my dinner companions.

Then I made the mistake of asking about autodog. It was actually soft ice cream, as I learned when one of the pilots demonstrated how it got its name. His craftsmanship with the chocolate ice cream made it certain that I'll never be able to use one of those machines again without thinking of a dog doing its business.

I left the dirty shirt and headed for the infirmary. To get there, I had to pass through the mess decks, where the sailors eat.

At the moment, there were hundreds of sailors eating at tables or standing in line to be served. Most were very young. All were dressed in denim, the Navy's working uniform. It looked, for all the world, like a prison. But they were mostly just kids, fresh out of high school, many on their first cruise. As I looked closer, I saw several young women scattered among the men. Definitely not prison.

Making my way aft, I began to comprehend the enormity of the challenge of feeding five thousand people three meals a day. Just the thought of washing all those dishes, pots, and pans, blew me away. I guess an occasional serving of overcooked mystery meat was to be expected.

Nurse Malerba met me at the door to Hoser's room.

"He's been much more active. Don't be alarmed, but we've had to use restraints on his arms and legs. It's so he doesn't pull out the IV."

"Is this normal?"

She gave me that nurse look. The one you get when you ask a dumb question.

"Nothing about a brain injury is normal. Look, it

could be a lot worse. All we can do is let the body heal itself and think good thoughts."

"Can I go in?"

"Sure. I want you to talk to him, like you did before. I think it helps, and it sure can't hurt."

"Thanks for taking care of Lieutenant Cole this morning," I said.

"She's had a tough couple of days. I think she's going to be okay, with a little help from her friends."

I heard myself ask, "What do you suggest?"

"Can you turn yourself into a woman?" She laughed at my expression. "She needs a sounding board. Don't be a man and try to fix things. Try to listen, not judge. And don't be too quick with advice." She eyed me, gauging whether anything had sunk in.

"Anything else?"

"Make sure everyone keeps their hands off her. She's vulnerable." To emphasize her point, she pulled a pair of surgical scissors out of her tunic pocket and snipped them menacingly. "If I find out anyone has taken advantage of that young girl, I'm going to perform a quick outpatient surgery."

"Yes, ma'am."

"Now go see your friend. I've got work to do." And off she strode.

Seeing Hoser strapped down was more unsettling than I expected. I felt the urge, and went ahead and snapped a picture, figuring to give it to him when he was healthy.

I was ready for him to wake up and demand a brewski, and I told him so. "Quit malingering, you old fart. I'm tired of tromping up and down six ladders just to watch you sleep."

I wondered what kind of world he was in. The instruments measuring his brain waves, pulse, and blood pressure, indicated that he was definitely engaged in some type of dream. Maybe he was back in Vietnam, flying downtown. Or he could be surfing an endless wave.

I flashed back to *The Wizard of Oz*. Thinking of Hoser as Dorothy made me chuckle.

"Sharing a good joke?"

Red-faced, I turned to meet the doctor.

"Relax. Nurse Malerba told me you'd be chatting away in here. It's a good idea. I'm all for it." He noted some readings on the chart and conducted a series of tests on Hoser's reflexes, shined a light in his eyes, listened to his breathing, and jotted it all down.

"The fractures appear to be healing nicely. Frankly, he'd be pretty miserable if he was conscious right now. I'm concerned about pneumonia. We'll keep an eye on that. Have you got any questions for me?"

"Let's say he does wake up soon. How careful do we need to be about the news he hears?"

"Oh. You mean about Lieutenant Mason's death? Was she one of his students, too?"

"Yes, one of his best."

"Let's keep that quiet until we can fully evaluate his condition. You're right to be concerned. The tendency is to want to fill the patient in immediately on everything he's missed. That can be traumatic and confusing. I'll want you to let Captain Santana set his own pace. Answer his questions, but in simple terms. If he wants more information, he can ask."

"You're speaking about just me seeing him. What about Lieutenant Cole?"

"I'll have to judge that at the time. My patient's health comes first. The watchword is no jolts, no shock, no surprises until we know what we're dealing with."

"Is Lieutenant Cole under a doctor's care? She said she was given something to sleep."

"Yes. Her flight surgeon, Dr. Barrett, is the one who prescribed for her. I know he's concerned about the pressure she's under."

"Do you know where I can find him?"

"Certainly. Follow me."

He led me through the infirmary to the other side of the ship, where we found Dr. Barrett doing some paperwork.

"Frank, this is Jack Warner. He's the friend of Lieutenant Cole's we discussed. Jack, meet Frank Barrett, a wanna-be pilot and a complete quack." They were obviously good friends.

Frank said, "Shove off, sawbones, and don't let the door hit you in the ass." After the surgeon left, he said, "Sit down, Jack. What can I do for you?"

"I hear you're concerned about Lieutenant Cole."

"I can't talk about the specifics of her case. But it doesn't take a brain surgeon to see that she's had three major events occur in her life in the span of four days."

"Three?"

"Count 'em: Captain Santana's injury, Lieutenant Mason's death, and by now she's got to realize that she's the Navy's last female fleet Hornet pilot."

"You think she's going to put too much pressure on herself because of that?"

"I'd ask you the same question. You know more about her than I do."

"I know that yesterday, when she was certain that Captain Santana was killed in an accident, right before her eyes, she kept her cool, was able to fly her jet, air-refuel, then land aboard this carrier."

Barrett nodded.

"Let me ask you a question," I asked.

"Shoot."

"Are you going to let her fly?"

"Does she want to?"

A damn good question. "I haven't asked. But, she's not a quitter."

"So I hear. Look, Jack, I'll be frank." A big smile made me suspect a pat line. "CAG is willing to give her some time, but with this Libya situation brewing, if she doesn't get back in the saddle right away, she's liable to be grounded for the whole operation. You can imagine what long-term effect that could have. She has two choices. She can come down here and demand to get back on the schedule, or she can admit that she's done and ready to get on with the rest of her life."

CHAPTER 26

Saturday, 19 Oct/1855

On the way to my room, I swung by the Comm Center and asked if the blackout on the mishap was lifted yet.

"Not yet, sir," said the chief. "Do you want me to call you, when the next-of-kin confirmation comes through?"

"If you can do that, Chief, I'll owe you one."

"No sweat, sir. I'll be the first person to see it. Go on back to your room, and you should be hearing from me tonight. And, sir?"

"Yes?"

"Never tell a chief you owe him one. I'll let you slide this time." He gave me a friendly smile as he closed the door.

I went to my room and straightened up. Then I called Randi and asked her to come down. She hesitated, but I explained that I couldn't leave because I was waiting for an important phone call.

She was there in five minutes, dressed in a flight suit.

"How's Hoser?" she asked, taking a chair.

"He's getting more active. It's a good sign."

"I should go see him."

I was about to offer advice, but the voice of Ms. Malerba rang in my head, *Just listen*. So I nodded, and let her talk.

"I should have gone earlier, but I couldn't seem to muster the energy."

"Maybe it's the drugs."

"Maybe." She sounded unsure.

"What else do you think it could be?"

"Well, I've been wondering about that. I feel like I hit bottom. To tell the truth, Jack, Amy's death hasn't affected me the way I would expect."

"What's different?"

"I'm numb, and I don't think it's the drugs. I think I've just processed as much bad news as I can. You could probably tell me I was grounded forever, and I wouldn't feel much different. Or you could tell me I was being promoted to commander, and I wouldn't get too excited. It's not that I don't care, exactly. It's that I can see that only a few things are really important to me now." She looked at me out of the corner of her eyes. "You think I'm ready for the funny farm, don't you?"

"Nope. You've reached some kind of threshold. Life is simple for you right now."

"That's close. I mean, I loved Amy like a sister. Losing her left a hole in my life. I love Hoser like a father. If he dies, or is permanently brain-damaged, it'll be terrible. But I can't do anything but accept it.

I'm still responsible for living my life. Do you know what I mean?"

"Yes."

We sat in a comfortable silence.

Her next question was right to the point. "Jack, do you think I should quit flying?"

"Not without some compelling reasons."

"I feel like I'm at a crossroads. Like I could walk away from flying and never look back. First my dad, and now Amy and Hoser. This business has taken three of the most important people in my life. Do I still need to prove anything?"

"Not to people who know you, and certainly not to any strangers."

Her eyes were wet. I knew this was about more than flying. "Randi?"

"Yes?"

"The time for you to prove things is over. That's all a trap anyway. You have only to be honest with yourself. Learn that, kiddo, and you get the rest of your life as a reward."

Her foot started tapping on the floor. She was getting antsy. "That makes sense. I can hear the truth in what you're saying." She stood and stepped closer. Looking down at me, she said, "You're going to think I'm nuts."

"Why?"

"Because I want to go fly. I mean, right now. I was born to do this. This Libya thing is hot, and I want to be part of it. But . . ."

"But?"

"I've got to convince the flight surgeon, my CO, and the CAG. And they don't listen like you do."

I stood up, silently thanked Nurse Malerba, and put my hands on her shoulders. "I have a hunch they will. Dr. Barrett is waiting for you. Go tell him what you just told me. Then go find your buddies in the mission-planning room. They'll be there most of the night unscrewing the mistakes of the senior officers. You'll probably be flying by tomorrow afternoon."

Before she could get mushy, I pushed her out into the corridor. "Take it one day at a time, sport."

"Roger that." She saluted, smiled sweetly, and left.

I watched her walk away, apparently taking my energy with her. As I closed the door wearily, I imagined that she, too, would die in an airplane, and I'd be the one who had pushed her back to the cockpit.

Saving that lovely thought for later, I polished up the article on Amy's mishap. It turned out to be what I call a Joe Friday piece. You know, "Just the facts, ma'am." The news that she died would hit my readers hard. They'd want to know what happened, but it was too early to share my suspicions about that. Besides, I didn't want to cloud the poignancy of the story of this Nebraska farm girl turned into jet jockey.

So I recapped the facts, provided a glimpse of her roots, and let the photos tell far more about the life and death of this young woman than my words ever could.

After finishing the article, I attached the photo of her parked on the elevator and the one of the ejection.

Then I zipped the file and put it on one disk. When the Comm chief called, I would be ready.

I made a quick trip to the head. The ship was definitely hauling ass. I could feel the pulsing from the engine room, and for a moment I imagined the tough sailors, they called them snipes, who tended the fires of the ship's massive boilers. Supposedly, some snipes rarely ventured above the third deck, not seeing sunlight for months at a time. Truth or fiction, it made a good story.

The phone was ringing when I reached the door of my room.

"Jack Warner."

"Don't use my name, okay? You told me to call you."

It was young Mr. Lawrence. He no longer tried to disguise his voice. "Can you talk?" I asked, buying time, so I could set up the tape recorder.

"Yeah. For all the good it does."

He was still in a funk.

I wasn't in a mood to humor him. "Last night, you told me to warn them. I did that. They said they'd be careful. There wasn't anything else I could do without some evidence."

"I didn't think they would kill her."

"Who's they?"

"You know I can't tell you that."

"Well, it appears that whoever *they* are, *they* did it. So what changed?"

"You."

"I don't understand."

"You, the press. They know this is going to be plastered all over every paper in the country."

"Wouldn't that be a good reason not to risk it?"

"C'mon, Mr. Warner, you're sharper than that. So are these guys. You being here, combined with the trouble in Libya, gave them the perfect excuse. All of America is going to wake up Sunday morning, read your article, and come face-to-face with someone's dead daughter."

His speech sounded well practiced, and he wasn't finished. "No, sir. Mr. and Mrs. America don't like to have their breakfast ruined by reading about somebody's beautiful young girl getting killed in a forty-million-dollar jet. Face it, Mr. Warner, you were the catalyst for this whole damn thing. That lieutenant would still be alive if you weren't here. And you have to live with the fact that you had the chance to save her, and you didn't do it."

The line went dead. The prick had hung up on me. My first urge was to go track down Lawrence and knock the living shit out of him. But it passed, replaced by a melancholy that put me flat on my back. I knew in my heart that whoever did it, whoever had murdered Amy, had done it because of the press coverage. And that meant because of me.

The Comm chief called at midnight. "You've been cleared to file your story, Mr. Warner."

"Thanks, I'll be right down."

I grabbed the disk and made my way down to the

Comm Center. The chief was bright-eyed, ready to talk. I was ready for sleep that I prayed would come easily. I made small talk while he set up the satellite link and launched the file on the high-speed data line.

It was chilly in the Comm Center.

"This place is like a meat locker," I said.

"Yeah, it's to keep the electronics from overheating. Come summer, we're the most popular place on the ship. So, Mr. Warner, you mind if I ask you something?"

"Shoot."

"Do you get to decide how the whole country feels about this Libya thing?"

My foggy head wasn't up to deciphering that question. "What do you mean, Chief?"

"I mean, all anybody is going to read about this operation is going to come from military press releases, which nobody believes, and your on-the-scene reports. Isn't that right?"

"No. Right now all we've got is a lot of posturing and talking. Back home, you've got those CNN experts yapping, and all those politicians leaking tid-bits to the networks. I'm small potatoes. We'll know if this thing is going to escalate when the prime-time press is crawling all over this ship."

"Aw c'mon, Mr. Warner, that's bullshit, and you know it. When we strike Libya, your by-line is going to be on the front page of every paper in the country."

The chief was eyeing me intently. Something in his expression jolted me wide-awake. "You just said, 'when we strike.' Are you trying to tell me something, Chief?"

"Of course not, sir. I'm just an old Comm chief. What would I know?"

A terminal buzzed to life. He stood up and walked to it, hit a couple keys, and read the screen. Without looking back at me, he said, "Your message went through, Mr. Warner. You have a good night, now, and we'll see you back here tomorrow evening."

I left, my head buzzing. The Comm chief had made a point of telling me earlier that he was the first person to see messages. Then he'd all but spelled it out for me that the strike was on.

I crawled into my bunk feeling overwhelmed. I'd gone from no prospects a week ago, to crashes, murder, and now, an exclusive on a budding war. Despite all that, sleep came with surprising ease. My body knew what I needed better than my overheated brain.

CHAPTER 27

CAG Office—
Sunday, 20 Oct/0730

After showering and catching breakfast in the nearly empty dirty shirt, I dropped by the CAG spaces.

Petty Officer Lawrence purposely ignored me, seemingly intent on some clerical duty. Commander Holmes was surprised to see me, but welcomed me into his office and graciously served me a cup of coffee.

"I'm glad you stopped by, Mr. Warner," he said. He appeared sincere.

Not expecting this reaction, I sipped my coffee to force him to continue.

"CAG has invited you to the noon briefings." He smiled. "We've been in contact with the Pentagon and gotten you cleared to listen in on some of the classified intelligence." He spread his hands in a gesture of revelation. "I'm sure I don't have to tell you what an incredible opportunity this is for you."

"What about my imminent departure?"

"Well, that's not going to happen until we establish some form of transport for you. In the meantime, you're the only press on board, and therefore a shoo-in to get an exclusive."

"Are you saying that there's likely to be something more to report on than the government's standard rattling of the scabbard?"

"All I can say is that Libya's actions are being taken very seriously in Washington." He pursed his lips. "Very seriously, Mr. Warner."

So, the Comm chief had been right. I shifted gears. "Has there been any news concerning the death of Lieutenant Mason?"

He honestly looked surprised that I'd brought it up. Again, not the response I'd expect from someone who wanted to plaster the papers with the news of her crash.

"We've collected all the film and maintenance records, and of course, the catapult logs and radio tapes. I'm afraid it looks like an unfortunate accident. Something caused that engine to self-destruct at the worst possible time."

I was baffled. No mention of pilot error or inexperience? I pushed harder. "I've left my readers hanging, Commander. First, I introduced them to Lieutenant Mason, and then she gets killed the very next day. Are you telling me I should report that it was an unfortunate case of bad timing?"

"But it *was* bad timing. A catastrophic engine failure on the catapult stroke, when the jet is loaded with two bomb racks and a centerline fuel tank, is just plain bad news.

"Off the record, I can tell you that Lieutenant Mason's inexperience most certainly contributed to the mishap. From observing the video, we can conclude that she grabbed the stick and overcontrolled the jet."

He shrugged. "A more experienced pilot hopefully would have had the presence of mind to let the flight-control computers compensate for the loss of thrust and the jettisoned weight, but it really doesn't matter, does it? I mean, she's dead, the jet is on the bottom of the ocean, and we're reemphasizing emergency procedures to all our pilots. Crucifying that young girl in the press won't do a bit of good. Besides, we'll never really know for sure, will we?"

I was dumbstruck. Holmes was doing everything but begging me not to put the blame on Amy.

I tried yet another angle. "Does this change how you feel about women flying Hornets?"

He seemed uncomfortable with the question and took time to answer it, rubbing his chin in thought. "I have to be honest with you. I did some soul-searching after that mishap. At first, a part of me was ready to stand up, point, and say, 'See? Do you see what happens when you send young girls to do a man's job?' But, it sounded so ugly, so harsh, that I had to admit to myself that it was wrong. I can tell you, unofficially, but without a doubt in my mind, that if half the pilots on this boat were in that jet, it would still have crashed. Not a nugget in the world could have saved it. Besides, who are we to say that the flight-control computers would have reacted fast enough? We don't have any flight test data on something like that. It's too dangerous, even for test pilots."

He looked at the bulkhead, silently considering his thoughts, before returning his gaze to me. "I can't take back the things I've said, and I still don't think bringing women out here is right, but what happened yesterday is not proof of anything. It is just a tragedy." Then he added with emphasis, "A brave American died defending her country. Her memory should be honored, not denigrated." He pushed his chair back. "And, Mr. Warner, if you'll excuse me, that's all I have to say on the subject." He stood and showed me out. "Remember, the memorial is at ten-hundred," he said as he opened the door.

I nodded and thanked him for his time. As I left, I caught sight of Lawrence, standing at the nearby copy machine. He turned his back to me and shuffled through the papers he was holding. From his position, he could have been listening at the door.

Just what the hell was going on?

Hangar Bay One—
Sunday, 20 Oct/1000

The memorial was well attended. One entire bay of the hangar deck had been cleared and was full of people. It took some work, but I managed to find a spot next to Lieutenant Commander Bradley. I had to see if he, too, had managed to have a change of heart. Maybe my suspects were just being careful.

Chaplain Hogan gave a solid, if uninspired, service. He emphasized Lieutenant Mason's sacrifice. Captain Morganelli offered a moving tribute to all those who had not returned from the *Ranger*'s many cruises. As he apologized for not having a more formal memorial, I realized that the ceremony was being videotaped. While the cameraman backed away and panned the enormous crowd, Morganelli concluded by saying that Lieutenant Mason's family on the *Ranger* offered their deepest sympathies to her family back home. In the background, the Navy Hymn played. Many sailors were dabbing their eyes, others waved sadly to the camera.

It was a touching moment, and I used it to prod Bradley. "Dizzy, do you think it will end up being called pilot error?" I whispered.

At first I thought he wouldn't answer me, but the guy really did think highly of his opinions. He motioned me over to a corner, but kept his eyes on the crowd. "Off the record?"

I nodded.

"Do I think it was pilot error? Yes. Absolutely. Do I think it'll ever be reported that way?" He turned to look at me. "No fucking way."

"You mean a cover-up?"

"Look, we all know she screwed the pooch. She grabbed that damn stick and ham-fisted it. Sure, it was a tough situation, but that's what we're trained for."

I couldn't figure it. If it was a conspiracy, they should both be on the same page. "Commander Holmes said that any nugget would have made the same mistake."

This seemed to surprise him. "Well, that could be, but it doesn't change the facts."

"And those are?"

"Women don't belong out here. This is a tough business, and people are going to die, no matter how much you train them."

I'd heard enough and disengaged myself. While waiting for the noon briefings I decided to go check on Hoser.

Nurse Malerba was off duty, but had left instructions to allow me into Hoser's room. When we were alone, I laid it out to him. As strange as it had seemed at first, talking to my comatose friend seemed like the most natural thing in the world.

"Hoser, you aren't going to believe all that's happened this morning. Remember, I told you that I had Holmes and Bradley all but nailed down for murdering Amy? Well, now I'm not so sure. I mean, they aren't acting the part. Guilty bastards almost always overcompensate by being too smooth, or if they can't pull that off, too nervous.

"Holmes went so far as to tell me that this mishap shouldn't be used in the argument against women on ships. Even if that was brilliant deception, and I don't think he's that shrewd, Bradley blew that by being his same old bigoted self. Frankly, I'm almost back to square one."

Again, there was no interruption or advice, and he was polite enough not to make fun of me. I wished him well and left to grab a bite to eat before the briefings.

The same crew was in place for the briefings, but this time, the CO and CAG were in the receive mode.

The CO of VFA–303, Randi's squadron, was first up.

"Good afternoon, gentlemen. I'm Kevin O'Hara, CO of the Hawks. I've been assigned as strike lead for contingency plan alpha, a daytime preemptive strike on the chemical-weapons-production facility, code-named Bertha.

"Recent satellite imagery indicates that Bertha is within thirty days of going on-line. Plan alpha is designed to target the three main buildings of the complex with precision munitions delivered from high altitude."

"Similar to the Desert Storm game plan?" asked one of the commanders seated in the second row.

"Somewhat. The idea is to establish air superiority, suppress their radar-guided air-defense systems, and stay out of range of their antiaircraft guns. This plan also has the benefit of keeping our strike aircraft out of any toxic materials released during the attack."

He turned to a chart that showed the Libyan coast. "Bertha is located in the foothills, fifty-five miles inland, southeast of Tripoli, near a town named Tarhaza. It was originally thought to be an agricultural-research facility and, in fact, is located in an area populated mostly by farms."

"What changed our minds?" asked someone in the front row.

The Intelligence officer stood up and uncovered another series of satellite photos and pointed to one with his pointer. "I can answer that. It was a combination of indicators. As you can see, these personnel that are handling the liquid off-load from this vehicle are wearing full hazardous-material protection suits, including respirators. When we cross-checked the delivery inventory, we found that they signed for five thousand liters of distilled water."

"Yeah, right," said a voice from the back.

"We can't divulge our sources, but we have substantial evidence of their intent to produce chemical weapons, including names of the research staff and inventories of equipment and raw materials. Gentlemen, this factory will soon have the capacity to produce several hundred chemical warheads a month. Combine that with the Scud missiles our friend Gadhafi is buying from North Korea and we have an emergent threat to the safety and security of the central Mediterranean."

O'Hara picked up the brief again and laid out the Libyan defenses. They were impressive. Their radar coverage totally enveloped the country. Most sites were located on mountaintops and had excellent fields of view. Surface-to-air-missiles (SAMs) were arrayed around cities, communications centers, power stations, and airfields. Their coverage was depicted on the charts with multicolored rings showing the distance they could "reach out and touch someone," as O'Hara put it.

From where I was sitting, there was no inch of Libya uncovered. It looked like a death trap.

"We'll use a rolling suppression tactic to create a safe corridor for our strike package. We'll employ a combination of decoys and see-through jamming to bring the sites up. Our decoy launchers will also be carrying HARMs.

I knew that HARMs were antiradiation missiles carried by the Hornets that would guide on the radar signals supporting the SAMs.

"Skipper, please explain the jamming plan," said CAG, with a nod toward the audience.

"Yes, sir. Our Prowlers will provide sufficient electronic jamming to convince the Libyans that they're under attack, but they'll still be able to burn through it to break out the decoys. We want them on their highest power settings to give the HARMs good targets. Our HARM shooters will be orbiting and launching at intervals designed to provide total coverage of the strike ingress and egress."

"What's the air threat?" asked Captain Morganelli.

"Sir, we have the MiGs flying out of the two coastal bases. They've got MiG–23s and MiG–21s. Neither presents a sophisticated threat. We'll plan on deploying a MiG Sweep and establishing a Barrier CAP for the duration of the strike.

"We are concerned about the recent purchase of Fulcrums. As you know, the MiG–29 is a match for our Hornets, particularly if we're loaded up with racks and bombs. But we've got no indication that their pilots have been trained, or even that they're operational. This is another good reason to strike as soon as possible."

"What's our threat of a counterstrike?" asked the captain.

"Well, sir, we know that Gadhafi would do almost anything to bag one of our aircraft or hit one of our ships. We'll have the *Arkansas* and her picket ships providing coverage and sanitizing the strikers on their egress. With our aerial-refueling plan, the *Ranger* won't need to be closer than two hundred miles at recovery and can pull back immediately thereafter.

"Our biggest threat comes from the Exocet cruise missile. Libya employs them on their MiG–23 Floggers, which can really haul the mail. They're not much of a fighter, but those scooters can cruise at seven hundred miles an hour on the deck. In addition to our own SAMs, we'll also have our Tomcats loaded out with Phoenix, Sparrow, and Sidewinder missiles. We're confident that our air-defense net can intercept and neutralize any over-water threats."

"Very well. Go on."

"We'll be using laser-guided munitions. Our objective is to render the site useless; therefore, we'll be dropping one-thousand- and two-thousand-pounders with delayed fuses.

"Will pilots designate their own targets?" CAG asked.

"Yes, sir. That's because of the three separate targets. We're scheduled to fly a practice mission this afternoon."

"What's your practice target?" asked the captain.

"One of the frigates, sir. She's agreed to hold position and be our target for the day."

"Make damn sure they understand the risks associated with lazing and have proper eye protection," warned the captain.

"Absolutely, sir."

"Are there any other questions before we get into the nitty-gritty stuff?" asked O'Hara.

I raised my hand, garnering several puzzled looks.

"Yes, Mr. Warner?"

"This is a fixed target. Why aren't you briefing a cruise-missile attack instead of sending the air wing over the beach?"

The captain answered me. "That's a fine question. There are several reasons for using manned aircraft. First, this complex is a hardened target. And it's very low profile, only one story high, with most of the important facilities arrayed underground. A cruise missile doesn't carry a sufficient warhead to penetrate and cause the kind of damage that one of Commander O'Hara's Volkswagens will."

Several people chuckled at his reference to the two-thousand-pound bombs as a small car. "We also have reason to believe that Gadhafi has taken steps to protect this facility from subsonic cruise-missile attacks."

He nodded to Commander Kopper, who unveiled one more photo. Everyone leaned forward to see the image.

"See these clamshell structures surrounding the complex?" He tapped on several sites.

"Are they gun emplacements?" someone asked.

"Very good. They're radar-guided, four-barreled ZSU–23s. But instead of being part of their anti-aircraft defense, their orientation and interlocking fields of fire have convinced us that they were built specifically to take out cruise missiles."

He turned to me and smiled. "It seems that some jobs still take the human touch, Mr. Warner."

I sat through two more briefs. Both were low-altitude attacks designed to slip the strike package into the target undetected. Both CAG and the captain rejected the daytime operation because of unacceptable risks. However, a night strike featuring the Marine pilots using night-vision devices was well received. It was a much smaller operation. The main objection was the exposure of the strike aircraft to the ZSU–23s. As one officer stated, a radar doesn't give a damn if it's day or night. There was also a significantly lower probability of target destruction. But, striking at night was one way to keep the Libyan Air Force out of the picture. Their nighttime flying capabilities were judged to be poor.

In the end, practice for both the high-altitude daytime and low-altitude nighttime missions was approved for today's flight schedule.

As the briefings wrapped up, the captain was handed a message from the Comm chief. Morganelli read it, stood up, and addressed the entire room. "Gentlemen, *Ranger* has been put on alert. Our mission could be approved for a go as soon as tomorrow morning. Take care of all loose ends today. Go ahead and brief your troops. No mail or unmonitored communications will leave the ship from this point forward, until our readiness status is lowered. Most importantly, take care of yourselves. CAG and I need you to lead, and for that you need to be rested and alert. I'm ordering each of you to get at least six hours of sleep between now and dawn. See Dr. Barrett if you are having trouble in that department. I'll be addressing the ship at eighteen-hundred tonight. See to it that your people hear it from you first."

"Attention on deck!" After he left, the room buzzed with conversation. "Sleep? What the hell is that?" someone asked.

I used the opportunity to find O'Hara. "Skipper, got a minute?"

"That's about all I've got. What's on your mind?"

"Lieutenant Cole. Is she going to be on your mission?"

"She didn't tell you?" he asked.

"Tell me what?"

"I guess that shouldn't surprise me. She really is a remarkable person."

"I'm afraid I don't have any idea what you're referring to."

"You remember that we were airborne during yesterday's mishap, right?"

"Yes. You were scheduled to fly ACM. You said you liked to get a feel for how the nuggets handle themselves under pressure."

"Yeah, that's what I said." He smiled. "She really didn't tell you anything?"

"No."

"Well, Mr. Warner, I've been flying for nineteen years. I spent the last eight years in F/A–18s. I've got over fifteen hundred hours in the Hornet. So when I take a nugget out for a little one versus one, I try to take it easy on them. On our first setup, I purposely gave her some angles, to see how aggressive she would be."

He looked down and cut his eyes at me, feigning embarrassment, before smiling. "Your friend was on me like a cheap suit. I was defensive from the git-go and couldn't shake her off my tail. When she got to guns range, I called a knock-it-off and set up again. This time, I gave her my best fight."

"What happened?"

"She matched me turn for turn. Neither of us got any angles, but she was consistently the first one to acquire radar locks and to get off shots in the face. Afterward, I went over her HUD tape. Every single shot was valid. She's a Phenom, Warner. Now you tell me she hasn't even bragged about it. To tell the truth, I was prepared to take a ribbing."

"I hate to push, but you didn't answer my question. Will she fly on your mission?"

He looked at me like I was an exceptionally slow pupil. "What do you think? She's one of the best ACM pilots in the air wing. I won't put her in the strike package. She's still got a lot to learn about the bomb-dropping business, but she'll be on the MiG Sweep or Barrier CAP."

I left them to prepare for the afternoon and evening missions and meandered the 0-3 level, wandering into several ready rooms. Morale was high. The ship was crackling with energy.

CHAPTER 29

**Lobo Maintenance Control—
Sunday, 20 Oct/1545**

Art Cardone was in his element. He was systematically driving his maintenance department into a fevered pitch.

I found a chair and watched the maestro at work. Questions were fielded deftly, big jobs were coordinated, and individual tasks assigned, all with a personal touch. He managed to convey to each sailor that his or her contribution was vital. He would chastise or cajole, depending on what worked, to convince his charges that they could do better with just a little more effort. All the while, he kept track of hundreds of details. But his real genius lay in his ability to coax help and favors out of the ship's other departments.

Art could use corny lines without sounding insincere, and he could charm the most obstinate of supply officers with a combination of banter and relentless coercion. I listened to him negotiate respots for his aircraft from flight-deck control.

"Handler? Yes, sir, it's Art. Gotta tough one. My

bird, five-oh-seven, is penned in on the six-pack. Yeah, I hear you. I told my MO you were overwhelmed, but he said to ask anyway. Oh yeah? Geez, that's a bitch. Say, what would it take to help you see it my way? Sure, I heard that. We could all use that, but what's a man to do? If I could just get this one respot, we'd be outta your hair, scout's honor. Five-oh-seven? It's a sweet machine, you've got my word on that, boss. It'll fly circles around Brand X. Okay? You mean it? Bless you and all the saints. Yes, sir. Adios."

He looked at me and winked. "Guy's a certified asshole. Nobody else can get the time of day out of him."

Art had the kind of street smarts that can't be learned in schools. It was quite a performance, and one that he seemed to relish.

In the midst of one of his flurries, he caught my eye and said, "Meet me here at seventeen-hundred. We'll go get some chow."

I gave him a thumbs-up and left him to his business. I'd promised to drop in on the Marine squadron down on the third deck.

The VMFA-461 Ready Room was plenty busy. After all, they had both pilots and backseaters, but I was welcomed in and given a good-natured ribbing.

"Wow, guys, the press actually found their way down into the bowels of the ship," said one of the pilots I recognized from the dirty shirt.

"Slumming it, aren't you, sir?" asked one of many young aviators sporting a shaved head.

"I can't help it that you guys like to fly when

everybody else is sleeping," I said. This resulted in a chorus of abuse making me feel right at home.

The pilot who invited me arrived and pointed toward a couple chairs after getting us each a cup of coffee.

"Heard you were at the brief," he said.

"Yup. Are you guys really eager to fly into that target?"

"Absolutely. That's what we do."

"I understand that night-vision goggles only provide a limited field of view."

"That's correct. We're trained to keep our heads swiveling." He demonstrated the technique.

"How low do you guys fly?"

"Below three hundred feet."

Three hundred feet! "Good Lord, how can you do that on a route you've never flown before?"

"Good planning." He smiled.

"So how do you plan to stay out of the possible toxic cloud from the factory?"

"We'll use retarded weapons."

I started to laugh, but he cut me off.

"No, sir. That's what we call weapons that deploy some kind of delay feature, like a parachute, or fins. They slow the weapons' fall time and give us a chance to get out of there before detonation."

"Are they accurate?"

"Yes, but not as accurate as laser-guided bombs."

"Are they as destructive?"

"Not for hardened targets. An LGB dropping in from three miles up is hauling chili. Our bombs don't have the benefit of all that gravity fall. But we'll drop several thousand-pounders from each aircraft; they'll do the job."

"What about the gun defenses?"

"That's why we've got to surprise them. If they get no warning from their air-defense system, we'll be in and out before they can get manned up."

That rationalization sounded suspiciously like whistling in the dark. What would happen if the guns were already manned up? I left that question unasked. We continued to banter back and forth until my host was yanked for mission planning. I left the Marines to their preparation and found Nurse Malerba.

"I think our boy is stirring," she said, when I arrived.

"No kidding?"

"Nope. C'mon, we're about to go see if we can get his attention."

Hoser was still strapped down, but his breathing was more energetic, and there was definitely more color in his face.

After the doctor took his vital signs, checked his pupils, and read the monitor, he said, "Captain Santana. Can you hear me?" Then he shouted, "Wake up, Joe!"

A tremor coursed through Hoser's body, but he didn't open his eyes. The doctor snapped his fingers, clapped his hands, and even jostled Hoser's uninjured shoulder. He looked at his nurse and shook his head.

She said, "Let his friend try."

The doctor shrugged and stepped back, signaling me to give it a shot.

"Tell him about something he likes," she said.

"Hoser. Hey, buddy, it's me, Jack. Are you going to sleep all day?" I grabbed his right hand; his left arm was in a soft cast. "Hey, man, the brewski is cold."

He moaned and rolled his head on the pillow. Instantly, the doctor was on the other side of the bed, watching intently. "Keep it up," he said.

Inspired, I leaned forward, and whispered into his ear. His head twitched toward me. I whispered again. Hoser's eyelids fluttered briefly and snapped open. I found myself staring into those amazing sky-blue eyes.

Hoser spoke for the first time since the mishap. "Jack?"

"Yes, buddy. It's me."

He tried to swallow. His throat was dry.

"Thirsty," he croaked.

Nurse Malerba stepped in and slipped a few ice chips into his mouth. He closed his eyes and smiled his gratitude at the simple pleasure.

He took a breath and tried to move his arms, frowning when he couldn't. When he opened his eyes again, the old Hoser was back. He looked from the doctor to the nurse and back again. "You'd better tell me what the hell is going on."

The doctor said, "You're in the hospital, Captain. There was an accident. I need you to answer a few questions, and then we'll catch you up on everything, okay?"

"Shoot."

"What's your name?"

"Hoser. What's yours?"

"Do you know what day it is?"

"Friday?"

Hoser had lost count of the days.

"How much is thirteen plus five?"

"Eighteen. Can I have some more ice?"

The doctor continued questioning Hoser. I stepped out when they began the physical evaluation. Finding a phone, I called the Hawk Ready Room, but Randi was manning up. I told the SDO the good news, and he promised to notify Randi as soon as she landed. Then I called the bridge. After a short wait, the captain came on.

"Morganelli."

"Captain, it's Jack Warner."

"Yes, Jack."

"Hoser just woke up. He's talking."

There was a slight pause before he answered. "That's the best news I've heard all day." His voice conveyed genuine relief. "When can I see him?"

"I'll have the doctor call you. They're evaluating him now."

"Listen, we're in the middle of flight ops. I'll have to get back to you. Thank you, Jack."

A few minutes later the nurse came out smiling.

"He's going to be okay," she said. "In fact, he's complaining already. Why do I think I'm going to long for the time when he was out cold?"

"I really can't see him being a model patient."

"Terrific. He wants to see you. Just a couple of minutes, though. We've got to give him some time to catch up to himself. And the doctor says no bad news, okay?"

"Yes, ma'am."

I was happy to see the restraints off. He was propped up, looking ludicrous in his gown.

"Hi, Jack."

"Hi, yourself. Damn, it's good to hear your voice. Are you in much pain?"

"Nothing to write home about. My ribs are sore, and my head hurts like hell. They tell me it was a pretty spectacular crash."

"What do you remember?"

"I remember bumping Amy from the cockpit. That's all. Everything else is a blur. What happened?"

"Captain Morganelli set it up for you to get three more traps to make your fifteen hundred. On the last one, the right mainmount collapsed, your hook slipped the wire, and you skidded into the JBD."

"Ouch. Was there a fire?"

"Yeah. Two firefighters, Douglas and Cates, got to you and pulled you out. I was standing on the bridge."

"I'll have to thank my saviors. Bet the jet is pretty bad."

"The captain had them dump it overboard."

He raised his eyebrows but didn't say anything.

"He kept right on flying. Said you can't buy training like that. He told me that you'd have done the same thing."

Hoser snorted. "Figures. Yeah, I just might have. Where the hell are we?"

"Off the coast of Libya."

"Get out of here. We had to have just in-chopped."

"That's true, but Gadhafi is at it again, and the air wing is briefing contingency strikes. Randi is flying a practice one right now." As soon as I said it, I could have bit my tongue.

"So, how are the girls doing? Have they flown at night?"

"Yup. Both have great landing grades." I needed to change the subject to keep from lying. "Randi even whipped up on her CO in ACM."

His eyes brightened. "No shit?"

"Commander O'Hara said she was on him like a cheap suit."

"Slick's not a hamfist. Hot damn. What about . . ."

"Hey," I said, tapping my watch. "I'm on strict orders. I've got to give you some time to get reoriented. I'll be back here this evening and bore you to death. You're not going anywhere, right?"

"Okay, sport. I get the message. Tell that little girl to come visit as soon as she debriefs."

"Wild horses couldn't keep her away. You know that. I'll be back." I started to leave, before he could ask any more about Amy.

"Yo, Jack!"

Too late. "Yes?"

"See if you can rustle me up a brewski. I'm so thirsty, I'd trade my left arm for one."

I laughed at the power of suggestion. "Got it."

The doctor met me outside the door.

"Well? Any signs of mental instability?" he asked.

"No. He seems to be right-on."

"Great. Look, I'm going to give him a series of standard tests to get a baseline. In a few days we'll administer them again. You can come back after dinner."

"I called the captain. When you're ready, he'd like you to brief him."

"Oh, of course. I should have thought of that. I'm afraid I'm still much more a doctor than a naval officer."

I shook his hand, careful not to squeeze those surgeon fingers, but he gripped mine and wouldn't let go.

"If you don't mind, Mr. Warner, I'd really like to know something."

"Okay."

"What was it that you whispered to him that made him wake up. It was really quite dramatic."

"Oh, that?" I laughed, remembering Hoser's instant reaction to my message.

"Yes, I'm thinking of writing his case up for a medical journal, and this kind of thing helps make it interesting."

"I'm not sure you're going to want to publish this, but I said, 'Surf's up!' "

It wasn't an answer he expected. "You mean, like surfing in the ocean?"

"The very same."

"Amazing."

CHAPTER 30

Chiefs' Mess—
Sunday, 20 Oct/1715

Art and I sat down to dinner with three other chief petty officers. I was stunned when a plate brimming with a lobster tail and a beautiful hunk of steak was set down in front of me.

The other guys enjoyed my reaction.

Ravenous for good food, I dug in. The meal was every bit as delicious as it looked. After polishing off the last of it, I looked up to find them all smiling at me.

"Art," asked one, "where did you find this guy? He's a human garbage disposal."

Another asked, "What's the matter, Jack? Those officers not feeding you?"

"Do you guys always eat like this?" I asked.

"Not always, but it's rarely bad," said the tallest of the group. "We do have a code, though."

"What is it?"

"You can't tell anybody what you've had, or you never get invited back."

"No problem. I'm a reporter, I can keep a secret."

For some reason this caused them all to burst out laughing. It almost hurt my feelings. After thanking my hosts and the chef, I walked Art back to his shop. On the way we discussed Mason's mishap.

"I checked with the hangar bay watch on the midnight to oh-four-hundred shift. She claims that nothing unusual happened around Lobo five-oh-nine that night."

"You sound skeptical."

"I am. She wouldn't look me in the eyes. She's not from my squadron—she's a Hawk—which means I can't press too hard. But I'm sure she's hiding something. Maybe she didn't see anything, but she could have nodded off or something else could have gone on. Something that she doesn't want revealed."

"What's her name?"

"Airman Johnson."

"I think I'll have a talk with her."

When we got to the Lobo spaces, I thanked him again for the great meal and left to find Randi.

She was in her stateroom and welcomed me with an enthusiastic hug.

"Isn't it great? I just got back from seeing Hoser. He looks fine, don't you think?"

"Yes, I do. We should have known that he was too hard-assed to let a bump on the head keep him down. How was your flight?"

"Solid. I'm on the BARCAP. We worked on our radar game plan, then did some ACM."

"What is a BARCAP?"

" 'BAR' stands for barrier. We have two pairs of Hornets stationed so that we can intercept bogies from either of the MiG bases. The other air-to-air Hornets are the MiG Sweepers. They'll preemptively flow through the threat sector, stir up, and hopefully clear out any bogies that might be waiting for the strike package.

"How did practice go?"

"It felt good out there. I'm psyched."

"Do you think the mission is a go?" I asked.

"I don't know. What do you think?"

My answer was interrupted by the bosun's whistle.

"This is the captain speaking. I want every man and woman to listen up. *Ranger*, we are about to embark on combat duty. At this moment, we are three hundred miles off the coast of Libya, whose leader, Moammar Gadhafi, has thumbed his nose at the United Nations and built an illegal chemical-weapons factory. We've been ordered to prepare to destroy this facility. That explains all the activity you've seen.

"Tomorrow morning we will be in position to launch air strikes. I need each and every one of you to be mentally and physically prepared to do your jobs. You can expect to be at General Quarters for an extended period of time. I won't mislead you. Our ship is at risk. We are a large target, and Gadhafi would do just about anything to hit us. But we're protected by our air wing as well as *Arkansas* and her picket ships.

"The decision to strike will come from the president. We have already been put on alert. For day shift, try to get a good night's sleep. For night shift, make sure you pay strict attention to detail. Everyone needs to square away their equipment. We can't afford any loose gear.

"If you have any questions about your responsibilities or procedures, especially those concerning damage control, now is the time to ask someone in your chain of command. Until we're taken off alert, off-going mail will be restricted and other communications will be strictly monitored. You can bet, though, that the eyes of the world will be upon us.

"*Ranger*, five minutes ago, I was proud to send a message to the Pentagon telling our superiors that we are ready. I urge you to make every minute count. That is all."

"Does that answer your question?" I asked.

"Yeah."

"Randi?"

"Yes?"

"Do you know an Airman Johnson, a female in your squadron?"

"That's a strange question. Yes, I do. Why?"

"She was on watch in the hangar bay where Amy's jet was parked Friday night. She says she didn't see anything, but one of my contacts tells me she may be hiding something or protecting someone."

"So you want to interview her?"

"Yeah. What's the best way to make that happen?"

"Well, she's just coming off duty right now. Let me call down to maintenance and see if I can catch her."

Randi made the call, and after a few moments, was told that Airman Johnson would stand by in Maintenance Control until we got there.

It was a short walk down the passageway to the Hawk spaces. Randi took me in to the maintenance officer and introduced us. He was an aviator and knew why I was on board. I told him I was doing background info for my articles on women in the fleet. He bought it.

"Johnson can surely give you a woman's perspective. You can use my office."

Something in the way he said it made me do a double take. He was smiling as if he knew the punch line to a joke I was just hearing. Before I could ask, he was called to answer the phone.

Airman Johnson was a petite brunette, who was what my mom used to call well endowed. She was wearing a white T-shirt, through which her low-cut bra and bulging breasts were clearly visible. She also wore more makeup than I'd seen on a sailor and had long, fake fingernails.

"Is this going to take long?" she asked after Randi introduced us. "I could really use a smoke."

Randy pounced: "It'll take as long as it takes, sailor. And during this conversation you will extend both of us proper military courtesy. Do I make myself clear?"

Chastised, the sailor nodded meekly.

Johnson and I sat in the room's two chairs. Randi

perched on the desk edge. I tried to lighten the moment. "No, it won't take long. I just wanted to get your opinion about being a woman at sea for a series of newspaper articles I'm writing."

Johnson's body language changed immediately. She crossed her legs, turned, and arched her back, the better to display her chest in profile. "Really? In the papers? Okay, sir, what do you want to know?"

"For starters, do you think women belong on combat ships?"

"Sure. I mean, it's not natural to put all these men out here without any women." She glanced at Randi, whose scowl deepened. Johnson gave me a flirtatious smile.

I dutifully wrote on my notepad, and asked, "What about the long hours, like those watches in the middle of the night. Don't you feel vulnerable?"

She frowned. "Sometimes. It gets scary at two A.M. and you're the only one on station."

She didn't use military time. This young woman was still more civilian than sailor. I tried to make the next question sound spontaneous. "How do you keep awake that long? I'd be afraid I'd fall asleep."

She was sharp, though. "What is this, sir? Why are we talking about watches all of a sudden?"

To keep her off-balance, I hammered away. "You were on duty Friday night in Hangar Bay Two. Lieutenant Mason was killed when Lobo five-oh-nine crashed yesterday. She manned five-oh-nine on the hangar deck. I'm investigating the possibility of sabotage."

She looked from me to Randi and back again. "Sabotage? You think I wanted to see a woman pilot dead?"

I kept silent.

"C'mon, Miss Cole, there's no way. I mean, I'll grant you I'm not really the Navy's idea of a good sailor, but I wouldn't do anything like that. Besides, I wasn't even there all the time . . ."

Her face reddened as she realized that she'd made a blunder. "I mean, anyone could get to that airplane. It's a big hangar deck."

It was time to bluff. "Listen, we know you aren't involved, at least with the actual act. Like you said, you weren't even there the whole time. Who was?"

She looked at her hands and shook her head.

Randi started to say something; I signaled her to stay quiet. I leaned forward, and whispered, "Let me tell you how this is going to go. You're going to cooperate with this investigation and Lieutenant Cole and I will protect you. Listen to me, Johnson, this is a murder investigation. You can't allow yourself to become implicated in that."

She looked up, tears in her eyes, no longer the spitfire. "Jamie said it would be okay. It was just thirty minutes. It was just a short break."

I caught the drift. "You and Jamie?"

"Yes." She sniffed and wiped her eyes with the back of her hand, spreading mascara. Out of nowhere, Randi produced a tissue.

"Thank you." She dabbed at her eyes, the tissue turning black with mascara. "Jamie and I have been dating for a couple months. He got one of his buddies to cover for me and we . . . we went to the boats."

"The liberty boats?" asked Randi.

"Yes. He had it set up with a blanket and candles. It was real romantic. But, it was just thirty minutes, I swear."

"What time was that?"

"About three A.M."

"Who is this friend of Jamie's?"

"Adam. Adam Lawrence. He works for CAG."

CHAPTER 31

Sunday, 20 Oct/2040

Johnson told us that she and Jamie had decided to cool it for a couple weeks and were now on different shifts. After swearing the sailor to secrecy, I let her go.

My first challenge was persuading Randi not to write them up. She was seething. I explained that, since Lawrence had shifted from source to suspect, I needed time to do some more investigating. Besides, it was getting late, and Randi had to get to bed. If the strike went tomorrow, she'd need her rest.

We stopped by Lobo Maintenance and pulled Art away long enough to update him. He assured us that Lawrence would not get near his machines.

"Don't worry about it. I'm tight with the CAG Admin chief. I'll make a phone call and tell him that his boy has been pissing in his corn flakes."

"Pardon?" I asked.

Art clapped me on the shoulder. "You're such a sand crab." Randi thought this was funny. "Lawrence will be kept very, very busy. He won't know why. It's a chief thing, Jack."

After dropping Randi off at her room, I made my way down to the infirmary. Hoser was grumpy, but I could tell he was happy for the company.

"How bad are you hurting?" I asked.

"Everything aches. My head, my chest, and my shoulder hurt like hell. The worst thing is being trapped in this damn bed. Hell, Jack, they make me pee in a jug." He held it up for my inspection. "Anyway, enough of that. I heard the captain speak. Tell me about the strike plan."

I laid out everything I could remember about the high-altitude strike. Hoser asked several questions, some of which I couldn't answer. He seemed frustrated.

"Listen, Jack. Tell Randi or Amy to come see me. I need to get a handle on some of the technical details. This sounds like it could be a cluster-fuck to me."

To derail a discussion of Amy, I asked, "Why do you say that?"

"Look, this plan is nearly identical to what we did in Iraq. Don't you think Gadhafi is smart enough to expect that? You've got to believe that he's developed countertactics."

Figuring Hoser might be giving the guy too much credit, I asked, "But what can he do about it? If his missile systems come up, the HARMs will take them out. Our jets are out of range of the antiaircraft fire, and his air force sounds outmatched."

Hoser sneered at my naïveté. "You'd make a first-class Pentagon admiral. It worked last time, so it's got to work this time, huh? Hell, Jack, that's exactly the kind of thinking that got our asses handed to us in Vietnam. Gadhafi hates us. He's got big bucks and little to lose. During the Gulf War, we showed the whole world our capabilities and tactics. Now, years later, we plan to fly the same damn mission profile.

"Jesus Christ, man, the gomers have a million options. What if they use new frequencies on their missile and radar systems that we can't jam or guide on? What if his air force has been training? What if the whole damn thing is a ruse, just to get us over the beach for God knows what?"

The night nurse came in, cast one eye on the monitor, and booted me out. I could hear him trying to soothe his patient as I left.

"Captain Santana, I'm going to have to give you something to calm you down. The doctor has left strict orders . . ."

Hoser's words haunted me as I climbed up the six ladders to my room. Everything he said made sense. But once again, there was a zero-percent chance that someone in a position to alter the plans would listen to me. And, because of the news blackout, I couldn't print it. For the second time in four days, I'd been given a warning I could do nothing about.

PART THREE

Feet Dry

CHAPTER 32

**Stateroom—
Monday, 21 Oct/0402**

The phone rang with teeth-jarring insistence. It was the Comm chief.

"Thought you'd want to know. You've got an e-mail from your editor. It looks important."

"I'll be right there." Mechanically, I slipped on my pants, a T-shirt, and flip-flops and trudged down the passageway, too sleepy to be more than mildly curious. When I got there, the chief handed me my e-mail. I shivered from the arctic temperature of the Comm Center.

She'd written to let me know that the wire service had picked up my series. My work was being read in a couple thousand newspapers. She also noted that the photos of Amy's mishap had caused an uproar. Several papers had refused to print them, but most had put them on page one. There were some nice words about my work, and she passed on an "attaboy" from the publisher.

What I found most interesting was her lack of

emphasis on the Libyan operation. She merely said that if things "heated up," I should be prepared to give her six hundred words on the carrier's preparation and role. Apparently, the Navy's ruse of keeping the *America* in port was working.

While I reread the message, the chief said, "All the brass are awake, too. There's been a steady stream of messages from the Pentagon since oh-two-hundred."

The implication finally penetrated my thick skull. "It's going down, isn't it?"

Instead of answering, he asked, "Do you know your General Quarters procedures?"

"No."

He looked at me with a big brother's combination of pity and disgust, took a deep breath, and grabbed me by the shoulders.

I struggled to pay attention.

"Listen up. The captain cleared you to observe from the Combat Center. It's right next door. It'll be cold in there, too, so wear a jacket. When they sound the alarm all foot traffic becomes one-way. On the starboard side, you go forward and up. On the port side, you go aft and down. They'll lock the watertight hatches, and post damage-control teams in the passageways. You'll only have ten minutes to find your way there, and it'll be hectic. Once you're inside, you'll be stuck, probably for most of the day. Make sure you have your computer and everything you need. You won't be able to get back to your room.

"You should go take a shower to wake up, then

get something to eat. The aircrew start their briefs in an hour, and GQ will probably go down about an hour after that. Got it?"

"Yeah. I think so." My head was spinning as I tried to remember all the details.

"What's the direction of foot traffic during GQ?" he asked.

"Uh, port side goes . . . down?"

He rolled his eyes. "Gimme your hand." He took my left hand and wrote, PAD, on the back of it with a black felt-tip. "Port, aft, and down. The starboard side is just the opposite. Can you remember that, or do I need to write it on your other hand?"

"I got it. I'll just be sure not to wash it off."

He smiled. "Not a problem. That marker's permanent."

I caught a quick shower, dressed in clean khakis, and gathered my laptop, extra battery, camera, and nylon flight jacket. The jacket had been a gift during my last Navy assignment; it was my favorite possession. Lugging all my stuff, I stopped by Randi's room, but she was already gone.

The dirty shirt was brimming. I grabbed some cereal, stuffed two muffins in my pockets for later, and found a seat at one of the tables. The mood was tense. Listening to the stilted conversations around me, I noticed there wasn't much eye contact being made. It reminded me of a locker room before a big game. Most of the aviators were picking at their food, several were just drinking juice and coffee. I recognized one of the Hornet pilots from my table as being the TOP-GUN graduate I'd talked with two days before.

Catching his eye, I asked, "Are you on the strike?"

"MIGSWEEP." Several heads turned in our direction.

"I'll be in the Combat Center. What's your call sign?"

"Vader. But our flight will be called, Lobo five-one and five-two."

"Who is your wingman?"

"Dizzy Bradley."

"Who's calling me?" Bradley arrived at our table. One of the guys got up to make room for him. When he noticed me he said, "Oh, Mr. Warner, you're up early."

"Good morning, Commander. Vader was just telling me that you're going to be on the MIGSWEEP. I told him I'd be in the Combat Center during your mission." If he was nervous, he was hiding it well. Unlike his peers, Dizzy seemed exuberant.

"Well, you've got box seats for a good show. We're going to kick some major rag-head ass, right, Vader?"

Vader gave a half smile, but he was clearly uncomfortable with his wingman's cocky attitude. "I'll be happy if we accomplish our mission and recover everyone safely. There's a lot out there that can bite us in the ass."

Dizzy didn't let a mouthful of eggs and toast prevent him from offering his opinion. "The only uncertainty is whether those desert rats are going to have the balls to come up and play, cause if they do, they're going down in flames, and that's a fact."

Since he was on a roll, I kept pumping him. "I hear that Lieutenant Cole is flying on the BARCAP. Isn't that unusual for a nugget?"

His face reddened as he struggled to swallow. After a quick look over his shoulder, he leaned toward me, and hissed, "Damn right it's unusual. It's fucking insane. When I asked Deputy about it, he said that CAG and the Hawk CO made the call." He glanced at his flight lead and continued in a louder voice, "Just what we need, a scared, trigger-happy nugget perched behind us. We'll be lucky not to take a Sparrow up the ass."

At the next table, an aviator wearing a Hawk patch heard the comment, snapped his head around, and angrily reached out to grab Dizzy by the shoulder. A second pilot stopped him with a whispered warning. They both gave Dizzy's back a hard stare and resumed their breakfast. Our table had become dead quiet. Bradley continued to eat noisily, completely unaware of his faux pas.

Vader stood, his face exuding tight-lipped frustration, and said, "C'mon, Dizzy, we've got to get to the brief."

Bradley wolfed down the rest of his food and joined his lead. Their departure led to a mass exodus, with Bradley oblivious to the hostile looks he was collecting.

I followed a crowd down to the Hawk Ready

Room and found an empty seat in the back for the brief. Randi was discussing something with the pilot I knew as Snort. Apparently, they would be flying together. I sat down without interrupting.

A few moments later, there was a flurry of activity as pilots were issued sidearms. The weapons were handed over by a tough-looking Marine sergeant, who admonished each pilot to keep the clip out of the pistol until after manning their aircraft. The pilots seemed excited by the prospect of carrying the 9mm automatics.

Before he left, the sergeant said, "Listen up, gentlemen!" Conversation stopped. "You are not soldiers or Marines. Because you are not experts, you have a much greater chance of getting killed by your own weapon than you do by the Libyans. Do not go cowboy on me; keep the damn weapon in its holster. In fact, I want you to treat it like a grenade. *Comprende?*"

There were a couple halfhearted answers.

The sergeant's voice took on a menacing growl. "I said, *'Comprende?'*"

This time all the aviators piped up, a few instinctively replying, "Yes, sir."

The Marine surveyed the room with unbridled disgust. "I am not a 'sir.' I work for a living." He let the door slam behind him.

The ready room erupted in chatter and catcalls until Commander O'Hara, the CO, quieted everyone. "That man is trying to keep us alive. You'd best heed his advice. Now, let's get our heads on straight and listen to the brief."

The SDO turned up the volume on the TV monitor, which soon displayed the smiling face of Bill Kopper, the Intelligence officer.

"Good morning, Air Wing Thirty. This is your oh-five-hundred brief for today's mission over Libya. If you thought this was the strike on Iraq, that'll be briefed at ten-hundred."

A couple of the pilots groaned at the early-morning stab at levity. The camera panned to a picture of a large-scale map.

"*Ranger* is currently two hundred forty miles north of Tripoli. Our launch position will be at two hundred miles, as will recovery."

The camera panned to a chart depicting the route of flight for the strike force.

"There will be both a strike force and an air-defense force." He used a pointer to tap the chart as he talked. "Our strike package consists of six distinct elements. We have the deception package of decoy and HARM shooters from VFA–305 and the Prowlers. They'll penetrate Libyan airspace first, at oh-seven-forty-five local. After the decoys are deployed and the second round of HARMs are inbound, the MIGSWEEP will proceed to clear the target area. One pair of Hornets, each, from VFA–305 and VMFA–461, will conduct the MIGSWEEP.

"Because of the potential for civilian aircraft flying in the area, rules of engagement require that, outside of visual range, bogies must be declared hostile by the E–2 before you can fire. We'll have two Hawkeyes airborne, one to control the strike package, and one to handle tanking and support the air-defense net.

"The third element will be the strike package itself, led by the Strike Lead, Commander O'Hara, from VFA–303. He will take four Hawks and two VMFA–461 birds into the target area at high altitude, while the MIGSWEEP aircraft contain the threat from the target south. In the meantime, our BAR-CAP, composed of two aircraft from VFA–303 and two from VFA–305, will deploy along the flanks of the strike corridor, here and here, protecting to the east and west.

"The fifth element will be composed of two recce-equipped Tomcats from VF–301, which will make a high-speed pass three minutes after the last bomb impact."

I remembered that Tomcats could carry a pod with sophisticated cameras in it. The Tomcat's high top-end speed and two-person crew made it a good platform for the mission.

Kopper continued. "Last, but not least, will be the combat search-and-rescue element. The SAR helos will be holding off the coast with their Hornet escorts from VMFA–461.

"Tanking for the package will be conducted en route by four KS–3s, which will shuttle from two Air Force KC–135 tankers positioned one hundred fifty miles off the coast.

"Ladies and gentlemen." He rapped the podium with his pointer. "If you are over water and heading north, you do not want to be below ten thousand feet after oh-seven-fifty. The air liaison officer from USS *Arkansas* assures me that she will treat all unidentified inbound traffic below that altitude as hostile, as will our Tomcats. This is especially important for our combat-rescue element. Make absolutely certain you are cleared to transit the free-fire zone before you turn your nose toward *Ranger* below ten K.

"Now, before we continue with the rest of our brief, here is our resident weather-guesser, Chief Trupin. Take it away, Chief."

A bespectacled chief petty officer came on the tube and described the weather for the strike. Over the ship, there was a solid cloud deck at five thousand feet, but it was clear on top. The strike route and target area were in much better shape, with only scattered clouds at twenty-five hundred feet. A pilot not going on the strike leaned over and told me that the weather was one of the key factors in the decision to go this morning. Trupin told us that the forecast called for a cold front to enter the area in the next twenty-four hours.

Kopper came back on and gave a quick synopsis of the international arena. "We have UN Security Council authority for this strike, with the exception of China, which chose to abstain. The media has been buzzing over this for the last several days. Almost all of the experts agree that there won't be a strike until both the *Ranger* and the *America* are on station. *America* has been held in port at Naples an extra day as a deceptive tactic. I have it on good authority that there are some unhappy campers on board."

The guy next to me chuckled. He said, "Man, that would suck. First, you do a whole cruise and miss out on the strike. And then they won't even let you go home. Brutal."

The rest of the brief covered hundreds of details: code words, IFF squawks, weapons load-out, lost-radio procedures, timing, the air-defense strategy, and contingency plans. Kopper briefed no-go criteria that included bad weather, broken airplanes, and inoperative weapons systems. The rules of engagement were briefed and rebriefed in detail. The sequence of the strike and the responsibilities and routes of flight for each element were spelled out.

There was real concern about preventing collateral damage. The strikers were given specific guidance not to drop unless their targets were clearly identified. The same caution existed for civilian aircraft. Though it seemed strange, there would likely be airline traffic into and out of Tripoli. There were also a couple civilian airstrips where small aircraft might be flying. Procedures were put in effect to prevent noncombatants from being accidentally shot down.

Kopper said, "All bogey calls will be referenced from the target, known as Bull's-eye. When a bogey is identified as a Libyan combatant, it will be called a bandit, which signifies clearance to fire."

Kopper gave way to CAG. Captain Andrews was blunt. "Every bone in my body tells me to lead this strike. But that would be my ego acting, not my brains. Slick O'Hara is the best man for the job, and that is why he's leading the strike. Air Wing Thirty and *Ranger* are the best team for the job, and that's why we're here and *America* is parked.

"Each of you has been handpicked to perform your role because you are the best choice for a specific job. That also means that you are trusted to stow your ego. Ladies and Gentlemen"—the camera zoomed in tight—"if I can do it, you can do it. Stick with the game plan. Be certain of your objectives before you climb into that cockpit. I want each and every one of you back here for chow tonight. Now, go kick some ass."

The TV screen went blank. Commander O'Hara stood up and said, "I want the strike force up here. BARCAP, head on down to Ready Four and brief with the Lobos. Alert crews can stay here. Everyone else, please clear out."

CHAPTER 33

Monday, 21 Oct/0600

I followed Randi and Snort down the passageway. Just before we headed in, I pulled her aside into a small cubbyhole, and whispered, "I've got to ask: How can we be sure your jet will be okay?"

She said, "I thought of that, too. First off, whoever killed Amy already accomplished their mission. From what I hear, your photos are on the front page of every paper in the country." She gave me one of those looks patented by my ex-wife—the kind where I'm supposed to squirm with guilt.

But I wasn't squirming. I said, "I hope you have a better reason than that not to be worried."

Her eyes flashed. "How about: Amy's jet was left alone and mine is covered with people? Good people. Nobody is going to screw with it, Jack. Look, I appreciate your concern, but I've got to go." She walked toward the ready room.

"Randi."

She turned. There was an edge in her voice. "Yes?"

"Be careful, okay?"

She grinned, and said, "Okay, Mom, I promise," and left me standing in the passageway feeling very old and useless. I longed for her confidence, but I was left with a churning hole where my stomach was supposed to be. It wasn't enough that this young lady had to risk her life just flying off and on the carrier. She had to share the sea with at least one woman-killer. To keep flying, she was forced to gamble her life on every launch. To top it off, she was preparing for combat.

I ducked into Lobo Maintenance Control and caught Cardone's eye.

"What's up?" he asked, when we'd stepped away from the desk.

"Art, how the hell are we gonna make sure that Cole's aircraft is okay for the launch?"

He put a meaty hand on my shoulder and squeezed. "That's why I like you, Jack. With a little work, you could have been a semidecent chief petty officer." He smiled. "Don't sweat this one. I had a meeting last night with my fellow master chiefs. I didn't spill the beans, but I gave them enough hints that we might have a problem to make sure that nobody screws with a jet. Don't forget, some of us have been through this before. Last night, every shit-bird in the air wing found himself busy with new duties."

I should have known. I thanked Art and hustled back to the brief.

Vader was conducting the brief for both the

MIGSWEEP and BARCAP elements.

"Here's the game plan. Sweepers will go feet dry at T-minus-fourteen minutes. This should be oh-seven-fifty local, if all goes well with the SAM suppression. Be prepared to slide our push times if the gomer radar sites remain operational. The BARCAP will flow to their stations at T-minus-nine minutes. The strike package follows two minutes after that.

"During ingress, the MIGSWEEP formation will be four abreast, with the Lobos on the west. We'll use standard radar coverage and channel separation. All calls will be relative to Bull's-eye. Dizzy and I, call sign Lobo five-one and five-two, will take threats southwest of Bull's-eye. Hulk and Tetro, Jester six-three and six-four, will work to the southeast. If we do not get engaged by the time we overfly the target, we'll split into two sections and run a racetrack pattern.

"On the BARCAP, Lobo five-three and five-four, will take the east, and Hawk three-five and three-six will cover the west. If bandits pop up during the strike phase, the closest section will prosecute. Keep your speed up and remember not to put the bandits directly on the nose. Always offset, so that you'll be certain on which side of the aircraft they'll appear. Any questions?"

There were none.

"Good. Randi, what can you tell us about the Fulcrum?"

A test question.

She stood, walked to the front of the ready room,

and picked up two aircraft models, each of which had been fastened to the end of a dowel. She cleared her throat, and said, "The MiG–29 is a category-five fighter with a one-point-one thrust-to-weight ratio. Performance is comparable to an F–16 in acceleration, and an F/A–18 in pitch rate. Unlike other MiGs, cockpit visibility is excellent. Additionally, the aircraft has exceptional slow-speed handling characteristics. Its weapons system is optimized for a dogfight. It has an infrared tracking system that allows it to track a heat source, like a Hornet, without triggering our warning gear. So beware of sneak attack.

"The aircraft's primary weapon is the heat-seeking Archer missile, which has outstanding off-boresight tracking and a very good flare-rejection system. The Archer is considered superior to our Sidewinder and may be launched well outside of our envelope. The gun is also quite good.

"Our best tactic against the MiG–29, if it's being flown by a capable pilot, would be to use our radar missiles to destroy him before we merge."

Using the models to demonstrate her point, she said, "In a knife fight, particularly over his territory, we must not allow him to swing our wing-line. If he gets behind you, expect to be defending yourself from missile and gun attacks. If you do get slow, below two hundred fifty knots, you're in real trouble. Before you get defensive, call for the cavalry."

"Geez, maybe we should call off the whole thing. These guys sound like supermen," said Dizzy.

Vader ignored the sarcasm. "Thank you, Randi.

That was excellent. I want to stress that we should consider every MiG pilot to be King Kong, until proven otherwise. The Libyan Air Force is capable and has many veteran pilots. Now, let's get down to the details."

He briefed everything from how they would join up, check each other over, refuel, and conduct weapons-systems checks, to what visual signals they would use if their communications were jammed. After all of that was spelled out, he went over procedures they would follow after the strike to check for battle damage. Then he covered their plan for a downed pilot, including coordinating the search-and-rescue effort.

I found it ominous that the planners had decided that no rescues would be attempted deeper than twenty-five miles from the coast. The threat to the rescuers was considered too great.

Finally, he stressed that the strike package was all Hornets, and once their bombs were dropped, they could be pressed into use against bandits.

Dizzy piped up, "Hey, I don't want to share!"

Again, he was ignored.

When the MIGSWEEP and BARCAP groups split up to brief their own procedures, I left to get myself situated in the Combat Information Center, or CIC. No sooner did I enter the passageway than the Klaxon announcing General Quarters sounded. Immediately, the passageway began filling with people, all of them moving fast. Fortunately, I found myself heading in the correct direction, albeit not as quickly, since I was carrying my gear and was still wary of knee-knockers.

Approaching the CIC entrance, I heard someone holler, "Make a hole!"

I barely had time to press my back against the bulkhead, when a column of ten Marines, all carrying rifles and wearing helmets and flak jackets, pounded through. One more second of hesitation and I would have been crushed. I silently thanked Lieutenant Irvine for the warning.

Admitted to CIC, after showing my ID, I was ushered through the darkness to an upholstered seat set upon a raised platform. From my perch I had a bird's-eye view of the various computer-generated displays. My eyes gradually adapted and I could make out, seated below me, several senior officers, including CAG. Each was wearing a headset.

Over the next several minutes, a flurry of announcements concerning the status of the ship's battle readiness were made. Every once in a while, we would hear the pounding footsteps of people running outside our little cocoon.

Flight quarters were already under way. The E–2s were shown as airborne on the flight-status board. It didn't take long until the Tomcats that would man the air-defense net were launched and vectored to join the Air Force KC–135 tankers. It was difficult at first to track the various radio calls being broadcast over the CIC's speaker system. Eventually, I began to make sense out of all the call signs.

The E–2 Hawkeye that had primary responsibility for monitoring Libyan airspace was called Steeljaw. Their reports were eagerly awaited by the group of men seated at the consoles. CAG was known as Alpha-Whiskey, apparently in reference to being the Air Warfare Commander.

"Steeljaw, Alpha-Whiskey."

"Go Alpha-Whiskey."

"Request snapshot."

"Roger. Steeljaw is still twenty minutes from station, but the weather is clear at both Miami and Tijuana. Looks like a fine day for flying."

I remembered from the brief that Miami referred to the eastern MiG base, and Tijuana was the western base. The clear forecast had nothing to do with the weather but with the lack of MiG activity. Even though they were communicating on supposedly secure radio channels, the strike force would use code words as a precaution.

"Alpha-Whiskey, stand by for dolly."

"Roger."

In a couple minutes a data-link circuit was established that allowed those of us in CIC to view the exact same display seen by the controllers in the Hawkeye. Using cursors, the battle staff could highlight a radar contact and request information, or direct an action, without using the voice radio. Over the course of the next twenty minutes the air-defense net filled in with Tomcats checking in as they arrived at their CAP stations and began to patrol, ready to pounce on an inbound threat.

The *Arkansas*, with her sophisticated weapons

system, was actually running the air-defense net. Her data-link information was also piped into one of the displays. With the exception of one Tomcat, whose IFF system was working sporadically, everything was on schedule. The spare F–14 was launched, and a very unhappy-sounding Tomcat crew was ordered to stand by for recovery.

I checked the monitor and saw Hornets taxiing to the catapults. It was the first time I'd seen the air wing armed with live weapons. Since this was the high-altitude strike, they were loaded with precision weapons. The laser-guided bombs, or LGBs, were particularly ominous-looking. These bombs had special fins installed that would be programmed by the laser seeker head to steer the bomb to its impact point. One of the reasons a high-altitude bomb run was desired was that there was plenty of time to make corrections as long as the bomb was released within aerodynamic range of the target. For today's mission, the bombs were tuned to specific laser frequencies that coincided with the emitters carried on the Hornets, so that each bomb was guided by the pilot who dropped it.

All of the Hornets were bristling with missiles as well. Randi was in Hawk 312. She was lined up behind cat two. The sight of her poised behind the catapult that had killed Amy and nearly killed Hoser gave me a jolt in the stomach. I busied myself by using my laptop to record my impressions of CIC.

A red phone mounted on a panel above CAG's

head rang. All conversations and activity in the CIC stopped while he answered it.

"Yes, sir. Roger that. Aye, aye, sir." He carefully replaced the handset and spoke to the room at large. "That was the captain. We have been cleared to launch the strike aircraft. We are to proceed with the mission and expect final clearance at oh-seven-forty local. Let's get to it, people."

The activity resumed amid the buzz of urgent conversations.

I examined the air-to-air display. The Libyan coastline was outlined on the screen along with symbols marking Bertha and the MiG bases at Miami and Tijuana. Over water, airplane silhouettes of the Tomcats could be seen orbiting their CAP stations, from which they would protect the vulnerable carrier, my home, from attack.

Occasionally, a symbol would pop up near Tripoli. In each case, the E–2 was able to confirm that it was a commercial airliner on the proper schedule and route of flight, but nevertheless, the Aegis cruiser would track it until the airliner flew out of range.

With a concussive shudder that vibrated my seat, the first of the Hornets was launched. It carried four HARM missiles, each of which was designed to destroy a radar or SAM site. It also carried two tactical decoys, small disposable gliders that emitted the radar signature of a full-sized aircraft. They were designed to fool the enemy SAM operators into launching their missiles and absorbing a supersonic HARM in return.

Also launched were the Prowlers, special electronic warfare aircraft that could detect enemy radar and communications signals and jam them. I'd covered a story a few years ago where a Prowler had accidentally shut down all communications in Seattle because of a mistaken switch position in the cockpit. Prowlers were especially deadly to SAM sites. They carried HARMs that the four-person crew could reprogram in flight, as well as several pods containing some of the world's most sophisticated electronic gear.

Together, these aircraft comprised the first element of the strike force. It would be up to them to deny the Libyan SAM and radar operators the chance to target and destroy the rest of the strike package.

The launch continued. I don't remember ever feeling as tense and helpless as I did when Randi taxied onto the cat. When she made it safely airborne, I felt like cheering, but kept it to myself. She still had men out there trying to kill her.

There were some more glitches with weapons systems and such, but all of the Hornets made it eventually. After the lone Tomcat with the faulty IFF was recovered, the captain pointed *Ranger* north to put as much distance as possible between us and the coastline until he'd have to reverse course for the recovery.

The radios were full of chatter as the strike package checked in and squared away their own data-link systems. Between the Tomcats on CAP, the Hornets, the *Arkansas*, and the Hawkeyes, just about everybody was sharing data via secure data-link with everyone else. It was amazing technology, but from where I sat, it looked like a royal pain in the ass to set up. When it was all said and done, at least one aircraft in each pair had a working data-link.

The next biggest headache was the tanking. One of the KS–3s went sour, which meant it couldn't refuel anyone. This created a great deal of concern and eventually led to the CAG requesting that the captain turn the big ship around and launch another KS–3. This did not make the captain happy, and some pointed exchanges took place. Begrudgingly, Morganelli made a U-turn, into the wind and launched another tanker, but stopped short of recovering the broken one. He'd have to wait it out and was given a holding position.

Though it looked like all the details couldn't possibly be coordinated in time, the strike package assembled piece by piece. At 0735, Slick O'Hara radioed that the six elements of the strike were in their holding positions and ready to proceed. CAG relayed the information to Morganelli, who passed it, via secure satellite link, to the Pentagon War Room. We waited.

CHAPTER 34

**Rabta Airfield, Libya—
Monday, 21 Oct/0736**

Dieter Graf had just finished his morning inspection of the alert aircraft and his ten-man maintenance crew. As he'd expected, the jet was spotless, despite the miserable sand and dust surrounding the small civilian airdrome. He was generally pleased, but consciously guarded against a letdown in discipline. His handpicked crew were restless with the rural lifestyle, as was he.

They'd been stuck at this remote field for a month as part of a package deal worked out with the Libyans when they purchased the Fulcrums. While ten of the aircraft were being repainted and prepped to form the training squadron, Dieter agreed to run this small detachment comprised of the two remaining aircraft. Ostensibly an instructor, his real mission, along with the allure of a big payoff, was to guard the Tarhaza complex from American attack. Dieter especially liked that.

As a former major in the East German Air Force,

he harbored a burning hatred against the United States. His father, a Luftwaffe pilot, had been horribly burned when his Messerschmidt was shot down defending the homeland. Dieter had long ago vowed revenge for his father's life of pain and disfigurement.

Given the chance to tangle with American pilots, he would have gladly taken this mission for free. The bounty of one million US dollars being offered by Ghadafi for bagging an American jet simply made the deal that much sweeter.

On the downside, his crew had been forced to cannibalize his spare jet for parts. It was now unflyable. He'd sent the other pilot back to the training base. There'd also been very few hours of flying over the past several months. Trying to keep fresh, Dieter spent two hours each day strapped in the cockpit, mentally executing the skills he'd honed in the skies over Europe. On the rare occasions that he did get airborne, carefully scheduled so as not to be observed by the American satellites, he crammed as much work into the mission as possible. It wasn't ideal, but it would have to be enough.

Dieter's prayers were answered when his crew chief activated the makeshift siren mounted on the roof of the dilapidated hangar housing Dieter's prime jet. The Americans were coming!

With practiced efficiency, he ran to the shed where his gear was laid out. Dressing, he heard his aircraft already being tuned up by his team. The rear hangar wall had been dropped to allow the jet's exhaust to escape.

Zipping up his G suit, he paused for just a brief moment to consider the odds against him. One man against the mighty American military. To survive and, moreover, to win would require an audacious plan. He knew he wouldn't have a chance if they used their radar missiles against him. For weeks Dieter had struggled with the problem of getting the Americans into a dogfight. The answer had come to him in the dark hours of a sleepless night. Once again, its boldness and cunning simplicity made him smile.

CHAPTER 35

Oh-seven-forty had come and gone without a go-ahead. The mood shifted among the officers on the console. Nerves began fraying. When Steeljaw asked for a status report, no doubt to answer the questions from the impatient strike pilots, the answer was a curt, "Stand by."

A ringing phone broke the tension in the CIC. CAG snatched it off its cradle.

"Yes?"

He nodded once. "Got it." Before he replaced the handset, he said, "It's a go."

The word passed quickly, amid a series of abrupt radio transmissions, culminating with the voice of Slick O'Hara ordering the SAM-suppression element to proceed. In the CIC, CAG spoke quietly, to no one in particular, his pain at not being airborne clear. "Good hunting, boys and girls."

With crisp efficiency, the suppression element pressed its attack. As expected, Libyan surveillance-radar systems quickly acquired the HARM shooters. The Prowlers waited until the first signs of target-tracking radar were emitted before they began their careful jamming. One by one, the Hornets released their decoys, which were set to glide inbound. The pilots then reversed their course and set up for the first salvo of HARM launches.

Meanwhile, the Prowlers monitored the Libyan defenses as they shifted to higher-power modes and different frequencies in their attempt to burn through the jamming. As the decoys crossed the coastline, their small, but powerful emitters began to supersede the purposely thin jamming. The Libyan SAM batteries, eager for a kill, took their radar locks and fired.

The speakers in CIC filled with the calls of the Hornet and Prowler crews coordinating their attacks. In less than a minute, a dozen HARM's were guiding on the unsuspecting SAM sites. Sixty seconds later, another dozen missiles were launched. Pilots reported seeing the smoke trails of SAM missiles fruitlessly guiding on the small decoys. From the electronic-warfare console, an officer signaled CAG with a thumbs-up. The HARMs were finding their targets.

CAG notified O'Hara, who cleared the MIG-SWEEP element to begin its run. We watched the display as the aircraft silhouettes representing Vader and his three wingmen closed on the shoreline. Meanwhile, the suppression element reset to their stations, and the Prowlers brought their jamming up to a maximum.

Steeljaw reported activity out of both Miami and Tijuana. Apparently, the alert MiG's were being launched. Soon, four red silhouettes popped up on the display, heading south toward the target area. The level of excitement in the controller's voice leapt with the news.

"Bandits airborne out of Miami and Tijuana! Possible four MiG–21s southbound.

Vader kept his cool. "Steeljaw, Lobo five-one, say bearing and range off of Bull's-eye."

This had a calming effect on the controller. "Steeljaw has two groups. Closest is, Bull's-eye, three-four-zero for twenty, angels low. Second is, Bull's-eye, zero-three-zero for twenty-five, angels low."

From the data-link display, I could see that the two MiG groups and Vader's formation were converging on Bertha, with the MiGs in front. It seemed doubtful that the MiGs knew they were in danger from behind and above. That was certainly the objective of the Prowlers, who were doing their best to comm-jam the frequencies used by the MiGs and their controllers.

As we watched, the BARCAP Hornets, including Randi on the west side, crossed the beach. The strike element, led by O'Hara, followed twelve miles in trail.

Vader split his forces to attack the MiGs. "Lobo five-one and five-two are hot for the western group."

"Jester six-three and six-four have targeted the eastern group."

"Steeljaw has possible civilian aircraft, Bull's-eye, two-three-zero for ten, angels low, squawking VFR."

Vader asked, "What's his ground speed?"

"One hundred knots. It's gotta be a puddle-jumper."

"Roger."

The display was now becoming cluttered with aircraft. The strikers were nearly feet dry, making a total of fourteen air-wing aircraft over the beach. A host of others were orbiting just off the coast. There were four MiGs and a civilian aircraft within ten miles of the target.

To add to the confusion, occasionally one of the Navy pilots would call that they were being painted by an enemy radar, whereupon the Prowler would coordinate an attack on the site.

Out of the darkness, the Comm chief slipped into the seat next to me, smiled, and handed me a phone whose cord stretched clear across the room.

"It's for you. Don't worry, I've got it on a separate circuit."

"Hello?"

The raspy voice was unmistakable. "Jack, give me the skinny. What's going down?"

"Hoser, you're supposed to be recovering. The doc said no excitement." I was whispering to keep from distracting CAG and his people.

"Knock it off, Jack. Lay it out for me. Are we across the beach?"

"Yes."

"Are the SAMs down?"

"Yes."

"Any MiGs up?"

"Yes. Two pairs. They're heading toward the target with Hornets on their tail." I scanned the display and saw that the strikers were already ten miles inland and the BARCAP had reached their stations.

"That's it? No other aircraft?"

"No. Except there's an airliner out of Tripoli. She's on schedule and on course, about a hundred miles west of us, and there's a civilian aircraft orbiting south of the target, but he's only going a hundred knots. The E–2 says it's a puddle-jumper."

"What are the MiGs doing now?"

"They're staying low, but they're closing on the target."

The speaker crackled with Vader's voice, "Hulk, looks like they're going to swap sides, stand by for a switch. Western bogies at Bull's-eye, three-five-zero for five, angels three."

"Roger. Eastern package, Bull's-eye, zero-one-zero for six, angels two. We're four miles in trail, staying high."

"Steeljaw concurs with picture. Recommend switch if they cross."

I briefed Hoser on the developments.

"What about that civilian aircraft?"

"It's still about eight miles southwest of the target, maybe six, it's hard to tell from here."

"They need to get an ID on that guy."

"They're pretty busy with the MiGs."

The radio barked again. Vader said, "They've

crossed. Switch, switch! Vader and Dizzy have the bandits at two, heading southwest."

"Copy Switch. Hulk and Tetro have the bandits heading southeast at three."

"Steeljaw copies."

"Dizzy, Fox-one on the northern MiG."

Hoser asked, "What happened?"

"They switched when the bandits crossed each other. Dizzy just called Fox-one. That's a missile isn't it?"

"Yeah, what's the range?"

"Maybe five miles."

"Too long. Christ, I hope Vader keeps in search mode. What's that civilian doing?"

"He's still heading at them. Just a minute, it looks like he's climbing."

"Aw, shit."

CHAPTER 36

Cockpit, MiG–29 Fulcrum—
Monday, 21 Oct/0759

Dieter had a solid infrared lock on one of the Americans. Soon he would be able to use his laser range finder. It had taken every ounce of self-discipline he could muster to keep the flaps down and fly the MiG–29 as slowly as possible. The stick was like mush in his hand, and he'd never felt so vulnerable and exposed. He rechecked his armament switches for the tenth time.

As soon as the MiG–21s flashed overhead, he plugged in the burners and programmed the nose into a maximum-performance climb. Though his airspeed was still low, with the flaps down the big engines gave him a phenomenal rate of climb.

Vader was pissed. Dizzy had taken a poor shot and, worse, had taken a single-target lock without telling him. As wingman, Bradley was responsible for keeping his radar in search mode to sanitize the area.

Vader had already selected his target, and now he had to break lock to acquire the other MiG. It caused him to waste several precious seconds. The bitch of it was that he knew that Dizzy had his eyeballs locked on his missile and wouldn't be visually checking their six. They'd have to count on the controller to cover them.

"Steeljaw, confirm Vader flight is clean."

"Vader, show you four miles in trail of bandits and holding. Wait. They're starting to turn north. You can cut them off! Recommend right turn to heading three-zero-zero."

It was a good call. Vader started the maneuver even as he radioed Dizzy to check right ninety degrees, but his training made him cautious. He was turning his tailpipes to that civilian aircraft, certainly no threat, but it bothered him just the same. He had to ask.

"Steeljaw, status of civilian?"

The controller's eyes flashed to the amber symbol he'd assigned to the puddle-jumper. The Hornets were on top of him. He had to change the display scale to break out the altitude readout.

Dieter couldn't believe his luck. The American F/A–18s had fired a missile at his *dummkopf* Libyan decoys and were so enthralled with getting a kill that the bastards never checked for other MiGs. They would pay for their arrogance. His Archer missile quickly acquired a seeker-head lock on the missile shooter. He had to be the mission commander. Better to dispatch him quickly, then he could concentrate on the less-experienced wingman. But just as he was about to squeeze the trigger, the second Hornet made an abrupt turn to the northwest.

Dieter knew his target would soon follow, and such a maneuver might sour the shot. He calmly switched to a different Archer, acquired a lock on the wingman, and fired. While the missile leapt after its prey, Dieter raised his flaps, carefully pushed the nose down, and let his speed build for the fight.

To hell with the wingman, he thought. This was much better. He would go head-to-head with the commander.

"Vader flight, Check Six!" Every person who heard Steeljaw's panicked call felt the thump of adrenaline slam into their heart, and knew, in the pit of their stomach, that something terribly wrong had just happened.

Dizzy's first clue that they were in trouble hit him when he pried his eyes away from his errant missile and looked over his right shoulder to find his flight lead.

In two seconds flat, the Archer was traveling at over a thousand miles an hour. Even with the synapses of his brain firing in nanoseconds, the time it took for Dizzy to correlate the white blur he saw with a missile, activate the radio switch with his gloved thumb, and phrase a warning, the Archer covered the remaining distance, followed its heat source

straight up the Hornet's starboard tailpipe, and deto-
nated.

Vader died in the fireball.

Dieter had trained himself for this moment. He
ignored the fantastic explosion and set his sights on
the other Hornet. Every second counted. There were
dozens of Americans, and many were no doubt on
their way. He rolled his aircraft slightly and activated
his radar in the vertical-scan mode. He was rewarded
with a lock and a flashing in-range cue. This was
almost too easy. He launched the second of his four
Archers.

CHAPTER 37

**USS *Ranger*—
Monday, 21 Oct/0800**

It was bedlam in the CIC. CAG was livid, demanding to know the status of Vader flight. But they were unwilling or unable to answer Steeljaw's beseeching requests.

"Lobo five-one, Lobo five-one, come in. Vader, what's your status?

Dizzy's voice broke through, high-pitched with fear, "Engaged Fulcrum! Vader's down." A burst of static, and then, "Help me!"

The controller recovered his poise. "Hawk three-five, snap one-niner-zero. Two groups. A pair of MiGs on your nose, low, twelve miles, northbound. Second group, a fur-ball, twenty miles. Target second group."

Snort's voice said, "Hawk three-five and three-six WILCO."

The controller continued giving directions. "Hulk flight break it off and reset to Bull's-eye. Lobo five-two, status?"

• • •

One heartbeat after Vader's explosion, Dizzy glimpsed the sinister shape of a Fulcrum cutting to his deep six. He saw the puff of smoke as another missile left its launch rail. Dizzy hit the flare button three times and buried the stick in his lap.

Twelve flares in groups of four were ejected from beneath the Hornet. The Archer's seeker-head sensed the rapid temperature rise and went momentarily dormant before trying to reacquire. Again and again the Archer's computer brain cycled through the flares, rejecting them and reacquiring the Hornet's engine exhaust. Dizzy had forgotten to pull his throttles back.

In the end, it was simply the pitch rate of the Hornet versus the pitch rate of the Archer. In this case, the aircraft won, by generating enough of an overshoot to cause the missile to fly a mere six feet aft of the F/A–18's twin tails. One millisecond after noting the change in closure on its target, the Archer's computer signaled its warhead to detonate, but it was too late for a kill. When the thousands of white-hot fragments exploded, nearly all missed their target.

Hoser demanded to know what was going on. I did my best. "A MiG jumped Vader's flight. It looks like he bagged Vader. He must have been posing as a civilian and waited for them to fly over. Now, they're sending Snort and Randi down to help. But, there's two MiGs in between."

"Can you hear an emergency beacon?" he asked.

"No."

"Vader's toast, then. They've got to nail those two MiGs before they get to the strike package."

Hoser must have read CAG's mind because Andrews told Steeljaw the same thing.

Steeljaw conveyed the new priority to Snort and Randi. "Hawk three-five, new vector. Snap two-zero-zero for ten, angels five. Two MiG–21s northbound. Cleared to fire."

"Roger that. Radar contact."

Randi's voice came over the speaker for the first time. "Snort, Randi's still got the southern group. Dizzy's defensive; let me press."

There was a slight pause. "You're clear. Steeljaw, Hawk three-five is engaging the first group, Hawk three-six is flowing to the second."

"Fuck!" Dieter swore when the missile failed to destroy its target. The Hornet's pitch rate was every bit as impressive as he'd been led to believe. But the American had traded all his airspeed for angles. He was slow; a deadly mistake against a Fulcrum. Dieter closed rapidly on the F/A–18, passing within a hundred meters of the American, and pulled straight up to build the separation he'd need for the kill shot. Expertly, Dieter pirouetted the MiG–29, on the lookout for more Americans, while his soon-to-be second victim struggled beneath him.

• • •

Randi tried again to get Dizzy on the radio. She had two contacts and had to know which was which. "Dizzy, are you high or low?"

Dizzy was terrified. He watched the Fulcrum take it up and knew he couldn't match him. He did the only thing he could and dumped his own nose to get some knots, while desperately trying to keep sight of the MiG. In the calamity, he missed the warning tone and never saw the caution light indicating that his upper UHF/IFF antenna, damaged by the near miss, was no longer working. Automatically, the Hornet's computers assessed the problem and switched to the lower antenna suite.

Where the hell is my help?

CAG was forced to decide whether to abort the strike or continue. He'd lost one jet, another was in danger, and there were two MiGs closing on the strike package. In an agonizing decision, CAG was forced to admit that his old friend was too deep in enemy territory to mount a rescue attempt, especially without an emergency beacon to signify that he'd survived. With grim determination, he answered O'Hara's query with a simple, "Continue."

• • •

Hoser was trying to climb through the phone lines. All I could tell him was that Randi was racing to defend Dizzy, and Snort was chasing down the MiGs threatening the strike group.

"She's by herself? Jesus Christ! She should have stayed with her flight lead. Goddamn it, what the hell is she thinking?"

Randi kept pushing the throttles hard against the stops, but she couldn't get to the fight any faster.

"Think, goddamn it!" she shouted. *Dizzy's lack of communication means that he is defensive against a pilot who has already downed one of our best. That means the MiG has to be on top!* At ten miles, she took a radar lock and selected a Sparrow missile.

Dieter topped out two kilometers above the Hornet. If the pilot was as lazy as Dieter thought, he had no doubt lost sight of the Fulcrum. A radar lock was unnecessary; just put the seeker-head on the Hornet, uncage it, and fire. Then go collect his two million dollars.

The Fulcrum's electronic-warfare gear was quite good and calibrated to the known American radar frequencies, but it couldn't determine range. When his display lit off, Dieter's heart jumped into his throat. In an instant, he was transformed from attacker to prey. Dieter pointed his nose at the ground and pounded the chaff button to eject a dozen bundles of specially cut aluminum foil designed to confuse the enemy's radar. He searched vainly for a glimpse of a missile trail or his attacker.

Dizzy had lost sight. His survival instincts took over and he kept his jet pointed at the deck, fire-walled the engines, and prayed for a chance to escape. Waiting for the missile to strike him was too much to bear. Too low for the antennas on the belly of his airplane to work properly, he didn't notice when his radios stopped receiving Steeljaw's calls.

In the E–2, the disappearance of Lobo five-two off the radar screen was met with disbelief. A desolate controller transmitted, "Steeljaw, lost contact with Lobo five-two."

Randi caught sight of a single dark shape and broke the radar lock to let the Hornet's hot radar mode search for the second aircraft. Scanning the area, she caught sight of the smoke rising from a crash site on a distant ridgeline.

"Hawk three-six is engaging the southern bandit. Wreckage bears one-eight-five for six from my position."

"Steeljaw copies. Your bandit bears one-seven-five, four miles. We've lost contact on both Lobos."

•　　•　　•

Randi adopted an old TOPGUN trick to locate Dizzy. Using the nose of the MiG as a pointer, she scanned the ground until she found the shadow of the aircraft he was chasing. It had to be Dizzy trying to escape. The MiG was closing and would soon be in range. Randi had to take him out, but the setup was terrible. She needed more look-down, but there wasn't time. With no choice, she took a lock and launched a Sparrow.

"Fox-one from Hawk three-six."

Dieter had seriously considered leaving the area when the American's radar lock was broken. But the sight of that coward running away infuriated him. If his own wingman had been shot down, he would have fought to his death to avenge him.

Instead of taking the safe route, Dieter used his altitude and superior top-end speed to run down the bastard. When the second radar warning buzzed in his headset, he knew he'd made a mistake, especially when he looked up and caught sight of a smoke trail coming at him.

"Scheis!" he said, as he pounded the chaff button and reefed his jet into an abrupt pitch-up. This he held for just a second before again pounding the chaff button, rolling the jet on its back, and pulling the nose down hard.

The Sparrow missile was having difficulty discerning the aircraft from the chaff and ground clutter. When the target momentarily appeared cleanly above the horizon, the missile's internal-guidance computer, confronted with a climbing target, immediately programmed the flight controls to intercept the MiG's new flight path. But when the Fulcrum again disappeared below the horizon amid a cloud of chaff, the Sparrow lost contact and flew blindly overhead.

As Randi watched the MiG's defensive maneuver, she had no choice but to keep her aircraft steady to provide the Sparrow with the best possible radar information. This cost her valuable altitude. But she'd succeeded in getting the MiG off Dizzy's tail. Now, if she could just get Dizzy to pitch back, they could bracket the Fulcrum and nail him.

On the chance that he could receive, but not transmit, she called, "Dizzy, pitch back! I'm engaged two miles at your six." Simultaneously, she tried to get a Sidewinder tone on the Fulcrum, but the MiG dropped a half dozen flares as the distance between them closed in a blur of speed.

This guy's a pro, she thought.

Randi's call, received because of their proximity, jolted Dizzy out of his fog. His hands reacted automatically to snap the throttles out of burner and pick the nose of his fighter up. He needed to scrub off some airspeed before he pitched back. But a quick check of his fuel state brought bile up his throat. If he got into a fur-ball, he might not have enough to get to a tanker.

What good will it do to end up like Vader? he thought. *Besides, there have to be other Hornets being vectored to help out the nugget.* He pushed the nose back down and called up the *Ranger* on his navigation system.

Without keying the mike, he muttered, "Better you than me. Yo-Yo, baby."

CHAPTER 38

**Four miles south of Bull's-eye—
Monday, 21 Oct/0802**

Randi saw Dizzy's jet pitch up in response to her
call and knew they could make quick work of the
MiG. All she had to do was tie him up, keeping her
foe's attention on her, while Dizzy maneuvered for a
shot. As the Fulcrum passed by, close aboard on her
left side, she executed a maximum-performance slice
turn into him, which the MiG quickly matched.

Dieter strained to remain conscious against the load of
9 Gs. He was gratified to see the Hornet try to out-
maneuver him instead of extending and using its radar
missiles. His fuel state was critically low, but that just
made him lighter and more deadly. As their matching
turns continued, he steadily began to gain angles.

Randi thought, *What's wrong? Dizzy should have fired
by now.* She knew there was no way he'd leave her. Yet,

as she watched the Fulcrum relentlessly march around the circle, she realized she must be alone.

Her foe was gaining angles every second. Randi forced herself not to pull more Gs. It would only make her slower and give the MiG a lethal advantage. Contorting herself in the cockpit, she released back pressure to preserve the airspeed she needed.

At least the bastard is too close to use his Archers, she thought. Randi concentrated with every fiber of her being as she prepared to defend against the upcoming gunshot.

Dieter expected the American to reef into him, which he was prepared to counter, but instead, the idiot allowed him to close into gun range. Eagerly, he selected his cannon and made a final pull to center his target. The gunsight settled on the cockpit of the American fighter.

"This one is for you, Papa," he said. Dieter pulled the trigger.

Randi waited until she could see down the intakes of the Fulcrum. Then she pushed the stick full forward, bunting the jet, in the process going from positive 4 Gs to negative 2 Gs. It was a brutal transition, momentarily blinding her as her helmet slammed into the Plexiglas canopy.

•   •   •

As the first rounds left his cannon, the Hornet simply disappeared from his windscreen. The tracer ammunition stitched holes in empty space.

"Was ist los?"

The MiG pilot's hesitation kept his jet in a left-hand turn two seconds too long. Randi rolled her wings level and pitched up to elude her enemy's line of sight. As the Fulcrum reversed his course to the right, she executed a barrel-roll attack, carving a graceful, spiral turn above and behind the MiG, her fingers unconsciously selecting guns and a radar lock.

Dieter snap-rolled the Fulcrum only to find empty space where the Hornet should have been. His first thought was that the F/A–18, like its partner, had used the maneuver to escape. Furious, he tilted his aircraft to search below for the tailpipes of the F/A–18.

When the radar warning alarm sounded once more, he cursed his stupidity. Even as the high-explosive rounds tore into his wings and fuselage, Dieter Graf begrudgingly acknowledged that the better man had won.

CHAPTER 39

**USS *Arkansas*—
Monday, 21 Oct/0803**

The captain cautioned his fire-control crew to stay vigilant. "This strike has turned into a goat rope. We've lost two Hornets, and we've got MiGs airborne. Keep a sharp eye out for low, fast flyers."

"Aye, aye, sir," said Lieutenant Sandra Day, the tactical control officer. She adjusted the scale of her radar display, bumping the coverage out another twenty miles, and was rewarded with a solid contact. A high-speed bogey was inbound.

"Bridge! Radar contact bearing one-eight-zero for sixty, angels low, heading three-six-zero."

"Is he squawking?" asked the captain, referring to the aircraft's IFF code.

"Negative."

"What's his ground speed?"

"Four hundred eighty knots." Excitement crept into her voice.

The captain picked up a handset to relay the information to the air staff on the *Ranger*.

"Are you in communication with any aircraft below five thousand feet, northbound? No? Roger that. If he closes within thirty miles, we're going to engage him."

Lieutenant Day said, "Sir, the bogey just went feet wet. He's forty-eight miles south."

"You're cleared to lock on and compute a targeting solution. Wait for my command."

"Aye, aye, sir."

Hoser insisted that I keep feeding him information.

I did my best. "It looks like both Lobos got bagged. Randi called out the wreckage of one just before she engaged the MiG. Snort is chasing the other MiGs, and the strikers are right over Bertha."

O'Hara's voice broke the silence. "Hawk three-three is in hot."

This was followed by similar calls from each of his wingmen. The strike package was in their bomb runs.

CAG hung up his handset and told one of the techs to bring up the data-link display from the *Arkansas* on the big screen. "We've got a bogey inbound," he said.

Everyone in the CIC watched as the red silhouette crossed the coast and entered the free-fire zone.

Randi had been trying to get a word in edgewise on the radio since she'd bagged the MiG, but the strikers had started their run and clobbered the radio. Despite being low on fuel, she took a calculated risk and dropped down for a quick pass on Vader's crash site. There was no sign of a parachute and no emergency-beacon signal. With a watchful eye on her radar warning display, she recorded the location with her navigation system and climbed back to altitude.

"What's happening now?" asked Hoser.

"The strikers are in their bomb run, there's no word from Randi, and there's a bogey heading straight for us."

"Tell me again what happened to the second Lobo," Hoser demanded.

"He called for help. I heard Randi call him once, but he didn't answer."

"Did she call to say we had two down jets?"

"No."

"Tell CAG that I think that bogey is our Lobo."

"I can't do that."

"Jack. Grow a fucking spine and do it."

"CAG!"

Captain Andrews shot me an angry look.

I spoke quickly, "Captain Santana says he thinks that the inbound bogey could be Lobo five-two."

Andrews turned around without comment. But a moment later, CAG keyed his mike, and transmitted, "Steeljaw, Alpha-Whiskey."

"Go Alpha-Whiskey."

"Make a broadcast on all frequencies warning anyone northbound, over water, below ten thousand feet that they will be fired upon. Copy?"

• • •

The tactical control officer forced herself to keep her voice steady. "Bogey is at thirty miles, sir."

"You are cleared to fire, Lieutenant."

An instant later, one of the Navy's newest weapons, a state-of-the-art SAM, left its launch rail amid a blast of white smoke.

"Missile away, sir."

"Very well."

During a pause in the radio chatter, the E-2 controller broadcast his warning. "Ninety-nine Ranger. Stay above ten thousand feet northbound. We have missiles in the air."

Randi's first thought upon hearing the warning was that the task force was under attack. Then she remembered Dizzy. He'd been northbound and might well have lost his radios. Both frequencies were still full of chatter. She reached up, switched on her emergency radio, and keyed the mike. As the only woman pilot over the beach, there was no need to waste time identifying herself. "Steeljaw, Lobo five-two last seen northbound at low altitude. Suspect no radio."

"Break lock!" With less then ten seconds to impact, its engine no longer producing telltale smoke, the missile lost its radar signal and plummeted into the dark waters of the Mediterranean.

Dizzy never saw it. He was too busy trying to find the tanker with his radar.

"The unidentified aircraft is climbing, sir," said Lieutenant Day. "We have a Tomcat closing in for an ID."

"Steeljaw, Inferno one-one."

"Go, Inferno."

"We have a visual on a Hornet. Side-number is five-zero-nine."

"Roger. That's Lobo five-two. He must be NORDO. Please escort him to the duty tanker."

"WILCO."

Inside the cockpit of Lobo 509, Dizzy turned the volume of his radio down so that he could barely hear it. The belly antennas were poor at low altitude. Now that he was climbing, his radio reception returned. He just realized that he'd busted the rules for returning to the carrier. They'd probably been calling him for the last fifty miles.

His luck was still holding, though. They'd sent a Tomcat to ID him instead of letting those trigger-happy goons on the Aegis cruiser shoot him down. He decided to keep the fact that his radios now worked to himself.

PART FOUR

Final Approach

CHAPTER 40

**USS *Ranger*—
Monday, 21 Oct/1000**

The captain secured General Quarters after the last of
the strike package and recce birds had landed. The
air-defense Tomcats were refueled and left airborne
to protect against a counterattack.

I'd spent the last hour hammering out an account
of the strike, leaving holes for a couple of pilot interviews. Both CAG and Captain Morganelli had
refused comment until they had a chance to debrief
the pilots and reconstruct the mission.

The word had spread like wildfire that Randi
had bagged the MiG–29 that shot down Vader and
damaged Bradley's aircraft. As it turned out, her
flight lead, Snort, had shot down a MiG–21.
Together, they had scored two kills for the Hawk
squadron. And the early word on the strikers was
that their bombs had been on target. I headed to
their Ready Room first.

The mood was ecstatic.

"Man, I put that LGB right in the front door!"

"I saw your building go before mine, Skipper. It just disappeared!"

O'Hara was beaming. When he saw me, he welcomed me with a shout, "Make way for the press!"

There were hoots and hollers as squadron mates pounded each other on the back. Randi and Snort were at the center of the group, both in sodden flight suits. Apparently, they'd been doused by their maintenance crews as they climbed out of their cockpits.

Randi saw me and pushed her way through to give me a hug. The guys backed away to give us some space.

"You scared the shit out of us," I said.

"Us?"

"Yeah, Hoser was on the phone to me in the CIC. He had some choice words for you when you left your lead."

She stepped back, and said, "It wasn't the best decision I've ever made. That MiG pilot was really good."

"But you were better?"

"I was luckier, that's for sure. Thank God, he'd never seen a negative-G guns defense. Otherwise, I'd be splattered in the desert."

"How's it make you feel to be the first woman with a MiG kill?"

She perched on the back of a ready-room chair and pushed her wet hair back. "You're going to quote me, aren't you?"

"No, Randi. Of course not. I'm just the first reporter to get an interview with the soon-to-be most famous woman pilot since Amelia Earhart, and I'm not going to quote you. C'mon, girl, give it up."

She laughed. "Okay." Then she leaned close to me, and said in a breathless whisper, "It feels fucking great." Poking me hard in the chest, she said, "Use that, smart-ass." Then she blew me a kiss, smiled devilishly, and sauntered back to her buddies.

By contrast, the Lobo Ready Room was hushed. They'd suffered their second death in three days. Pilots filled out their reports listlessly. I wanted to corner Bradley, but he wasn't there. I did find the CO, and asked if there had been any word on Vader.

"Until the Libyans confirm it, we're listing him as missing in action, but it doesn't look good."

"I was in CIC for the strike. It looked like your folks did a great job in SAM suppression."

He brightened. "Thank you, Mr. Warner. I'd appreciate it if that was reported. It's a tough job, but our pilots and weapons systems were up to it. The fact that the strikers didn't lose a single jet to SAMs is a testament to that."

"What would you like me to tell the world about Vader?"

His eyes teared up, but he didn't try to hide it. "He was a good friend. Please tell your readers that one of our finest has sacrificed himself for his country. Vader was special. He was the epitome of a professional naval aviator. He left a wife and three kids, Mr. Warner. If you want to tell people something, tell them that we gave him our toughest mission because he was the best we had."

"I guess that goes for Lieutenant Commander Bradley, too."

Jaw clenched, he said, "Vader is a hero. That's all I have to say." He spun on his heel and left the ready room.

I made my way down to the Intelligence Center. It was time to see what the recce birds had found.

Kopper escorted me into the back room. "The imagery is just coming out. Petty Officer Wilson, here, is the best photo analyst in the Navy."

The film was on a giant spool mounted on the end of a long table. The surface of the table was illuminated from underneath. Wilson was bent over the film, slowly advancing it with a hand crank, inspecting the frames through a magnifying glass.

"Here we go," he said. Then he whistled. "It's good and clear. Yup, we've got major hits on all three buildings."

"Shit-hot!" said Kopper. He patted me on the shoulder. "I'm going to find CAG and tell him the news on the battle damage. See you back here in fifteen minutes."

I noticed Wilson was cycling the film back and forth. He seemed agitated, and was mumbling to himself.

I stepped closer. The guy was talking to himself. "What the hell?"

"What's wrong, Wilson?"

He spoke without raising his head. "There

should be debris scattered everywhere. There'll be tons of crap from an explosion this powerful. But I don't see any desks, or chairs, and there's no equipment. Where's the fricking lockers, clothes, books, and cardboard? There's nothing. *Nada*, zilch! And check this out." He tapped the film. "There's no cars or trucks in the parking lot, either, and not even one body. I'm telling you, these damn buildings were completely empty. I say we've been had."

CHAPTER 41

Monday, 21 Oct/1045

Before Wilson turned around, I was gone. Twenty
years of journalism had primed me for this moment.
Kopper said fifteen minutes. In that time I had to
draft a new lead and figure out how to get my bomb-
shell of a story off the carrier before they shut down
communications.

At the Comm Center, the chief said that the NOK
notification on Vader had just come through. Using
their phone, I called Lieutenant Irvine, the ship's
Public Affairs officer. He agreed to come down and
clear my first press release. He also said that I was
scheduled for a television link-up with CNN, using
the ship's broadcast crew. It would go down at 1700
(5:00 P.M.) tonight so that we'd make the early-
morning news on the East Coast.

*How was I going to get Irvine to release the
truth?* There was no way he would approve of the
changes I would write. Then a devious plan popped
into my brain.

I gave the chief a disk containing my first draft of

the story, telling him that I also had a photo I wanted
to add. While he printed out a copy of the text for
Irvine to proofread, I left, ostensibly to get the photo.

I raced to my stateroom and cranked up the laptop to rewrite my lead.

Navy Pilot Feared Dead in Combat Strike on Phony Target

USS *Ranger*, Mediterranean Sea.

Two hours ago, the United States conducted a
secret bombing mission, striking deep inside
Libya, to destroy a suspected chemical-weapons
plant. Launching at dawn, a dozen Navy attack
bombers flew into the teeth of one of the world's
most heavily defended landscapes. Their mission
was to destroy buildings thought to contain hundreds of chemical weapons. The complex was
destroyed by laser-guided bombs. One of the
Navy planes was shot down; its pilot has been
declared missing in action.

This reporter has learned that post-strike photographs reveal that Libya's so-called chemical-
weapons factory was completely empty.

Word aboard the carrier is that the govern-
ments of the United Nations, especially the United
States, were the victims of an elaborate ruse per-
petrated by Libya's leader, Colonel Moammar
Gadhafi.

A technician, described by his boss as, "The
finest photo analyst in the Navy," ascertained

from post-strike photographs that the three buildings destroyed by the bombers were vacant. "I
don't see any desks, or chairs, and there's no
equipment . . . not even one body," he said,
before concluding, "we've been had."

This reporter was present in the Combat
Information Center, the scene of mission coordi-
nation, during the entire strike.

Lieutenant Commander Richard "Vader"
Corbett, 36-year-old married father of three, has
been listed as missing in action. Pilots on the scene
report that no parachute was sighted, and there
has been no radio contact. His commanding officer said, "Vader was given the toughest mission
because he was our best pilot."

Corbett was the victim of a Libyan Air Force
deception described as "extremely cunning" by
one of the ship's senior officers. The American battle staff was dumbfounded when one of the
world's most lethal aircraft, an advanced MiG–29
fighter, executed a sneak attack on the first pair of
Hornets to enter the target area.

The MiG–29 pilot, described as "a pro" by
the Navy, fooled the entire battle staff into thinking he was flying a harmless civilian aircraft. The
Americans were lured into the trap by a pair of
older-generation MiG fighters acting as decoys.

After his leader was shot down, Navy pilot
Lieutenant Commander Dennis Bradley cornered
deep in enemy territory, desperately radioed for
help. His aircraft had already been damaged by a

second missile fired by the MiG pilot, who was closing in for another kill.

The closest Hornets were flown by Lieutenant Miranda Cole and her flight lead, Lieutenant Commander Gregory Neary. In addition to the imminent danger to Bradley, there were two more MiG fighters threatening the American bomber formation. The Air Wing Commander chose to vector Neary and Cole to engage the two MiGs, leaving Bradley on his own.

Cole surprised the controllers by requesting permission to go to Bradley's aid—alone. It was granted.

In the next three minutes, Cole and Neary each scored kills, and both the strike group and Bradley were spared. Cole becomes America's first woman MiG killer.

That she tangled with and shot down a pilot in a better dogfighting jet, who had already destroyed one Hornet and damaged another, makes her achievement even more impressive. Expect supporters of women in combat to point to Cole's victory today as vindication.

Opponents, who include Lieutenant Commander Bradley in their ranks—at least until this morning—must face the claim that America's hottest combat pilot is now a woman.

The situation is even more complex for Libya's enigmatic leader, Moammar Gadhafi. Though his motives are unclear at this point, it appears Gadhafi achieved his long-standing goal of making the American government look hostile and inept. But all may not be well in the Colonel's palace.

Gadhafi's vaunted air defense system fired dozens of surface-to-air missiles at the American strike force and failed to hit a single aircraft. Although he can claim a victory for shooting down an American F/A–18, he lost two of his own MiGs.

Worst of all, for the Libyan leader, cultural experts contend that there can be no greater shame for a Muslim warfighter than to lose to a woman.

Whatever his objectives, Colonel Gadhafi may end up the laughingstock of the Middle East, while on the other side of the Atlantic, the Pentagon scrambles to explain why Navy pilots were put at risk to bomb empty buildings. (Pam— back me up on the Muslim thing—I don't have time to confirm. JW)

Instead of saving it as a text file, I converted the screen to an image file and downloaded it on a disk. Then I gave it the same name as a photo I'd taken of Randi earlier, which I put on a second disk. With a little razzle-dazzle and some luck, I hoped to be able to slip it past Irvine.

When I checked my watch, my heart jumped into my throat. I had less than two minutes. I jogged down to the Comm Center, but composed myself before entering.

"This is a great piece," Irvine said, waving the first draft at me. "No problems, I told the chief to launch it, but he said you wanted to send a photo."

"Yup. Here it is." I showed him the bogus disk.

"Well, you know I have to check it out, sir," he said, with a deprecating smile.

"Of course." I slipped the disk into the laptop and turned the machine around so he could see it.

"That'll work. Chief, let's get going. The captain wants our story hitting the morning papers."

Standing at the console, the chief said, "Roger that, sir. I've already got us on-line." His fingers danced across the keyboard. "In fact, there goes the article. Just hand me that disk, and we'll get the photo off, too."

My pulse raced, but I forced myself to calmly extract the disk. I palmed it and handed over the real one. The chief snatched it from me and slipped it into his computer, but his eyes were glued on me.

The phone rang, melting my cool facade. Despite the chilly temperature, a bead of sweat trickled down my spine.

Irvine answered it. "Yes, sir. He's right here. Say again, sir? Nothing? But, we just sent the draft I approved."

I was so screwed. Instead of a world-class exclusive, my first draft, dead wrong, would hit the streets. The best story of my life, and I'd missed it by a couple seconds.

"Chief, kill that transmission! We're in a blackout."

His expression inscrutable, the chief deliberately hit a key. He flashed me a thumbs-up out of Irvine's sight. "Too late, sir."

Irvine looked like he'd been punched. "Sir, the story and a photo of Lieutenant Cole have already been sent. Should I follow up with a message telling them to disregard?"

The young man winced, pulling the phone away from his ear, before answering, "Yes, sir. Right away, sir."

"Damn it!" Irvine slammed the phone down. "What the hell do they expect me to do?"

"What's the matter, Lieutenant?" asked the chief.

"The captain has stopped all of Mr. Warner's communications. Same with the crew. I don't know what the hell is going on, but for some reason, I'm number one on the shit list."

He turned to me. "I'm sorry Mr. Warner, but I need to show the captain what was sent. Can you come with me, and bring your computer?"

"No sweat."

As Irvine walked out, I turned to the chief and mouthed the words, "I owe you."

Handing me the disk, he said, "You better believe it."

CHAPTER 42

Monday, 21 Oct/1115

Morganelli and CAG were seated in the captain's wardroom. They were as grim-faced as a pair of morticians.

Morganelli spoke first. "Have you got the report?"

Irvine handed him the copy of the draft.

"And the photo?"

I fired up the laptop and pulled up Randi's smiling photo while Morganelli read the bogus draft.

When he finished, he handed it to CAG, and said, "Looks okay."

I spun the laptop around, and they both checked out the photo.

Morganelli took a deep breath and sank into his chair with a sigh. "What a day."

CAG finished scanning the article and seemed much relieved. He glanced at Morganelli, then looked at me. "Bet you're wondering what got us all fired up."

"I'm a reporter. I wonder why people do anything."

"Well, we're just very concerned that all information that leaves the ship about this strike is accurate."

Yeah, right. "Any problems with what you read there?" I asked.

"No, not at all. You're a damn good writer, Mr. Warner. It's easy to see why the Pentagon wanted you out here."

Morganelli said, "CAG is right. In just eight hours, every American who gets a morning paper will be reading your piece. We had to be sure it was absolutely correct."

Some things never change. The way they were pounding smoke up my ass, these two guys could have been any of dozens of politicians I knew. And they sure as hell weren't my friends. When it came down to it, they were perfectly willing to let me take the fall for publishing a bogus story. Right now, they were just another couple government officials sharing the mantra, "God forbid the truth be told."

"So why the news blackout?"

Morganelli said, "We've got a downed pilot."

"But the next of kin has already been notified."

"Yes, but his status remains unclear."

"You mean you think he is still alive?"

"We don't know. But we have to assume so until we find out differently."

"When can I talk with Bradley?"

CAG said, "We're still debriefing him. It'll be a while."

"What about the photos of the battle damage?"

Both men reacted tensely. CAG said, "All three buildings were destroyed. Kopper tells us you saw that yourself."

. "Does that mean you're calling this mission a success?"

Morganelli said, "Of course it was." He held up the draft of the bogus article. "Just like you reported it to thousands of papers around the world."

I had to bite my tongue to keep from spilling the beans just to wipe that smug smile off his face. "Tell me about this CNN thing."

Morganelli looked up at Irvine and back at me. "Well, I'm afraid there's been a change of plans. You were going to get to conduct the interview, but we've just received word that a CNN crew is en route by COD. I'm sorry, Mr. Warner, but that decision was made above my pay grade. On the plus side, you'll be happy to know that both you and Captain Santana are scheduled to leave on the return flight."

"When is that?"

"Fifteen-hundred. That's three and a half hours from now."

I asked CAG, "I don't suppose Bradley will be available for an interview before then?"

"Probably not. But you can check with Commander Holmes."

I turned back to the captain. "What about that other matter?"

He spoke to Irvine. "Lieutenant could you give us a few minutes?"

"Yes, sir."

When the door closed, Morganelli said, "Take a seat, Mr. Warner."

"I prefer to get screwed standing up."

"Screwed?" He tried to look amazed.

I kept silent.

"You're going to have to enlighten us, Mr. Warner. Didn't you just get an exclusive report that will put your by-line on every paper in the country?"

"I'm the media pool reporter. What you have in your hand is a piece of fluff. It doesn't answer any of the hard questions. Now you've got the television hot dogs coming aboard, and you're kicking me off before I can finish my work. I thought we had an agreement."

Morganelli nodded toward CAG, and said, "He knows all about it. I briefed him. Tell him what you told me, CAG."

Andrews said, "There's no fucking way someone sabotaged that jet, Warner. It's too much of a risk. Think about it. If Mason had followed procedure, she'd have recovered it, and we'd be able to inspect the engine. Nobody could be sure she was going to grab the stick. And I resent like hell that you would imply something like this without any proof."

"What kind of proof are you looking for?"

"A witness. A confession. Fingerprints, hell, something tangible, Warner, instead of innuendo and your vague suspicions. Look, I know you followed that mishap investigation on the West Coast last year. Now that this operation is over, we'll reopen our investigation. If there's anything, *anything*, to what you're saying, we'll find it."

As far as these guys were concerned they'd put me in a box. In three hours, I'd be out of their hair. The empty buildings and the sabotage stories would be buried forever.

"Gentlemen, I've got to go pack and say my good-byes. Will I see you again before I leave?"

Morganelli rose and said, "Certainly, Jack. We'll be down to see both you and Hoser off. If you need any help with your gear, just let Lieutenant Irvine know."

CHAPTER 43

Monday, 21 OCT/1145

What little compunction I'd felt about sneaking my story off the ship evaporated as I left that room. They'd made it easy for me.

By now, back in San Diego, Pam had pulled up my picture of Randi and found the embedded story. After picking her jaw up off the floor, she had no doubt called a meeting of the paper's big guns. Even now, they were probably developing a strategy to leverage their scoop. As the wire-services feed, the *Herald* was obligated to distribute the story, but if my guess was correct, the brass would keep it on ice for a couple hours. They'd use the time for layout and to put together several companion pieces. Other papers, particularly those on the East Coast, would barely have time to draft a headline and plunk the story onto page one. Of course, had they been in the *Herald*'s position, they would have done the same thing, newspaper publishing being the nice, wholesome business that it is.

As big as the empty-building story was going to

be, I wasn't about to quit without nailing the bastards who killed Mason. If I had to, I'd call Admiral Russell first. But I hoped that I could do it without stirring up that hornet's nest.

Art Cardone was behind the maintenance desk. I gave him the high sign and waited for him in the passageway. He came out a minute later, and we walked to my stateroom. When we were alone, I asked, "How are you holding up?"

He looked worse than yesterday. "I don't know. I've been at this nearly thirty years, and I never lost two pilots back-to-back. I know this sounds shitty, but those were my two best jets, too. I don't know what we're going to do for up aircraft for the next six months." He sat down heavily.

"Well, the captain is sending Hoser and me off on the fifteen-hundred COD."

"What about the sabotage? You're not going to cave in, are you?"

"No. But I only have a couple hours left, and I need time with Lawrence and Bradley."

"I can't help you with Bradley, but I can have that little maggot Lawrence down here anytime you want."

"I was hoping you'd say that. Do some of that master-chief shit."

Art made a phone call, explained that he needed Petty Officer Lawrence immediately and would come to get him. I outlined my plan, and he left to go get the kid.

My options were limited. All I had on Lawrence

that was solid were the two phone calls and, of course, my own skill at bullshitting. It would have to be enough.

I placed the miniature tape recorder on the desktop and set up my laptop so that only I could see it. When Art knocked, I was sitting with my back to the bulkhead.

"Come in." Lawrence entered first. He was nervous. "Sit down, Petty Officer Lawrence."

"What's this about?"

"Sit down!" bellowed Art. The kid immediately sat in the chair I'd provided. Art prowled behind him. Lawrence looked furtively over his shoulder, then back at me.

"What is it, sir?"

I didn't answer. Instead I reached over and clicked on the tape recorder. Despite his attempt to disguise it, Lawrence's voice was recognizable, "You've got to warn them."

His eyes widened. Then he rallied. "So what? You can't prove that's me."

Art started to pounce, but I warned him off by holding my hand up. The kid flinched.

When the tape finished, I made a show out of pulling it out, flipping it over, and putting the little machine on record. "That's not why I brought you here."

I hit a couple keys on the laptop and pretended to be intrigued by the screen.

Lawrence stared at the recorder as if it were a snake. "Hey, I've got rights. And you're just a civilian." He started to stand.

Art's hand, fingers as big as sausages, pushed the kid back into his chair and held him there.

"Ow!"

"Sit still, young man. I'm not going to tell you again."

I typed a couple more commands. "You know something, Lawrence?"

"Sir?"

"I asked my people to run a background check on you." A few more keystrokes, then I banged one extra hard. "Newspapers employ some of the best investigators in the world, by the way. Ex-feds, IRS agents, those types." Then I gave him what my ex-wife called my evil smile. "And it's the damnedest thing what they came up with."

The kid was sweating buckets. He was hiding something that terrified him. Of course, I had no clue what it was, but he didn't know that.

I shifted gears. "Where were you at oh-two-hundred on Saturday morning?"

It caught him off guard. "Uh, asleep, I guess."

"You guess?" asked Art, hissing in his ear.

"Well, yeah, I was asleep."

I typed his response onto a blank screen, waited for a moment, and played my trump card. "You're lying. We know all about you pulling the hangar bay watch for Airman Johnson. Don't we, Master Chief?"

Lawrence's eyes followed my glance. He encountered Art's face scowling above him, dripping with pure venom. He quickly looked back at me, clearly frightened.

I patted the recorder. "I just wanted to get you on tape denying it." I decided to take a huge gamble and closed the laptop. "You can go now."

He looked around unsure. Art cut me a look like, *Boss, what the hell are you doing?*

Lawrence stood uncertainly, then grabbed the doorknob.

"Lawrence!"

He turned to the sound of my voice. I snapped a flash photo from my camera.

He stopped, frozen in place like a deer caught in headlights. "What are you going to do with that?"

"Well, son, that's a good question. But you're smart. If you'll give it just a little thought, I'm sure you can figure it out."

"You're not going to publish it, are you?"

"Since you asked, I'll tell you. I'm going to take this photo, these tapes, the material my investigators dug up, and Airman Johnson's testimony, and I'm going to write a little article. Then that little article is going to be sent to my newspaper, which will forward it to the wire services. With any luck, Lawrence, you're going to be plastered on the front of a few thousand newspapers tomorrow."

"But you can't do that!"

Art laughed at him. "What the hell do you think he's doing out here? He's a reporter, for Christ's sake."

"That's right, Lawrence, and I've got a scoop. Navy petty officer sabotages jet to kill first Navy woman Hornet pilot. It's good and juicy, don't you think?"

He took a step toward me. Art intercepted him and guided him back into the chair. This time he didn't fight. He started crying.

Between sobs, he managed to say, "But I tried to warn them. I even called you. I told you, Mr. Warner, they made me do it."

"Who made you?" Art was now a dad. He had his arm on the kid's shoulder. "Who made you tape those coins to the engine?"

Lawrence jerked like he'd stepped on a hot wire. "How do you know that?"

Art played his role perfectly, managing to sound almost bored. "We know all about it, son. It's over. We just need you to tell us who made you do it. We want them, not you. This is your only chance not to take the fall for the whole damn thing."

The moment of truth. Lawrence took a deep breath and let it out while biting a knuckle. "You'll never believe me. Nobody will."

"Try us."

"It was the chaplain and his crew." Lawrence cringed as if we were going to laugh him out of the room.

"Go on," I said. Art's eyes were as big as saucers.

Encouraged, he spilled his guts. "A few months ago, Deputy CAG invited me to join their worship group, 'The Brothers.' I didn't want to, but he was insistent. I mean, I work for the guy, you know?"

I kept quiet.

"Anyway, they meet every Monday evening when we're at sea. At first it was kinda cool. They're

all officers, and here I am just a third-class petty officer. They really seemed to care about what I thought.
But then it got weird."

"What do you mean?"

"Well, they kept talking about God's will being
that only men should fight wars and that it is was sin-
ful to have women on ships. Once, I tried to argue a
little. That didn't go over too good."

"How so?"

"Well, everyone got real quiet. Then Chaplain
Hogan asked me if I believed in God. It was spooky.
I felt like I was on trial. I didn't go to the next couple
of meetings. I made up an excuse about having to
work on my correspondence courses."

"What happened next?"

"I was outside on the flight deck one night, just
catching some fresh air, when two of the 'Brothers'
walked up behind me. Next thing I know we're all
standing on the catwalk. Standing in front of me is
Chaplain Hogan and between us someone has taken
off a section of the deck grate. I was looking straight
into the ocean. These guys kept inching me toward it.
Mr. Warner, I was scared to death."

"What did Hogan say?"

"I'll never forget it. He was shining a flashlight in
my face, but I knew it was him. He said, 'Lawrence,
before you take the next step in your life, I want you
to think about it very carefully. You can continue the
way you're going and fall into the godless abyss'—
and he pointed the flashlight at the hole—'or you can
step over to the brotherhood.' "

Reliving the experience had Lawrence shaking. Art got him a glass of water from the tap. He gulped it down.

"Then what happened?"

"Chaplain Hogan stepped back, and said, 'What's it going to be?'"

"No," I said. "I mean what did he say before that?"

"I don't know what you mean."

I reopened the laptop and pretended to read the screen. "Lawrence, we know he was blackmailing you. What did the man say?"

He exhaled sharply as if I'd punched him. His eyes welled up again. The words came out in a monotone, "He said, 'We know you're a dirty little cocksucker. We know you lied on your enlistment. We know you're homosexual.' Then he said I had three choices."

"And what were they?"

"He said, 'You can go turn yourself in and go to jail. You can die like a man, right here. Or you can step across and join our brotherhood and swear allegiance to God's work."

"What happened after you stepped across?"

"He took me down to his room, and we spent all night praying. He told me that he was willing to do anything to save my soul. The way he said it made me want to believe him."

"Who were the two officers?"

"Lieutenant Cummiskey, he's a supply officer, and Lieutenant Commander Bradley, he's a pilot."

"Who else is in the group besides Hogan, Holmes, Bradley, and Cummiskey?"

"There's about five other guys, but I don't think they're involved in the accident."

"What makes you say that?"

"Because the chaplain explained that only Bradley, me, and him were God's chosen soldiers. That's what he called us. He used to say that the others were too weak. Especially Commander Holmes."

"When did you get the orders to tape the coins into the engine?"

"That came from Bradley, on Friday afternoon."

"How did you know what you were doing?" asked Art.

"I used to work in the line division before I got orders to CAG. I've dived engine ducts hundreds of times. Anyway, Bradley told me what Hogan wanted done. He promised me that the engine would quit and scare the pilot, not kill her. But he was lying to me, wasn't he?"

There was no need to answer.

"By the way, he's one sick bastard."

"Bradley? What makes you say that?"

"He laughed when he gave me the coins."

"And?"

"And they were Susan B. Anthony silver dollars. You know, the chick? He said he'd been saving them for a special occasion."

CHAPTER 44

Stateroom—
Monday, 21 Oct/1240

While Lawrence crawled into the top bunk and lay down, Art and I agreed that we had to get the kid off the ship. It was for his own good. Our next problem was to figure out how to smuggle a sailor out from under everyone's nose.

"I got it!" said Art. "You know the doc, right?"

"Yes."

"Get him to send our boy along as a corpsman for Hoser. With a helmet and goggles on, nobody will recognize him."

Leave it to a master chief to come up with a devious plan. When we landed in Naples, I could call Russell and arrange to turn Lawrence over.

"That still leaves one thing undone," I said.

"I'm afraid to ask."

"I want to interview Bradley. I need to know what happened out there today with Vader and Cole."

"You said they were keeping him under wraps. It's not worth risking this for"—he pointed at

Lawrence—"is it?"

"No. But my gut tells me that something went on out there that is being covered up. Something only Bradley knows."

"What about his HUD tape?"

"Say that again?"

"The Head's Up Display videotape. I'm sure he had it on. It records all communications, even what the guy says to himself."

For crying out loud, of course! "Art, you gotta get me that tape! I'm begging you, buddy."

"Let me see what I can do. What about him?" he said, pointing with his thumb at the top bunk.

"Have you got someone you can trust to sit with him?"

"Yeah. I got just the guy. Wait a couple minutes. I'll send down Big Pete."

While I was waiting for Cardone's man, I packed my gear and called the infirmary. Nurse Malerba answered.

"Infirmary."

"Hi, this is Jack Warner."

"Well, hello to you, too. I hear we're going to be sharing a plane ride."

"Does that mean you're escorting Captain Santana off the boat?"

"Boy, you are as sharp as a twenty-gauge needle. I don't know why everyone says reporters are so dumb." She laughed.

"How's our boy?"

"He's raring to go. That nice young lieutenant is

down here with him. Is she really going to be a hero?"

"Tell you what. I'll come down there right now and let you read tomorrow's headlines."

"That sounds like fun."

"But I need a favor," I said.

"Then it better be a really good story." She hung up.

There was a heavy knock on the door. When I opened it, a behemoth stood before me. His shoulders filled the gap between doorjambs.

"Mr. Warner?"

"Yes, you're Pete, aren't you? I recognize you from the hangar bay."

"Yes, sir. Master Cardone told me to give you this." He handed me a videotape with a yellow Post-it attached.

I let him into the room while I read Art's note. It said:

> *The schmuck told everyone his tape player broke. He even wrote a gripe on it. But the tech says it works fine. My para-rigger saw him stash this in his locker. Not anymore! See you on the flight deck. —Art*

After saying a quick prayer to the gods that the tape machine worked, I briefed Pete to keep watch on Lawrence, who was doing a good imitation of sleeping. For his part, Pete was happy to have a quiet place to read the well-worn paperback he produced from his back pocket.

"Don't answer the phone on the first two rings. If

it's me, I'll hang up and call back."

"No sweat, sir."

I had to ask. "Aren't you curious as to what this is all about?"

"Nope. Master Chief told me that you and him were going to bust some officers what done wrong. If Cardone says it's okay by him, it's okay by me."

I left him settled comfortably in a chair. He gave me a thumbs-up as I closed the door. He locked it behind me.

CHAPTER 45

**Medical Spaces—
Monday, 21 Oct/1320**

Randi and Hoser were deep in a discussion about her fight with the MiG. They were both using their hands to talk and seemed determined to analyze every single detail. I used the opportunity to negotiate with Nurse Malerba.

After letting her read an excerpt of the article that discussed Randi's victory, I asked, "How does this patient-transfer thing work?"

"Well, it's real tough. We put Santana, me, and my gear on the number-one elevator and run it to the flight deck. Then we get on the airplane. Then the airplane takes off."

This woman could make "hello" sound sarcastic, but I liked her. "No corpsmen?"

"Nope. Just me. Now why would you care about corpsmen?"

"Can you keep a secret?" I asked.

"Sure."

"I've got to get a material witness off the ship."

"Why?"

"Because he knows that someone on this ship sabotaged Lieutenant Mason's jet on Saturday."

She absorbed this without changing her skeptical expression. "And?"

The woman would make a good reporter. "And he's in danger until we can get an investigation started."

"Why aren't you turning him over to the captain?" she asked.

"He's not going to want to hear the names this kid has to say. That's all I can tell you. Please believe me."

"What are you going to do with him when we get to Naples?"

"I'm going to call CNO and hand the kid over to protective custody."

"You're just going to dial up the Pentagon and ask to speak to the big guy?"

I pulled CNO's card out of my wallet. "He's the one who put me on this assignment. Here's his private number. He'll take my call."

"What do you want me to do?"

"Give me a set of scrubs for the kid to wear and keep him under your wing until we get airborne."

"Go see your friends, I need to think about this. I'll let you know." She left me standing at the nurses' station.

I had no choice but to trust her. It wasn't a pleasant feeling.

When I went back to Hoser's room, Randi was

fiddling with a video player and monitor that had been rolled in on a wheeled stand.

"Jack!" Hoser bellowed. "Good timing. We're just about to see Randi's MiG kill."

She said, "Don't blame me. The old goat said he wouldn't leave unless I showed him my HUD tape." She hit the play button. "I think it's cued to the call we got from Steeljaw vectoring us on that pair of MiG–21s."

The camera was mounted to record the view looking straight out over the nose of Randi's F/A–18. The black-and-white image was clear and captured the graphical information she would have seen through her Head's Up Display, or HUD. The audio was very sensitive, picking up both her microphone and the radios. At first, there was some low-volume radio chatter in the background, and slightly louder, the sound of Randi breathing into her oxygen mask.

"That's my number-two radio," Randi said. "Number one is tuned to the fight freq."

On what must have been the fight frequency, Steeljaw transmitted, "Hawk three-five, new vector. Snap two-zero-zero for ten, angels five. Cleared to fire."

Neary's voice, "Roger that. Radar contact."

Then Randi's voice, "Snort, Randi's still got the southern group. Dizzy's defensive; let me press."

After a pause, "You're clear."

Hoser said, "Stop it right there." After Randi hit the pause button, he grilled her. "What the hell is running through your brain?"

She turned to look at him, her eyes narrowing. She spoke in the precise tone I'd heard when she briefed the flight this morning. "I painted both groups with my radar. Bradley was in trouble. I knew Snort could handle the MiG–21s. It was a snap decision. I wanted to go help if I could."

Hoser said, "It was the wrong decision. You should have known from the geometry that the strike package was threatened. What if Neary's weapons system malfunctioned? Your assumptions would have been catastrophic. Weren't you taught never to leave your leader?"

"Even if somebody could die?"

"The mission was to protect the strike group. They were the most vulnerable and most important element. Vader and Dizzy were the MIGSWEEP. They engaged a single MiG. It may sound shitty, but even if they were both eventually bagged, they accomplished their mission, which was to keep the MiG away from the strikers. More importantly, you and Snort are a team. You don't go freelancing over enemy territory, Randi. Not when the mission is on the line. I need to know. Do you understand what I'm saying?"

She was staring at the floor. With her head down, it was impossible to see her face. She put her hands on her hips and took two deep breaths. When she looked up, her jaw was clenched, and her eyes were slits. "I do understand. And next time, I'll think about the mission first. But I don't regret it, and I'm not promising I wouldn't do it again. I'm sorry, Hoser, but that's the way I feel about it. You're going to have to accept that."

They stared at each other for several seconds. Teacher and pupil locked in a battle of wills. In the end, it was the teacher who backed down.

"That's all I'm asking for. Hit the tape, let's see this gun's kill."

The next transmission was Randi's voice saying, "Dizzy, are you high or low?" Her breathing on the intercom became rapid. The airspeed indicator climbed to six hundred knots. After several more seconds, the display on the HUD changed. She had locked up a target. The range was ten miles. The cues for a Sparrow missile popped up.

"Watch this," Randi said to us, pointing at the display. The target's altitude suddenly plummeted. "The guy dived for the deck. I also think he pumped out chaff. I couldn't take a shot."

The controller transmitted, "Steeljaw, lost contact with Lobo five-two."

"I caught sight about here," Randi said to us. We watched as the radar broke lock.

Her voice again, "Hawk three-six is engaging the southern bandit. Wreckage bears one-eight-five for six from my position."

Hoser said, "That was a great call under the circumstances, Randi. I'm impressed."

Randi allowed herself a small smile.

"Steeljaw copies. Your bandit bears one-seven-five, four miles. We've lost contact with both Lobos."

Quickly the display changed again. Another

radar lock, then a flash of smoke. The missile, a white blur, raced away from the camera. "Fox-one from Hawk three-six."

Randi paused the tape. "I didn't want to take that shot."

"Why not?" asked Hoser.

"Not enough look-down. I should have stayed higher instead of boresighting the bogey."

"That would have been a good move. But the shot was technically okay. You're in range and within parameters. You say you've got both of them in sight now?"

"Yeah. Dizzy is about three miles in front of the MiG."

"So, he was about to take one up the poop chute, right?"

"That's what I figured."

"Then it was a terrific shot."

Randi looked surprised.

"I'm serious. That MiG should have left you two in the dust. As soon as you targeted him, he should have hightailed it out of there. But the bastard was going to get himself another Hornet come hell or high water. Randi, we taught you how to take the high-percentage shot, but nobody can teach you how, and when, to waste a shot. That's instinct. It's what separates the women from the boys." He smiled for the first time.

Randi spun around to resume playing the tape, but not before I caught sight of her blushing from the unexpected praise.

The HUD display changed as Randi selected a Sidewinder missile. Then she radioed, "Dizzy, pitch back! I'm engaged two miles at your six." Her attempts to get the Sidewinder to lock on to the MiG were fruitless. In the HUD field of view, the MiG ejected six or seven flares. Within just three or four seconds, the MiG grew from a black dot into a large predatory shape that flashed by on her left side.

"Stop the machine. What were you thinking there?" asked Hoser.

"I saw Dizzy's jet pitch up. I assumed he heard me. It was a big mistake, because I decided to tie up the MiG in a high-G fight."

"What else could you have done?"

"I *should* have extended, gotten some separation, and pitched back myself. Then I could have nailed him with a Sparrow."

"But instead?"

"But, instead, I groveled with the guy."

"What did I teach you about groveling with a Fulcrum?"

"You said it was like rolling in mud with a pig. You both get dirty, and the pig likes it."

"Good. Now, go on."

The audio of the next forty seconds was tough to listen to. Randi strained hard against G forces that peak at 7.3 Gs. Her breathing became raspy and labored. She grunted several times, a technique a pilot can use to keep the blood pressure up. Gradually, the accelerometer decreases until she was pulling only 4 Gs. Through it all the aircraft's nose tracked smoothly across the horizon.

"Here it comes," Randi said to us.

After at least two full circles, there was an explosive guttural exhalation from Randi. Simultaneously, the jet stopped its left-hand turn, and, without rolling, the nose pitched thirty degrees in the opposite direction. The G-meter snapped from positive 4 Gs to negative 2 Gs.

After a slight pause, the aircraft snap-rolled to the right sixty degrees and pitched nose-high. I recognized the next maneuver as a barrel roll. I remembered my own feeble attempts. I'd found them impossible. In contrast, Randi's jet carved a perfect arc in the sky.

"Beautiful," said Hoser.

In the next frame, the MiG appeared in Randi's windscreen. In less than a second, the gunsight popped up, and the pipper settled just behind the canopy. The picture vibrated, and smoke erupted in the windscreen. I could actually see the cannon rounds finding their mark. Dozens of small explosions dotted the skin of the MiG. As the firing stopped, the aircraft started to break apart at the wing root. Randi's jet rolled and pulled up and away from the target. She hit the PAUSE button.

"Any chute?" Hoser asked, matter-of-factly.

"Nope. It went up in a fireball."

"The guy was in your knickers pretty good."

"I'll say. I was staring down his intakes when I put on my guns defense."

"How many rounds did you fire?"

"Two hundred seventy. You think that was too much?"

"Nope. Just right."

The way these two were unemotionally analyzing the kill was uncanny. They were actually wondering if she had used too many cannon rounds to obliterate another jet. It fascinated me.

I asked, "What were you thinking? Were you scared?"

"Honestly? I was concentrating too hard to be scared. Don't laugh, but I do remember hearing the words from the back of that photo Hoser gave me."

"Oh, yeah?" Hoser asked.

"Don't you remember? *'Jink or die.'* It was weird. The words just popped into my brain. Daddy sure had that right, didn't he?"

"He sure did, sweetheart."

CHAPTER 46

**Medical Spaces—
Monday, 21 Oct/1340**

"What's that in your hand, Jack?" asked Hoser.

"I don't know. But it came from Bradley's locker."

He didn't reply but arched his eyebrows.

Randi said, "Dizzy's tape malfunctioned. It's too bad, because it would really help us to piece together what happened out there. Jack, I think that must be an old one."

"There's only one way to find out." I handed it to her.

Randi put it in the machine and rewound it. When she hit play, a view of the flight deck flickered onto the screen. For a couple seconds, the screen was covered in numbers.

"What the hell?" asked Randi.

"What is it?" I asked.

"That's today's date and mission code. Jack, this is a tape of today's mission."

"Fast-forward to the fight." Hoser's voice had an edge to it.

Randi forwarded the tape until the counter matched her tape. Then she hit play.

The jet was flying very low, barely two hundred feet. Ground filled the bottom half of the screen. The airspeed was pegged at 580 knots. Bradley's breathing was erratic, almost panic-stricken.

"No radios. I don't hear any radios." Randi said. "He didn't hear me." She sounded relieved.

"Hush-up," Hoser said.

Suddenly her voice burst through on the tape, "Dizzy, pitch back! I'm engaged two miles at your six."

The nose of Bradley's fighter pitched up thirty degrees and the speed bled off.

I watched Randi for a reaction. She stared open-mouthed at the video. "He did hear me," she said under her breath. Her tone was incredulous.

"Son of a bitch!" Hoser jerked bolt upright, his face contorted in anger.

The door to Hoser's suite opened, and Nurse Malerba stormed in. "What is going on in here?" Nobody answered.

On-screen, Bradley climbed to fifteen hundred feet, paused, then pointed his fighter back at the ground. The heading remained unchanged. He was fleeing. In doing so, he abandoned the pilot who had saved his life.

For the first time we heard his voice. Quiet, barely more than a murmur, nevertheless, it filled the room. "Better you than me. Yo-Yo, baby."

Hoser exploded. "I'm going to kill that chicken-shit son of a bitch!"

Randi looked like she'd been hit by a truck.

Nurse Malerba moved toward her patient.

I walked over to the machine, found the pause button, and rewound it. I played it again. And again. Then I asked, "What is he saying? *Yo-Yo?*" Nobody answered. I rewound it, but before I could play it once more, Randi grabbed my hand.

"Please don't. I can't hear that again."

"What's it mean?"

Randi said "Yo-Yo?" Her lips parted in a smile, but there was no humor in it. "It's radio code. Yo-Yo is short for, '*You're on Your own.*' That prick left me out there to die, Jack."

CHAPTER 47

Monday, 21 OCT/1350

The nurse kicked us out of Hoser's room, and with
the aid of a burly corpsman, gave him a sedative.
When she came out, she motioned me to follow her
into a supply closet. Closing the door behind us, she
got right to the point. "Does that tape have anything
to do with Lieutenant Mason getting killed?"

"Same guy."

"That bastard killed Mason, then left that girl
alone in combat?"

"Yes."

"And this sailor you want to smuggle off the ship
can prove it?"

"Yes he can."

She nodded. "How tall is he?"

"Five-ten, one-sixty."

She rummaged through a shelf holding scrub
clothes and picked out a set of pants and a top. "Here.
You'll have to get him to the hangar deck in thirty
minutes."

"What about the other medical personnel? Will

there be a problem when my kid tries to slip in?"

She was incredulous. "Listen, buster, this is my shop, my people. You just get him there. Now vamoose, before people start yapping that I'm getting some on the side."

Randi had gone back in to sit with Hoser. When I entered, he was battling to stay awake.

He motioned me to his bedside. "Jack, I've got to talk with the captain," he said. "We've gotta get that sumbitch."

"The captain isn't in the mood to listen. He's kicking us off the boat, Hoser."

"Why?" His eyelids drooped lower.

"You're going to have to trust me. We can't say a word to anyone. I'll tell you all about it on the plane. Catch some sleep."

The sedative finally won. Hoser dropped off. I signaled for Randi to follow me outside. She stroked his forehead and whispered something I couldn't hear. Then she bent over and kissed him. We stepped out into the corridor.

"Do you think he'll wake up before you go?" she asked. "I want to say good-bye."

"Probably not. Besides there's no time. You have an appointment."

"For what?"

I couldn't help pulling her chain a little. It was payback for that unusable quote she gave me. "Just go get a shower and get cleaned up."

"Are you saying I smell bad?" she asked, ready to be offended.

"In a word, yes."

She stepped closer. "Are you going to tell me what kind of appointment I have, or do I have to get tough?"

"CNN is flying in. You're going to be on TV in about an hour. You'll be seen by several hundred million people."

Her eyes did an Orphan Annie. "Oh, shit."

"Try not to say that on the air."

"What do I say when they ask what happened out there?"

"Play it like you never saw Bradley's tape. Just tell them the story from your cockpit. The rest of this will come out later. Right now, America wants a hero. And you're it, sweetheart."

"Oh, fuck."

"You really need to work on that."

"Oh, God."

"That's not much better. Hey, can I make a recommendation?"

"Please."

"Put on some lipstick and a little makeup. And wear a flight suit, don't get into a uniform. Allow yourself to be feminine, okay?"

She looked puzzled. "Why is that important?"

"It's to keep everyone off-balance. Some people are going to want to assume you're some kind of man-hating Amazon. When they see your pretty smile and then try to imagine you shooting down a MiG, it'll blow their minds. You ever see that woman drag racer with the pink car?"

She smiled. "Sure. She was a kick. I remember telling my mom and dad that's what I wanted to do when I grew up."

"Well, you're about to become ten thousand times more famous than her. And you can do the same thing for other little girls. This is your chance to make the world understand that you didn't have to become a man to do what used to be a man's job."

She stared at me for several seconds. I thought she might burst out laughing.

"What?" I asked, feeling self-conscious.

"You constantly amaze me, Jack."

Then she leaned forward, kissed me softly, spun on her heel, and walked away.

CHAPTER 48

Monday, 21 Oct/1405

After grabbing Bradley's tape, I raced up the six ladders to my stateroom. Pete said there had been no calls. I rousted Lawrence. It was time to get him ready.

First to go was the scraggly mustache. He wasn't thrilled but acquiesced when Pete offered to pull it out by the roots. Then we got him into the scrubs. Pete suggested using a magic marker to write a name on the pocket. We picked Jackson.

It dawned on me that something was missing. I looked around for my bags, but they were gone.

Pete said, "Master Chief sent some guys down for your gear. I made them leave your computer, camera, and jacket. They're over there."

"What about my stuff?" asked Lawrence.

"Master Chief says we'll pack it up after you're gone." He produced an envelope. "Here, write down the address you want it sent to, Jackson. I hope you don't have too much, fella, cause it's gotta fit in there." Pete laughed heartily at his own joke.

I briefed the two of them on where and when to meet Nurse Malerba. Pete already had a helmet and goggles for Lawrence—Jackson—to wear.

The speaker mounted outside my room kicked on. The bosun's whistle was followed by the words, "Stand by for the captain."

"Good afternoon, *Ranger*, this is your captain. I want to congratulate each and every one of you on a highly successful mission this morning. *Ranger's* air wing destroyed a chemical-weapons facility. There is no telling how many lives we've saved in the process. You can bet that the entire free world will sleep better tonight thanks to you. On that note, we will soon host a television crew from CNN, who will broadcast a live report to all our friends and families.

"I'd also like to single out two individuals for special recognition. Today, Lieutenant Commander Neary of VFA–303 destroyed a MiG–21 that was threatening the bombers. While he was scoring his kill, his wingman, Lieutenant Randi Cole, engaged and shot down a MiG–29, one of the world's best fighters. She becomes America's first woman MiG killer. This has truly been a historic day.

"On a sadder note, *Ranger* lost one its best pilots. We've received word from the State Department that Libyan authorities have confirmed that Lieutenant Commander Corbett, of VFA–305, was killed when his F/A–18 was destroyed by hostile fire. There will be a memorial for our shipmate tomorrow morning at ten-hundred on the flight deck. All hands not on duty are expected to attend.

"I've just been informed that the COD carrying the network people has checked in. It's time for flight quarters. Keep up the good work, *Ranger*. That is all."

I didn't have much time, but I stopped by the Comm Center.

The chief greeted me, "I didn't think I'd see you again, sir."

"Well here I am. I told you that I owed you one."

He smiled. "As a matter of fact, you do."

"Then what can I do for you?"

He reached into his desk drawer and pulled out a couple sheets of typewritten paper, stapled together. "You know that file you had me send off the ship a few hours ago?"

"Yeah." Despite the cold, a bead of sweat dripped down my spine.

"Well, you should have encrypted that photo, Mr. Warner. That is, if you didn't want anyone to read the little surprise you put in it. It was a slick idea though."

Oh, shit! I *had* forgotten to code the text when I embedded it in the image file.

He stared at me with an amused expression, like a big cat toying with a mouse.

"How'd you get a copy of it?" I asked.

"Easy, I just sent a copy to myself. It went up to the satellite, raced halfway around the world, and plopped right back onto my machine in a few seconds. Technology is amazing, ain't it?"

I nodded. "What would you like?"

"How about a trade?"

"What kind?"

He walked over to me. "This little document for your flight jacket. I always wanted one of these." He whispered, "And we're about the same size."

A mortal blow. I thought he'd ask for money or some kind of professional favor, like a job when he got out. But my flight jacket! He couldn't have picked anything more painful for me to part with. Still, I had no choice. I peeled it off and handed it to him. He handed me the paper. I watched him put on my jacket and remembered how perfect it had felt the first time I'd slipped it over my shoulders.

After a couple seconds, he said, "You okay with this?"

"Yeah. It's not like you didn't warn me. You said that I should never tell a chief I owed him one. Now I know why."

"It could have been worse," he said. "Have a good flight, Mr. Warner."

"Have a good cruise, Chief."

CHAPTER 49

Monday, 21 Oct/1440

As I left the Comm Center, an aircraft slammed into the flight deck a mere two feet above my head. Instead of jet engines spooling up, the high-pitched whine of propellers announced the arrival of CNN. On impulse, I entered the CAG spaces.

The door to his office was closed. "Is the deputy in?" I asked the Admin chief.

He eyed me warily. "Yes, sir, but he left word not to be disturbed."

"That's okay," I said, walking quickly to the door, "I'm sure he won't mind."

"But, sir!"

Nobody was going to stop me. After checking that the flash was off, I palmed the digital camera in my left hand and put my thumb on the shutter release. I grabbed the knob, opened the door, and shouted, "Commander! It's Jack. I had to say good-bye."

Three astonished faces stared back at me. Holmes, Bradley, and Hogan. I continued to speak loudly, to cover any sound the camera might make as

I snapped a half dozen pictures. "Sorry to barge in, fellas, but it's time to go. I just wanted to thank you all for being so helpful." I held out my hand to Bradley and said, "I'm glad you made it back, safe."

As we shook, he said, "Uh, thank you. It was pretty hairy out there."

Next was Hogan. "Chaplain, I'm real sorry you have to do another memorial service. Good luck with that."

"Thank you, Mr. Warner, but don't be concerned for me. Doing the Lord's work is its own reward."

"And, Deputy, good luck with the mishap investigations. I hope you get to the bottom of it."

"I'm sure we will, Mr. Warner." As I turned to leave, he stood. "Let me say that I'm sorry that you're leaving us. I hope we've given you something good to write about."

I took one last look at the three of them. Their surprised looks had given way to familiar smugness.

"You've given me terrific stuff. And don't worry, I'll make sure I spell your names right."

They laughed as I closed the door behind me.

CHAPTER 50

Monday, 21 Oct/1450

Cardone met me in the passageway.

"Thought you'd need some help finding the flight deck."

"Hey, I'm a cruise veteran. I can handle it."

He laughed. "Then maybe you could use some company."

"Thanks, my friend." We made our way to the flight deck by way of the hatch I'd stumbled upon the night before Amy died. It seemed like eons had passed since that evening.

It was gorgeous outside. The sky had cleared, and the ocean mirrored brilliant blue. I licked my lips and tasted the salt in the air. We walked toward the hole in the deck left by the number-one elevator. As we rounded the island, we caught sight of the CNN crew, already shooting. Cole and Neary were being interviewed. Morganelli and CAG stood on either side of them.

"Shit's going to hit the fan in a couple hours. Are you going to be all right, Art?" I asked.

"Sure. Don't worry about the lieutenant, either. I'll keep my eye on her."

"Anything you want me to do when I get back?"

"Yeah. Call Liz. Tell her I'm okay. She'll be worried that I'm holding myself responsible for losing those jets."

"So that's how you do it," I said.

"Do what?"

"Stay married forever. She worries about you, and you worry about her worrying. I never would have thought of that."

He shrugged. "What can I say? I'm well trained."

The quiet was shattered by a Klaxon.

"Here comes our boy. Look, I hate good-byes. Take care of yourself, Jack." He patted me on the shoulder and headed aft, probably to check on his aircraft. How the same Navy could attract men like Cardone and scum like Bradley remained a mystery to me.

The elevator rose quickly, silly-looking with only three people on it. I was happy to see that Hoser was awake. He was seated in a wheelchair. Nurse Malerba had "Jackson" pushing it while she carried a large satchel. Several feet away from them sat a rectangular crate. As I walked closer, I saw that it was labeled. Ten-inch letters, stenciled with military precision, declared, HUMAN REMAINS. Apparently, Amy Mason was also flying home.

Hoser nodded toward the box, and asked, "So who's the stiff?"

Nurse Malerba flashed a warning at me with her eyes.

"It's a long story. You can buy me a beer, and I'll tell you all about it."

A pair of sailors escorted us to the waiting aircraft. A loading ramp had been lowered from the rear of the plane. While we waited for the crate to be secured, Morganelli and CAG walked over to say good-bye. Lawrence stiffened.

"Relax," ordered Malerba. "They can't see your face."

Both men shook Hoser's good hand and gave him a hard time.

"Never would have thought I'd have to COD your ass off my flight deck," said Morganelli.

"And I had a Hornet all set for you, buddy," added CAG.

"Well, get me some gear, you two pudknockers. I can still fly circles around anybody you got out here." Hoser started to stand up.

Nurse Malerba placed a firm hand on his shoulder and pressed him back into his chair. "Remember our agreement?" she said. Then she looked up at the two captains, and added, "If he gives me a hard time, he gets an enema as soon as we land."

Everyone laughed.

Lieutenant Irvine wandered over with one of the CNN crew. I recognized him from the tube. Because everyone was still chummy, I knew CNN hadn't been briefed on the phony-target story. Surprising myself, I decided to slip the guy the copy of my article the chief had traded for my flight jacket. It went against every instinct I had, but with the killer stories I was sitting on, I could afford to be generous.

Morganelli made the introductions. "Jack Warner, meet Greg Vasquez. I'm sure you've seen him on television."

"Yes, I have. Many times. Nice to meet you, Greg," I said.

"Warner?" Acting like he'd never heard my name, he gave me a dead-fish handshake. "Oh, sure. You were the *pool* reporter out here, right?"

The prick was taking a shot. "That's right."

The loadmaster signaled for us. Malerba herded Hoser and Lawrence up the ramp.

Vasquez saved his best for last. "Well, thanks for standing in for us." His plastic smile begged for a right cross. Then, pointing at the aircraft, he said, "And try not to get airsick on the way home." He was the only one laughing.

I slipped the article back into my pocket and shook hands with CAG, the Skipper, and Irvine. Vasquez tried to match my grip, but it was no contest. Before I let go, I said, "Yo-Yo, Greg."

It caught him off guard. "What the hell is that supposed to mean?" he asked, wincing as he pulled his hand away.

I took one last look at the flight deck, turned, and joined my three friends and star witness for the ride home.

He could read about it in the papers, just like everyone else.